OUTLAWS

By:

William O. Weldy

Outlaws, Copyright © William Weldy, 2012

isbn: 978-1-61937-8490

Published in the United States of America
Editor: Megan Embry
Cover Design: Kelly Shorten
Interior Book Design: Coreen Montagna

Warning:
This e-book contains adult language and scenes. This story is meant only for adults as defined by the laws of the country where you made your purchase.
Store your e-books carefully where they cannot be accessed by younger readers.

Dedication

To my loving wife Pamela and my son Joshua, may he rest in peace.

With appreciation to the critters at Internet Writers Workshop for all their help with this novel.

OUTLAWS

Chapter One

Josh Grant's reliable internal clock awakened him just before dawn. He sat up and swung his feet to the cool wood floor, rose and walked naked to the small bathroom where he relieved himself. Whistling softly, he washed his hands and splashed cool water on his face. Feeling the stubble of a week's growth, he reached for the soap mug and brush.

Can't go to town all scruffy. He stropped his straight razor and scraped the whiskers off his face. He ran wet hands through his hair and shook his head violently, like Beau always did after a swim in the lake. He let his hair fall wherever it pleased.

Back in the bedroom, Josh pulled a dark-blue T-shirt over his head, then tugged a fresh pair of Wrangler jeans over his bare rump. Sitting on the edge of the bed, he put on socks and boots. Beau, his yellow Lab, approached and laid his head on Josh's thigh.

"Good morning, boy." Josh ruffled the dog's head.

The dog twitched his head up and chuffed.

Josh snorted a laugh and shook his head. "Sometimes I think you can understand English." Beau's massive tail wagged agreement.

Beau gazed at him, awaiting a command. "Come on, boy. We've got work to do." Josh rubbed Beau's head again.

The door from the bedroom led directly into the spacious kitchen, by far the largest room in the small log cabin. Josh bent to open the firebox door of the ancient cast iron cook stove. Some old embers still glowed. *No need to build up the fire today. Won't be doing any cooking.* A stainless steel thermos sat atop the stove with last night's fresh-brewed coffee, still piping hot.

He poured a cup and sat at the round wooden table. Before taking his first sip, he held the cup up and recited his daily greeting to the heavens.

"Good morning, Ellie. Good morning, Jimmy. I made it through another day without you. Thank you, Lord."

Just as he tilted the cup to his mouth, Leghorn, the alpha rooster of the barnyard, let go with his first raucous crow of the morning.

Beau looked at Josh with anticipation. His heavy tail beat a staccato rhythm against a chair leg.

"Not today, boy, we have to go to town. You never catch that old rooster anyway."

Beau's tail beat faster — Josh smiled. "No," he commanded. "Just settle down, Beau."

The dog drooped his head and flopped onto the floor with a hurt look on his face.

Josh finished his coffee while gathering a few supplies for the trip. He packed a knapsack with a peanut butter sandwich, deer jerky, some dried fruit, and the thermos. "Come on, Beau, let's go to the barn and feed the stock."

At the rear door, Josh snagged his hat from a wall peg and held the door for Beau.

After feeding the riding horses, he turned them out to pasture with the cows and hitched the Belgians to the wagon. The horses, Dick and Dan, stood placidly as Josh attached the yokes and harness. "Good boys." He patted the team as he worked. "We're going to town. Maybe I'll buy you guys some candy."

The calmness of the gentle giants, so out of place with their size, always amazed Josh. He whistled softly as he worked.

Climbing onto the wagon seat, Josh gazed in reverence at the eastern mountain range across the emerald green lake. The sun rose earlier this time of year — the end of May, with its crisp spring air and budding wildflowers painting the hillsides. "I hope Ross has our supplies ready."

Leaving the farm at six o'clock would put Josh at the Platte Junction general store by noon. Plenty of time to get back before nightfall.

He took a deep breath of clean mountain air and clucked the horses into motion. As the team started to move, Beau jumped in the back of the wagon and curled up on a tarpaulin.

Josh was eager to get to Platte Junction. He craved normal conversation with real people, like Ross, the store owner. His recent habit of talking to his animals had started to concern him. The other part of him, as usual, dreaded the long boring trip. Clicking air between his teeth and cheek and a soft flick of the reins, Josh said, "Hi on, boys."

Beau woofed his agreement.

They faced a rugged four miles up and down abandoned logging trails before reaching a real road, and then only gravel and hard-packed clay for another three or four miles. Only an ATV or horses could manage these mountain trails. The four-wheel-drive pickup he'd used when he'd built his cabin had worked, but Josh preferred the peacefulness of horses. The worst part of the trip would be the last couple of miles along the state highway. Motorists paid little attention to slow-moving horse-drawn wagons.

Josh embraced what others might consider the hazards of his chosen lifestyle. The few hardships, like traveling all day just to buy supplies, were well worth the effort it took to maintain his peaceful little mountain farm. The satisfaction he experienced from being in harmony with his surroundings, and the tranquility he absorbed on a daily basis made any hardships seem small by comparison.

His little isolated corner of the world continued to heal the memories of the deaths of his wife and child. Each day added a little peace to his heart. He had no desire for the city life he'd left behind.

Josh was brought back to reality when the horses skittered alert. A deer, in a blur of motion, burst from the trail and bound into the deep woods. Josh tightened the reins then chuckled, urging the horses on. Bo barked.

Josh looked forward to talking to the gruff old storekeeper to catch up on current events. The latest news always reassured him the way he chose to live was the right way. He hadn't seen Ross since his wife died several months ago, and wondered how he'd been getting along. Painful memories of his own wife slithered back into his consciousness. Don't go there, he silently admonished himself.

The reminder did little good. He struggled to focus on the trail and his surroundings. He tried to think about additional supplies he might need. But his brain wouldn't cooperate. Pictures of Ellen and Jimmy in their caskets forced their way into his head. Faces dull and lifeless. No semblance to the smiles and laughter that filled their lives before. Melancholy crept into Josh's mood as it always did when he thought of his wife and child.

He had tried the so called civilized life. In his mind, he had attacked it, yet he felt he had failed. He'd never had much impact on crime, and he sure hadn't prevented the murder of his wife and son. Much easier to give up and start over— here in this isolated corner of Idaho.

A bird flushed from a nearby bush and flew directly over the wagon, drawing him out of depressing thoughts. Josh shook his head and gazed at the majesty around him. The inner peace he now felt was something he hadn't realized was missing from his life until he experienced it. Although still new to him, he welcomed the change from his former existence. The serenity of his new world, an all engulfing high that sustained and awed him every day. He never regretted his choice to live reclusively on his simple farm. As Josh guided the team around a switch back in the trail, he relaxed his grip on the reins and eased back against the wagon seat. He turned and saw Bo already curled up on the tarpaulin in the back. He grinned. *How can that dog sleep at the drop of a hat, and the next instant be totally alert?*

The trip was peaceful, and driving the team not necessary. They couldn't stray from the deeply gouged tracks of the old logging roads, unless they wanted to careen down the side of the mountain. Horses aren't too smart, but they're smarter than that.

With little to do until they reached the highway, Josh relaxed and absorbed the sights, sounds and smells of his mountains.

To the East he could see for miles. The lush green mountains and valleys peeked through the misty morning. To his left, majestic Red Cedars towered above the Douglas Firs and undergrowth so thick full sunlight could barely penetrate. Josh breathed in the fragrance of conifers, wild flowers and forest loam, and smiled. His surroundings never failed to transform him into an almost hypnotic state of tranquility.

Chapter Two

Platte Junction

Ross Folkreth didn't like motorcycles. Cars and trucks he tolerated, but motorcycles intruded on his rural Idaho serenity. Motorcycle riders, he liked even less. So when they roared into his general store parking lot in a plume of dust, with annoying engine revving and loud crackling exhausts, he glared out the window, gritted his teeth and shook his head in disgust.

Four burly men in leather and oily denim strode toward the store. The door burst open amid shouted obscenities, pushing, and shoving. One man hip bumped another into a display rack toppling it. Ross felt his ire boiling as they split up down aisles.

A short fat biker opened a bottle of juice, took a sip then closed the lid and put it back on the shelf. "This is piss water," he spat, his upper lip peeled back into a snarl, baring broken and yellow teeth. The others laughed. Ross stood momentarily frozen in disbelief.

Down another aisle, two more roamed, scattering items off shelves at random, and howling like wolves at a kill. One shoveled chips into his mouth, peppering his beard with crumbs. His open denim vest exposed chest hairs poking through holes in his dirty T shirt like weeds from sidewalk cracks.

Ross' lip curled. Filthy bastards, think they own the place. He spread his feet and stared at the group, hands on his hips. He couldn't hide his contempt for their arrogance. He squared his shoulders jerked his chin upward and yelled, "Hey, what the hell do you guys want?"

He didn't need their business, and sure didn't need their crap. What the hell kind of scum are these guys? Never come across men like these in his world. Can't beat simple farming folk. These bikers made the "Wild Ones" look like a Boy Scout troop.

The man nearest the counter turned, glared at Ross and said, "Whatever the fuck we want old man, we'll just take."

"Like hell you will!" Ross started around the counter as if he were about to eject a youth for snitching a candy bar.

Without warning, the man closest to Ross, barrel chested with a pony tail and a large belly, hit Ross with a powerful punch to the face. Ross fell heavily to the floor. Blood streamed from his nose and ran down his chin and neck.

Sitting up but still disoriented, Ross' eyes watered from the intense pain. He touched his nose and felt sticky blood. Looking at his hand, he panicked. What the hell? He had been in his share of fights in his younger days, but none like this.

Still stunned, he tried to get back up by grabbing at the lead biker as he walked past and around the counter. Heavily tattooed arms lifted Ross easily to his feet. The evil looking man displayed a cruel grin and wild eyes. With a glint of pleasure in his eyes, he showed Ross the large knife in his hand.

Paralyzing fear gripped Ross' body. This can't be happening. He wasn't nearly as afraid of the knife as what he saw in the hollow, lifeless eyes staring at him. "What…" he started. Realization settled in — he was about to die.

His mind raced. Jolene. Oh God, no!

* * * *

The cold-eyed biker watched for a reaction in Ross's eyes, then quickly thrust the knife upward at the base of Ross's sternum and twisted it. Ross's warning cry to Jolene choked in his throat, throttled before it escaped his mouth.

The tattooed man pulled the blade out and casually wiped it clean on Ross's shirt. He dragged Ross farther behind the counter, as another hoodlum sauntered past them both to the cash drawer. While he emptied the till, one of the men in the aisles pulled a six-pack of Coors from the cooler and pitched them one at a time to the others. They all raised their beer bottles high in salute.

The pack of scavengers then set about collecting whatever else they wanted from the store. As they gathered around the beer cooler, one of them noticed a closed door. With a finger to his lips he motioned for the others to be quiet. They fell silent and listened. Country music and soft feminine humming wafted through the closed door.

* * * *

Ross' daughter, Jolene, stepped out of the shower and toweled off. The hair dryer buzzed as warm air fluffed her long hair into miniature black whips snapping silently. She smiled thinking how only a couple of months at home had begun to make her feel worthwhile again. Her mother's death last winter had taken its toll on her and her dad, and her divorce three months ago had turned her world upside down. Her return home had been a blessing for both.

She dressed in jeans and a light sweater, and went into the living room to use the big mirror to put the finishing touches to her hair. She hummed along with a country song playing on the radio, as she brushed her hair into place.

She stopped abruptly and cocked her head. What was that noise? Maybe Dad dropped something. She called out, "Daddy?"

The door to the living quarters burst open with a crash, and she screamed.

Chapter Three

The village, what little there was of it, sat quietly with its usual deserted appearance. A few scattered homes along the road and a General store, in the middle of nowhere. The sun, higher in the sky, promised a warm day. Josh turned the team from the highway onto the road running through the settlement.

He pulled the Belgians to a stop in the empty parking area of Ross's store, got down from the seat, stretched his lanky frame, and adjusted his hat further back on his head. Bo woofed at no one in particular.

"Hush, Bo. You're disturbing the peace. You'll get us arrested." He grinned at the dog. Bo stopped barking, but continued a muted growl of protest.

"Don't argue with me. And stay here…" Josh smiled at the dog. "And don't you go chasing any cats."

Bo looked at him, but continued a low throaty snarl. Josh smiled and shook his head.

Josh entered the store and looked for Ross behind the counter. He wasn't there. Odd. "Hey, Ross, you got paying customers on the premises. Get your lazy butt out here and pop me a cold one before I take my business to the next town."

No reply. "Ross?..." Josh stopped and focused his ears. Something didn't feel right. He looked around the store. Darker than usual. No lights on – only ambient light from the windows. He heard muted music from the back of the store where Ross lived, but it wasn't country, and Ross always listened to country music. He turned toward Ross's quarters.

Josh felt his sphincter muscles tighten, as icicles crept up his spinal cord. Something was definitely wrong. The store itself appeared deserted, and that wasn't like Ross either. He's usually right there behind the counter. Josh moved toward the apartment.

His body tensed. Was he just being paranoid? But he knew better than to ignore his instincts. They had saved his butt too many times on the streets of Detroit. His right hand automatically dropped to his hip. The comforting feel of polished leather and cold steel weren't there to greet him. He had little use for the Glock nine millimeter around the farm, although he still kept it in a trunk in the loft. Right now he yearned for the familiar feel of his duty belt and pistol.

Josh's mind raced. Was he over reacting? But what had caused Bo to growl? Had the town seemed even more deserted than usual? How could it? It was always deserted.

He thought he heard muffled sounds mixed with heavy metal music somewhere in the back of the store. It had to have come from Ross's quarters. Listen to your instincts, he reminded himself. Something's not right here. He looked around. What could he use for a weapon if needed? His brain flitted from one thought to another.

He eased his way through the rows of grocery and hardware items. Shelf items littered the floor. Uh-oh, Ross wouldn't let that be. His nerves tingled with a new intensity.

He knew the door in back led to Ross's apartment; he'd been there before. His eyes scanned the aisles while all his focus directed to his ears. He heard acid rock music, louder now. He thought he could hear muted conversation, but couldn't tell if it might be a television or radio. He couldn't call the Sheriff. The only phone is in Ross's apartment, and what would he tell them anyway?

He spotted a push broom leaning against a counter near the closed apartment door. Ross never closed that door. He couldn't hear the phone from up front with the door closed, and he couldn't hear customers if he were in his living quarters.

The broom handle might work. He slowly and quietly unscrewed the handle from the broom and hefted it. Not as heavy, and a little longer than a regular bow he's trained with so many years in the Dojo. Will this skinny stick have the speed and power of a regular bow? Too long and too light, but it'll have to do.

He propped the broom handle next to the apartment doorframe where he could get it quickly if needed. He took off his hat and put it on a shelf. Placed his hands over his open eyes, and stood still for a minute or two to allow his pupils to dilate in case it was dark in the interior of Ross's house. He listened intently for any sounds that might indicate what he was about to get into. He definitely heard heavy metal music and muted talking.

Slowly, he twisted the doorknob. How many entries had he made during his police career into unknown dangers? Yet this was different. He didn't even have the right to be snooping around like this. What if he were wrong? What if old Ross had come across some lonely widow and managed to talk her into his bed for a romp? It's not unusual that no customers are here. The store didn't do a booming business.

But Josh had that old feeling of danger. This is all wrong. He'd learned to trust his instincts.

He weighed his options. Sometimes it's better to slam the door open and make a surprise entry with a lot of noise and confusion. Sometimes it's better to sneak in. Here he had no information from which to operate. Usually he had some part of a story to go on. A witness would alert him to a problem, and shed some light on it, or the dispatcher would have some facts about what to expect. Now he had nothing to go on.

Damn! He took a deep, calming breath.

Chapter Four

Josh eased the door open and stepped quietly into the dimly lit living room. In the middle of the room he saw a young woman, wearing snug jeans and nothing else, standing next to an equally bare-chested man who definitely was not from Platte Junction.

Despite Josh's quiet entry, the man looked up and glared in his direction. He moved slightly behind the girl. His behavior and the look of him confirmed Josh's suspicions. They did not belong here.

The woman made no attempt to cover her bare breasts. Josh saw a bra and sweater lying at her feet. She looked stiff and frightened. But that could be because he had interrupted them. The stranger's eyes squinted and his brow tightened. He had an evil looking scar on his cheek. His hard glare conveyed his attitude. He was not happy with the interruption.

The man was huge, with a barrel chest and a large belly. His arms were massive, his entire upper body covered with jailhouse tattoos. One heavily muscled arm draped casually over the woman's shoulder, the other hidden behind her. Could they have been dancing when he interrupted them? No. She's scared.

Josh quickly surveyed the rest of the room. Three other scowling men stood by the curtained window to his left, holding long neck beer bottles. Although they appeared casual, their eyes said otherwise. The one with his back partially turned to Josh wore a faded denim jacket with the sleeves cut off. Josh immediately recognized the skull logo stenciled on the back.

He felt a rush of adrenalin surge through his body as it always did when he was scared. It felt pleasant in a way. It was familiar, comforting even. Adrenalin addiction flashed through his mind as his body tensed.

Not a doubt in his mind – Josh knew these strangers. Maybe not individually, but he knew the colors they wore. The skull and crossed pistons were embedded in his memory. He had dealt with their kind enough in his past.

The Outlaws, like the Hell's Angels before them, were trying to sell a more legitimate image these days, but Josh knew they were still involved in every violent, illegal activity and vice they could dream up. They were the organized crime mobs of the Midwest.

What in the hell were they doing way out here in his new world? And where were their bikes?

Josh scanned the room. He knew Ross's living quarters. He had spent the night a few times. The kitchen lay straight ahead through an archway, and three doors lined the right side of the room leading to two bedrooms and a bathroom. From this vantage point, he couldn't tell if anyone else was in the apartment.

"What the hell do you want? You're interrupting a private party here," the man with the girl said, his voice low, gravelly and mean.

"Sorry," Josh hung his head, to give the impression he was no threat. "I just came in for supplies and no one was in the store."

"Store's closed," the stranger snarled. "Now get the hell out of here."

"Okay", Josh stalled. "Where's Goodwin?" He purposely used a wrong name to watch for a reaction. "He was supposed to have my supplies ready."

"He ain't here. He left us to watch the place. Now get out."

The woman had a puzzled look on her brow, despite the fear showing in her eyes.

Thoughts flashed like a slide show. His nerve ends tingled. He thought he'd left all this behind him. Could he still do it? In a few short minutes, uncontrollable circumstances had thrust him into a situation he didn't want to experience again. Fate was dealing him another blow. It had let him claw his way back to being almost whole, only to beat him back down.

Now here he was in a familiar, yet unknown, position with no plan and no backup. But he had to try. What else could he do? He couldn't just walk away. He couldn't just demand they release this woman, whoever she was. Hell, she could be one of them for all he knew. No, he knew better.

She didn't fit the biker girl mold. He could see she had no tattoos and her hair and jeans were clean. No doubt she was scared. But what's she doing here? One thing he knew for sure, these bikers did not belong in Ross Folkreth's house.

Where is Ross?

Josh's thoughts whirled. Should he even be here? Are they armed? Did he have this all wrong? No. He knew the nature of these men. He had no doubt they were evil. He also knew good doesn't always conquer evil. His experience had taught him some harsh lessons about that. It was all just movie crap. What it boiled down to was pure, simple, dumb luck.

Oh well, here I go. Hope I get lucky.

Chapter Five

The biker's cold glare accentuated his threat, "I said, get out."

Josh struggled to keep his face meek. He mumbled, "Sorry," again, and turned as if to go back out the door. He stopped abruptly in the middle and looked back in. His right hand reached around the doorframe and grasped the broom handle.

"Hey, could you guys see if my dog's still out there?" He asked the men by the window. When they automatically turned to look out, Josh shouted, "Bo, come!"

With that lame distraction, Josh rushed back into the dimly lit room. The bare chested man reacted quickly, with plenty of confidence. He grinned, flashing a large hunting knife he had hidden behind the girl. He shoved the girl away and crouched with the knife pointed at Josh. An evil grin stretched his face.

Josh twirled the stick so fast it was practically invisible. Surprise registered on the goon's face milliseconds before the broom handle circled under his right wrist. Too late. The staff cracked a numbing blow to the hand, and the knife fell to the floor. The staff didn't hesitate. In a blur, Josh brought the circling tip down hard. It struck a stunning direct hit to the man's left collarbone. The hoodlum screamed in rage and pain. His left arm sagged. Almost instantly the opposite end of the long stick crashed into the thug's rib cage as Josh moved in. The blow caused the man to grunt and bend slightly. Before he could recover, Josh moved to his right and brought the other end of the staff crashing into the biker's left temple and jawbone. The Outlaw collapsed into an unconscious heap. In less than five seconds it was over.

Momentarily stunned, the other three didn't move quickly enough. Josh twirled the long broom handle over his head, and then with a tight figure eight, tucked one end neatly under his left arm as he faced them. The staff made a swooshing noise as it moved and a loud pop when it came to rest at his side.

The man in the Levi jacket pulled a switchblade knife from his boot, clicked it open and rushed at Josh. The staff came out with a flick of Josh's wrist. Timing the biker's rush perfectly, Josh lunged one step at the attacker and thrust the staff forward. The end of the broom handle caught the Outlaw square in the throat. The man's feet came off the floor and he fell to the ground with a heavy thud. He laid there, hands to his throat, writhing as he choked.

Josh turned when he saw movement. The other two thugs had maneuvered between him and the door. If they thought he would try to escape, they were wrong. The menacing look on their faces melted when they saw the staff swirl and again come to rest pointed at them. They made their move, but it was an abrupt turn. Both fled out the open door.

Josh heard Bo's low growl and then a yelp of pain from one of the men. Bo barked fiercely. A few seconds later Josh heard the familiar roar of Harleys racing away from the rear of the store.

So that's why he hadn't seen the bikes. Bo continued to bark.

Josh sighed in relief. His tense muscles relaxed a little. Thank God they didn't have guns.

He leaned the broom handle against a wall and turned to the girl. "Are you all right?"

With that, she turned away from him, sank to her knees, and started sobbing. Josh went to the couch against the wall, and pulled an afghan from the back. He gently draped it over the woman's back and knelt beside her.

"It's all right now. They can't hurt you; they're gone. It's going to be okay."

She wept. He reassured her knowing his attempt would have little effect until she'd vented some of the built-up fear and tension. As he soothed her, Josh's eyes darted back and forth from the woman to the downed men. When her breaths came more regularly, he assisted her to the couch and turned full attention to the two men.

The first biker was still unconscious, and judging by the way his arm had fallen during the fight, had a broken clavicle, but he would live. Josh checked the remaining man, but knew what he would find. He had seen the staff bury in the hollow at the base of the neck. Probably broke the hyoid bone. It would cause massive swelling and cut off the air supply. Josh sighed with the knowledge.

When he got to the man, he was still alive, his eyes frozen open, a look of fear and horror on his face. His eyes told Josh he knew his fate.

Josh knelt beside the dying man. That old helpless feeling washed over him. How many people had he watched die and nothing he could do about it? And this one caused by his own hand. A few seconds later the biker choked to death. No action short of a surgical tracheotomy could have saved him.

Surveying results of the melee and the sobbing girl, Josh wondered what had happened to Ross in all this confusion. Suspecting the worst, his heart turned cold. He looked down at the dead man. The remorse he had felt, now gone.

Josh gathered up the two knives, being careful to use his handkerchief to touch only the blades, and put them on a nearby table out of the reach of the unconscious man.

The girl's crying had slowed somewhat. Josh drew close to her. She looked up at him, her eyes at first soft and then they slammed open with new fear. "Oh God, where's Daddy?"

Chapter Six

Puzzled, Josh looked at her, and said, "I don't know." He shifted his head around the room. "Where was he?"

She sucked in a few halting breaths and tried again to gain control. "I think they must have done something to him." Her face pinched in anguish. "I was back here, and I heard a noise out in the store. When I started to go out and check on Daddy, they came crashing through the door."

"Wait a minute," Josh interrupted, "You mean Ross? He's your dad?" He jerked his head as if to look for Ross. "Where is he?"

"Yes, Daddy," Panic crept into her voice. "I don't know. He was out in the store."

"Call the Sheriff's office, now. And tell them what happened here. I'll go check on Ross."

Before he left the room he jerked the electric cord out of a nearby lamp and bound the hands and feet of the outlaw with the broken collar bone. When he jerked the cord tight, the man came to. He cried out in pain, followed by string of obscenities.

Josh went cautiously out into the general store. It didn't take long to locate Ross behind the counter. His heart sank. He checked for vital signs, but the pool of blood and Ross' color told him he was dead. He remained kneeling beside his friend as his mind flooded with memories of similar scenes, mixed with memories of Ross. Anger welled inside him. He wondered how he was going to tell the girl. "God damn it", he cursed.

Josh composed himself for the ordeal of telling the girl. He dreaded the task.

When he thought his face looked neutral, he returned to the living quarters, but she gasped the minute she saw him.

"No!" she cried. "Oh no. Please not now." She buried her face in her hands.

Josh looked at his feet, unable to say anything. His heart felt like a block of ice in his chest. The woman sank back into the couch and sobbed. She then launched into a piercing scream that trailed off to a fluctuating mournful wail. Suddenly she leaped from the couch and made for the door screaming, "Daddy!"

Josh grabbed her as she went by, clutched her to his chest, and said softly, "No, you don't want to go out there."

She struggled but after a while her shoulders sagged. They sat back down and Josh continued to hug her to his chest, rocking gently while she wept. He was thankful that she had pulled a sweatshirt over her bare chest while he was in the store.

Between sobs she managed, "Is... He..."

Josh didn't let her finish. "Yes."

"Are... you sure?"

He didn't want to answer, so he just nodded.

Her agonized howl trailed off into a series of sobs. She continued to cry softly with intermittent wails. After a time, she controlled her breathing and dabbed her reddened eyes with a tissue.

She sat silent for several moments, a bland defeated look on her face. Josh noticed tension ease back into her body. She glared at the bound biker and said, "He told me he'd kill me if I screamed."

Josh watched her face transform from forlorn helplessness to rage. Jolene jerked upright, and in one swift movement snatched a small candy bowl from the end table, and flung it at the tied- up biker. Her aim was fairly true, missing his head by inches. He yelped when the bowl hit his shoulder, glanced against the wall and broke.

Josh touched her arm. "I know how you feel, but that won't do any good."

"I know, but it felt good for a minute." Eyes squinted; she continued to stare at the thug.

Taking a deep breath, she turned back to Josh. "I'm sorry, I didn't thank you for coming in when you did. They would have killed me. Or worse," she added. Her face again registered fear and hurt. She sucked in a few jerking breaths. When she had calmed herself somewhat, she said, "Who are you, anyway?"

"Name's Grant. Josh Grant. I'm a friend of your dad. I just don't get in here very often for supplies. I knew he had a daughter, but I thought you lived in Seattle or some other big city."

"I do — I did," she paused. "It must be a long time since you've been here. I've been back for a couple of months now. My name is Jolene."

"Yeah, I remember now. Ross told me about you." Josh paused, his memory jogged to some specific conversations with Ross. His mind flashed to the possibility of other victims. He sprang to his feet. "Where's your husband?"

"Husband?" Her brows furrowed. "Oh, we're... ah... divorced." She looked at her hands but offered no more.

Josh's shoulders relaxed. "Sorry. Ross told me you were married... I didn't mean to pry."

There was a momentary lull in conversation. Jolene started to nestle back into his chest, but the instant her head touched his body Josh felt her stiffen and jerk herself back upright again.

"It's okay," he said, sensing her embarrassment. "You've been through a lot."

She remained quiet for a while then said, "Why would they do this? We didn't do anything to them. Who are they?" She started to softly cry again.

Josh put his arm around her shoulders. "I don't know who they are, but I sure know the type. I recognized their colors."

"Colors?" She had a confused look on her upturned face.

"Colors," he repeated. "That's the identifying marks of a motorcycle gang. This one is spread throughout the Midwest. They're called the Outlaws. I don't know how the hell they got all the way out here, but I know this is typical of how they operate."

She sucked in a breath. "I was so afraid..." she faltered, and looked down.

Josh tried to ease her fear, "Look, I don't think they targeted you. Usually they're just opportunists and probably didn't have a particular plan in mind." At least I hope not, he thought.

His mind turned to what he remembered about the Outlaws and their methods of operation. "His kind," Josh nodded his head toward the tied up biker, "are a different breed of people. They have no feelings for anyone other than their biker brothers."

"Fuck you!" the biker growled.

Josh ignored him, but Jolene jerked involuntarily.

Josh continued, "They're just lowlifes with no care for the rest of humanity." He paused again as his mind kicked into gear. "They usually travel in larger groups though..."

Josh felt the muscles in his back tense. He gently eased Jolene from his shoulder and rose. His mind abruptly changed focus. Two of the gang members had escaped. The fear and alertness returned. The thought of more being in town set his danger sensors off. He knew the gang would be more heavily armed than these four had been, especially if they were warned. He looked around the room.

"Does Ross keep a gun around here?" he asked, without looking at her.

"Why?" she started, and when Josh looked at her, a new fear registered in her eyes. "Do you think they'll come back?" her voice rose.

Josh saw the growing concern on her face. "No, probably not," He tried to sound confident. "But there'll be a lot more members in the gang, and if they get reinforced... Well... Do you have a gun?"

"Daddy has a couple of shotguns in his closet and a couple of rifles too."

"Get me a shotgun and some shells if you can find any." Josh glared at the tied-up man. "And shoot him," pointing to the downed outlaw, "if he moves or says anything else. Okay? I'm going to check outside."

"Oh, I will," she said, staring intently at the man.

When Jolene went into the bedroom, Josh thought of interrogating the biker but knew he would get nothing from him. Instead he checked the rear windows to see if he could spot anything. Nothing out of the ordinary. He walked back to the store, retrieved his hat and looked cautiously out the front. The parking lot and street all clear, except for his team and wagon. He slowly walked outside, scanning all directions.

"Bo, come!" He shouted.

The big retriever ran to his side and licked his hand.

With Bo at his side, Josh slowly rounded the rear corner of the store where he saw a large dumpster. Behind that, sat two Harley choppers. Between glances at the woods beyond, he rummaged through the saddle bags. He found a snub-nosed Smith and Wesson thirty-eight revolver in one, and a Star twenty-two semi-auto along with a bag of white powdery substance in the other. They must have felt confident they wouldn't need their weapons, he thought.

He picked the guns up by the checkered grips and tucked each into his belt. He might need them if the Sheriff didn't get here soon.

Josh and Bo checked the rest of the surrounding property but saw nothing out of the ordinary. As Josh turned the final corner of the building, he heard a piercing scream from inside. His heart pounded as he bolted for the front door. Had he missed one of them? Had the tied one gotten free? Damn, he should have checked the other rooms.

Running full speed through the open door, he almost missed Jolene kneeling at the end of the counter by the body of her father. The agony of her grief-stricken sobs tore at Josh's heart.

Gently he grasped her shoulders and urged her up. "You don't want to do this, Jolene."

"But Daddy... Oh, my God... How could they?"

"Come on, let's go back inside."

She started sobbing again as Josh led her back into the apartment.

Josh settled Jolene back on the couch and sat next to her trying to comfort her, but knowing his efforts did little good.

Josh saw an over and under double barrel shotgun leaning against the wall and a box of twelve gauge shells on the end table.

After a long cry into the crook of her arm resting on the back of the couch, she sat up and tried to compose herself. She looked at Josh. He saw anguish on her face and in her eyes. Finally she said, "Where were you?" Her voice had a touch of fear and relief at the same time.

"Checking outside," he replied. "It looks clear."

Bo ambled to the couch and sat at Jolene's feet looking at her with a cocked head.

Jolene jerked slightly, and her eyes widened in surprise when she saw the dog.

Josh said, "This is my dog, Bo. He was outside. I hope you don't mind if he comes in."

"No, of course not," she said, bending over to pet the dog. Bo nuzzled closer, somehow sensing her need.

After a moment Jolene looked up and said, "I called the Sheriff, and then I just couldn't stand it so I went out to the store and..."

Her face twisted again, but she managed to stifle the emotions by taking a deep breath. "They said they'd come right out."

"Okay good. I know it's a big county, but I sure wish they'd hurry," Josh said, hoping to keep her mind off her father.

Chapter Seven

The sound of a vehicle skidding to a stop in the gravel parking area brought Josh to full alert. He arose from the couch and grabbed the shotgun. Jolene sprang up from petting Bo, and jerked her head back and forth as if looking for a place to hide or run. Bo growled.

Josh slipped two shells into the shotgun breach, slammed the barrels shut, and pushed the safety button off as he stepped in front of Jolene. She grabbed the back of his shirt and held on.

A moment later a voice called out from the store, "Sheriff's office! Anybody here?"

Josh felt his neck and shoulders relax as the tension waned. Jolene expelled a loud sigh, and Bo wagged his tail. Josh clicked the shotgun safety on, and leaned the weapon against the wall. He swung the door farther open and called out, "We're back here."

"Did you folks call?" the approaching deputy asked.

"Yeah," Josh answered. When the deputy stepped into the room, Josh said, "You'd better get some assistance here deputy. I'm afraid you've got a major crime scene on your hands."

The deputy looked around the room. His eyes widened and he jerked back slightly when he saw the two bodies, one tied up the other obviously not moving. His hand reflexively dropped near his holstered gun and his eyes narrowed. "What the hell happened here?"

Josh knew the look. "There's more," he said offhandedly. He felt a minor satisfaction being the one knowing what had happened for a change. He'd been in the deputy's shoes and knew the deputy would have to wait for the information to unfold at its own speed.

Josh identified himself as a retired Detroit cop, and quickly rattled off the bare essentials of the crime. He waited while the deputy called for assistance on his portable radio. When he signed off with the dispatcher, the deputy looked at Jolene and asked, "How'd they get in?"

"The apartment door wasn't locked," Jolene said. "They were in the store and they just burst in here and grabbed me." Tears welled in her eyes.

Before the Deputy could ask another question, Josh asked, "Jolene, would you please get Bo a drink of water? He hasn't had any since we left home. I'll fill the deputy in until you get back."

"Oh, of course," She wiped her eyes and started toward the kitchen. "Come on Bo." Josh gave a slight hand signal, and the dog followed Jolene.

After she entered the kitchen, Josh lowered his voice. "I didn't want her to think any more than she has to about this, but there's more. Come with me."

He led the Caribou County lawman out into the store to show him Ross's body, being sure to point out the blood spots on the old wooden floor and the drag marks from Ross's boots. They surveyed the scene as Josh supplied more details of the crime from his perspective. The deputy jotted notes in his book.

When he finished the details Josh said, "Look, I know you have to question the girl, but try to go easy, okay? She's holding up real well under the circumstances, but she's in a tough spot, you know?"

The deputy seemed to take offense at first, then softened and said, "Yeah, I know the drill. I'll go easy."

They returned to the apartment and found Jolene sitting on the couch petting Bo. New tears slid down her cheeks. The deputy sat down beside her and softly asked if she could tell him what happened from the beginning.

She told her story, action by action, with precise details that impressed Josh. When she stopped a few times to suck in shaky breaths, the deputy gently asked questions to put her back on track. Josh was pleased by the deputy's manner.

"Which one actually attacked you?" the deputy asked.

"That one." Jolene nodded toward the tied up biker. He put a knife to my throat and told me he would cut my head off if I made a sound. It was so quick… He cut my sweater with the knife and took it off and my bra too. They were all making obscene jokes and gestures… They said the most horrible things they were going to do to me…" She paused and her breath came in small jerks. "They laughed telling each other what they were going to do. They said they would pass me around…" She lowered her face to her hands. The deputy waited in silence. Josh laid his hand on her shoulder.

She looked up at Josh and continued, "Then he came in and… It all happened so fast. I was so scared. He could have just left, but he didn't. And they had knives." She glanced at Josh. "He could have been killed."

She paused for a breath. "I think I might have blacked out for a moment or had my eyes closed, because I didn't see all that happened. But I did see two of them run out the door, and I heard the motorcycles."

The deputy turned to Josh. "Do you know which way the ones who got away went?"

"Don't know," Josh said. "They ran back out through the store. We heard the hogs roar away, but I never saw them. I was a little busy in here." The deputy nodded. "It's a good thing that you have more troops coming." Josh continued. "If I know the Outlaws, they could be on their way back here with the whole gang. These guys seldom travel in small groups."

"Oh, I wouldn't worry too much about them," the deputy said. "We'll round them up soon enough."

Josh didn't say anything, but he hoped the deputy's overconfidence wasn't shared by the entire Caribou County Sheriff Department. If it were, they'd all be in trouble.

"By the way," Josh said, "there are a couple of bikes out behind the dumpster. They must belong to these two. I found these weapons and a bag of dope in the saddlebags." He pulled the two guns from under his shirt and handed them to the deputy.

"You moved them? I thought you were a cop." The deputy sounded incredulous.

"At the time, I thought I might need them, and I sure didn't want the others to come back and have more guns than they already have."

The deputy seemed to think that over. "Yeah, I guess I would have too."

For the next three hours the deputy, a detective, and an evidence technician perfunctorily performed their duties processing the crime scene and periodically asking questions. A coroner's wagon came and hauled the dead biker and Ross to the morgue and another deputy took the prisoner.

Josh and Jolene sat at the kitchen table to stay out of the way of the officers. He tried to steer the conversation away from the event, but Jolene had questions about what would happen next.

"What will they do with Daddy?"

"They'll take him to the coroner for an autopsy, then they'll release him to a funeral director of your choice."

"Oh." She hung her head staring at her hands in silence. After a moment, she started talking softly as though Josh weren't there. "It's just not fair. Not now. We were both getting better. And now what'll I do? Nobody's left." Her tone filled with defeat. She wept, sucking in small breaths.

Josh pulled her against his shoulder and whispered, "You'll make it. I know it's rough, but you'll make it. You'll see."

After a long silence, she took a deep breath and asked, "Do you really think the others will come back?"

"No, probably not now that the cops have showed up," Josh said, trying to allay her fears. But his mind thought differently. That old nagging fear came back. He knew the Outlaws thrived on ruthless vengeance

.

* * * *

"Well, that about wraps it up here folks," the detective sergeant said. "We have your statements, but I'm sure the county prosecutor will be contacting you about your testimony,"

"Did the deputy tell you I only have a post office box here, and that I only get in to check it about four times a year?" Josh asked.

The sergeant shuffled through his notes trying to find that information, and finding nothing said, "Don't you have a phone?"

"No," Josh answered. "I live up in the mountains. There's sure no land lines there."

"How about a cell phone?"

"I had a cell when I first came here, but that didn't work in the mountains. If you can give me a time and date, I'll come down, but otherwise I'm hard to find."

The sergeant looked at Josh, a dumbfounded expression frozen on his face. His upper lip curled and his mouth opened as if to say, huh?

"Look," Josh started to explain, "I've got a CB radio I use to call Ross once in a while for special supplies or equipment, when I can get through, but it doesn't work all that well either. I'll try to keep it on and monitor channel fifteen. Maybe we'll get lucky and the signal will get through."

The sergeant looked at him as if he were an alien. "Is that your wagon out front?"

"Yes."

"You don't have a car?"

Josh sighed. "No. I don't have a car. It would be useless."

"We could send a car for you."

"Listen, I don't mean to be rude, but you guys haven't been listening. I live out in the sticks. The only way to get there is by horse or on foot for the last half, and it's at least three more hours from there. You could get there with an ATV or maybe a jeep, but you'd have to know exactly where you're going. There are a lot of switch backs and side trails," Josh said. Then pausing… "There is a bald hill on the other side of my lake where a helicopter could land, but that would take a while to find without me to guide you."

The sergeant's brow furrowed and his lip curled again, "Why the hell do you want to live that far out?"

"Long story," Josh said, and then added, "Look; I'll stay in town tonight. I can sleep in my wagon, and Jolene might need some help around here anyway, so if you can get the prosecutor to give a date and time and let me know tomorrow, I'll come back in then to meet with him, or for the trial, whatever. Okay?"

"Well, we don't have much of a choice now, do we?" He turned and followed the last evidence technician out to the parking lot.

Josh and Jolene followed to the end of the parking lot and watched the line of sheriff vehicles wind down the short street and onto the state highway. They stared after the cars for a while until they disappeared.

Josh scanned the tree line along the road.

Chapter Eight

Josh watched Jolene as she stared toward the highway. Her face blank, but Josh saw empty hopelessness in her eyes. He gently asked, "You going to be okay?"

Her head twitched, and her eyes focused back to him. She said, "Oh... Well, I guess so. I just don't know what I'm going to do." She looked back toward the highway.

"You look a little worried. Want to talk about it?" He took her arm at the elbow and turned her toward the store.

"More than a little," Jolene said. A deep breath preceded, "My head's in a jumble. Whenever I think about things, I get all shaky inside. I get so scared, and then I get so mad." She raked her hair over her right ear. "One minute I want to cry, and the next I want to run away. But there's nowhere to go. And crying just makes me think of Dad... And those men might come back and..." She stopped and turned to Josh.

"Damn it," she stomped her foot. "I'm not like this. I deal with things..." she faltered. "But I don't know how to deal with this." She lowered her face to her hands.

Josh put his hand on her shoulder. He couldn't relieve her anguish, so he didn't say anything. Her face held a defeated look. He again gently urged her toward the store.

Jolene took a deep breath and said, "Things like this only happen in movies. It's so surreal."

Josh patted her shoulder, "It'll get better, you'll see. It's going to take a while, but you'll get a handle on things. For now you're safe, and that's all that matters."

"No it's not. Nothing makes any sense."

"I know, Jo."

She stopped. Her breath abruptly changed to a series of small jerks, and new tears appeared in her eye. She looked up at him with sad eyes and compressed lips, obviously in despair, and softly said, "Daddy always called me Jo."

Josh's shoulders sagged. "I'm sorry..."

She looked at him, sighed, and then took another deep breath with her eyes closed. "It's okay," she finally said, opening her eyes, "I can't fall apart every time I'm reminded…"

"You're doing fine under the circumstances. Most people couldn't cope with what you've been through today."

Josh put his arms around her shoulders. She leaned into him as they trudged up the steps to the general store in silence.

Once inside, Jolene seemed more composed. She turned to Josh and said, "By the way, I heard you tell the deputy you would stay in your wagon tonight. That is not going to happen. We have a spare room, and I won't take no for an answer." She looked at him. "Besides, I don't think I could stand being here all alone right now."

Josh gave a slight nod and touched the brim of his hat. He allowed himself a hint of a resigned smile. "Why thank you, ma'am. I wasn't looking forward to waking up covered with dew, but I don't want to put you out."

"Don't be silly."

"Okay, I've actually stayed here with Ross a few times before." He saw her face twitch. He realized he shouldn't have reminded her of her father again.

She took a breath. "Good, it's settled then."

They turned and walked slowly back to the apartment. "You hungry?" she asked when they entered the living quarters.

"Well, I packed some sandwiches and dried fruit for the trip but most of that's gone." He looked at the lowering sun through the window. "Yeah, I could eat something, but I know there's no restaurant in this one-horse town."

"Again — no debate. I'll rustle us up something. I'm not known to be a great cook, but I can make something hot. It might help take my mind off of… things." She took another of those cleansing breaths. "You make yourself at home and I'll see what I can find in the kitchen."

Josh smiled. While Jolene busied herself in the kitchen, he went back into the general store. He located the supply closet in the rear and grabbed a mop and bucket. Using the outside spigot, he filled the bucket and set about mopping up the blood behind the counter. He didn't want Jolene to have to endure that job.

Finished with that chore, Josh moved outside to his wagon and unhitched the team. He led the horses to the large open field at the rear of the store and hobbled them so they could graze.

Back in the store, he found a stack of boxes with a handwritten bill on top. 'GRANT' printed in Ross' bold printing stared back at him. Josh sighed. There were several cardboard boxes and four fifty pound bags of oats. How far ahead had Ross packed up his supplies? He usually didn't know exactly when Josh was coming to town, but he knew the basics of his order. Again Josh hung his head; his mind whirled with thoughts of his friend. He absently walked the aisles picking out items other than the staples he knew would be in the taped boxes. He put these items with the other supplies.

When he finally returned to the living area he called out, "Can I help with anything?"

"Can you cook?" asked Jolene.

"Better than Beau."

"No," she said. "I've got it under control. How do you take your coffee?"

"Black."

"Coming right up."

Jolene set the cup on the table. "I made a casserole. I hope that's okay. It's in the oven. It'll be ready in half an hour."

"Of course it's okay," Josh stared at his coffee. "It's a lot better than okay. Sounds great."

"I have to take a shower," she continued. "I haven't felt clean since those animals touched me." Her arms and shoulders gave a slight shiver.

"Don't worry about me," Josh said. "I know where to find something to read."

She turned to go to her room, and Josh went to the bookshelves in the rear corner next to the back door. He surveyed the books as his mind turned to Ross. Ross had been so well organized and very particular in his selection of books. Josh perused the alphabetized collection as he had during prior visits. Ross had all of the classics in hardback as well as a complete section of Louis L'Amour paperbacks. He ran his fingers along the books.

On a lower shelf he noticed a scattering of paperback novels he hadn't previously seen. He suspected they belonged to Jolene. He grinned, thinking how Ross would scoff at the selection of modern fiction. He and Ross had often traded books since their tastes were similar. On a whim, he selected a new hardback by Barbara Kingsolver.

On his way back to the table, Josh opened the door to Ross' bedroom where he would sleep and turned on the light. He looked around the room. The wall facing the foot of the bed was filled with framed pictures of Jolene. Toddler Jolene in a tutu, adolescent Jolene on a horse, Jolene the cheerleader, Jolene in a wedding gown next to Ross. No wonder he had never seen a picture of her. They were all in Ross' room.

He returned to the table and opened the book, but he couldn't stay focused on the words. His mind flitted back and forth through the recent events, and then to dangerous possibilities of the future.

The group's name, Outlaws, sure fit their behavior. His last encounter with the group back in Detroit had been at a biker funeral. One of the Detroit chapter members had died in a crash, and members from other chapters around the country had gathered for the traditional grave urination ceremony. It was a week of drunken parties, gambling, and fighting.

At one point in his stakeout Josh had watched as a group from Canada auctioned off one of their women so they could get enough gas money to return home. She had stood proudly naked and encouraged the bidders with obscene gyrations and remarks.

Hearing the shower running triggered thoughts of Jolene's naked breasts. He tried to banish the pictures from his head, but his mind kept re-entering the room where he'd first seen her. *Topless. God have I always been so coarse, or just been too long in the woods alone?*

* * * *

"What will you do now?" Josh asked over his second cup of coffee after they'd finished eating.

"I don't really know. I have nowhere to go but here, but I don't want to stay here either. I couldn't leave now even if I wanted to."

"Don't you have any family around here, or someone you could stay with?" Josh couldn't remember Ross ever talking about other family members.

"No. They're all gone." She looked away. "I'll be all right."

"I'm still worried about the motorcycle gang," Josh said, thinking out loud. "It's not their style to just let something like this lie. They'll want to avenge their fallen brother."

"They wouldn't come back knowing the Sheriff is looking for them would they?"

"Honey, they eat small departments like that for breakfast. Hell, they outnumber and outgun most county sheriff departments. It's only a matter of time. If they're stupid, it could be quick. If they're smart, they'll wait until after the trial. That way they can try to get the one arrested off on some technicality. They wouldn't want to draw any attention or criticism until after the trial." Josh tried to work it out as he spoke.

"But the Sheriff will arrest the ones who got away and probably the others too, won't he?"

"No. First off, the ones who got away are long gone from these parts and won't be seen until it's all over. As for the others, as far as the law is concerned there's no evidence the rest of the gang even knew of this attack. Until the others violate a law there's nothing the local Sheriff can do."

Josh continued, "My advice to you would be to find someplace where you can start over as soon as you can."

Her brow furrowed. Uh oh, he'd caused her more anguish, so Josh quickly tried to allay her fears. "Look, I don't think they'll spend much time looking for you. They won't have any vendetta against you."

"Well, you keep saying they'll be back. What do they want?"

"Me. I killed their brother."

Chapter Nine

Outlaw Headquarters

"What in the Fuck's wrong with you idiots?" the leader of the Outlaws Idaho Falls chapter screamed at the two returning members, after they told him what had happened in Platte Junction. "Why the hell would you try to pull off such a stupid stunt as that? We can't afford to draw attention. Drugs are our business. Not petty rip offs. At least Jake should have known better."

"But Snake," the smaller biker, Frank said, "that old man was going after Jake and he had to defend himself."

"Oh, bullshit! Jake's almost big as me, and mean as a badger. An old man, Christ. And you guys just had to kill him?"

"We didn't kill him, Snake. Jake did," Frank offered. "Then once he did it... Well, we just figured we might as well get something out of it."

"You sure got something out of it, didn't you? Hell, there couldn't have been more than fifty bucks in the till. Now we got cops to worry about. And all you assholes if full colors, Christ!"

"Oh yeah there was, Snake. There was like eighty bucks," the squat biker with a beard responded.

Snake glared at Toad, contemplating whether to kill him or not. "You're actually pleased about that. You asshole. Now we've got ourselves a big problem. Jake and Pete are either in jail, hospital, or dead. How could you two just up and leave two downed brothers?"

"But Snake," Frank interjected. "That other guy was good – real good, and he had this big stick..."

"And a big mean dog," Toad added.

"Oh, big stick, my ass, and a dog, fuck!" Snake let them see his disgust. "Where the hell was your guns?"

"Uh… with the bikes," Frank murmured. They both looked at their boots. "We just went in for some beer. Then things went bad. Me and Toad knew we had to get out of there before they called the sheriff. We couldn't go back in, Snake."

"You two motherfuckers make me sick. I don't know why I put up with you. Jake and his dope's bad enough, but you two…" Snake shook his head. They were stupid, but they were sworn brothers.

"Look Snake, we were all pretty high, especially Jake, and once we found the girl… well he just had to have some fun with her."

"You guys… just get the fuck out of my face. I've got to figure something out."

* * * *

The next day's newspaper confirmed Snake's fears. Pete dead, and Jake in jail. No chance they could break him out. Snake knew he could call on the Chapter's lawyers. There was always a chance they could get Jake off on a technicality, but of course, that would all take time. Meanwhile, they had to do whatever they could to eliminate witnesses and at the same time avenge the brotherhood. They couldn't just let this pass. Snake mulled over several possible plans. He finally decided the two idiots needed to redeem themselves.

Snake yelled out into the clubhouse for someone to find Toad and Frank. He had a mission for those assholes. Maybe he'd get lucky and they'd get themselves killed.

Chapter Ten

"If it's you they want, Josh, what'll you do?" Jolene asked, her face pinched with concern. Josh rose from his chair and went to the stove for the coffee pot.

"Oh, after the trial I won't be too worried. You heard me tell the deputy where I live. They'll have a tough time finding me, and since there isn't much excitement around these parts, they won't spend a long time. Besides, up in the high country they'd be out of their element." Josh poured more coffee in each cup, and returned the pot to the stove.

"Just where do you live anyway?"

Josh raised his brows. "Do you know where Long Run Road is, off of Highway Thirty, about five miles north of here?"

"Yeah, but that's a dead end road. Daddy and I used to hunt up there."

"Really?" He looked at her and smiled. "Well then, "almost to the dead end of that road, there's several old logging trails leading up into the mountains. Mine goes off right after a big lone cottonwood tree. It's heavy woods and brush and hard to see. Each trail splits off a few times, and some of them just peter out into nothing. After a few miles up and down my road there's a plateau valley. I built my cabin in that valley near a lake. It's hard to find unless you know what to look for."

"I think I saw that lake once from the top of another mountain when we were deer hunting."

"Deer hunting, huh?"

"Don't look so surprised. Out here, girls hunt too."

Josh smiled and held up his hands. "Guilty as charged."

"And you like living that far away from civilization?" Jolene asked, then added, "Not that this, she waved her arm, is really civilization."

"Yeah, I do. It's comfortable, and my only responsibilities are to my animals. My grandparents were Amish and I loved their lifestyle. So…" he shrugged his shoulders and arched his eyebrows.

After a pause, Josh asked, "What are you going to do about this place?"

"Well, I don't know for sure. Try to sell out maybe. If it weren't for Daddy, I never would've come back here, and I never intended to stay when I did."

"There are worse places," Josh said, while looking into his coffee cup.

"You didn't grow up here," Jolene said, and then paused. "Oh, it has its good points I guess, but it's so limited. No people, no jobs, no future, no stimulation."

Josh continued to stare into his cup. "It's beautiful, it's quiet, and it's clean."

"And it can be hard and unforgiving when it wants to." Her voice had a hard edge. But her expression softened when she looked at Josh. "I feel stupid. I should be the one defending my home — not you."

"It's my home too now," Josh said softly.

They sat quiet, each staring at their coffee mugs.

"It's none of my business," Josh started, "but why did you come back here if you don't like it?"

She paused. "Daddy needed me, after Momma died, and..." She looked away. Her face registered a pitiful faraway look.

"Sorry," Josh said. "I should just shut up. Keep saying the wrong things."

"No you're not saying the wrong things, it's okay. I just can't seem to stop thinking about... things. Besides, it's not a secret or anything. It's just a little painful to talk about."

"What?" Josh furrowed his brow.

"Well," she took a breath, and tucked a strand of hair behind her ear. "I left when I went off to college... My goodness, that seems like a long time ago. Anyway, I married Bradley right after that and we moved to Spokane. We were real busy with our careers and all. We only came back here for Christmases."

Jolene paused, "When I got divorced... I just couldn't stay in Spokane, so I quit my job and came back here. That was right after Momma died and I knew Daddy needed me as much as I needed him." She trailed off and looked around the room. A forlorn look had slowly worked its way back onto her face. Josh felt another pang of guilt.

"Any children?" Josh asked, looking at her eyes.

They softened. "No, Brad never wanted kids. If I'd have known that when we got married…" She looked away again.

After a long awkward pause, Josh changed directions, "By the way, Ross had my quarterly supplies all packed and ready to go. I found them out in the store. The bill's on top. I'll settle up whenever you're ready."

"Like hell you will. If it hadn't been for you I'd probably be dead, or worse, by now. I won't take a cent of your money."

"One thing has nothing to do with the other," Josh tried to argue, "I pay my way."

"I understand that, but please accept the supplies. It'll help me feel better." The corners of her mouth turned down and her eyes pleaded at him.

Josh appraised her for a moment. She's playing me, but it's cute. A smile crept to his lips. He didn't want to make her feel bad by refusing, but it went against his grain not to pay.

"Okay." he finally said. "But I owe you a dinner when we go to trial."

"You're on."

"After they let us know when to meet with the prosecutor, maybe we can stay in touch by CB," Josh suggested. "I'll leave my set on when I get back, and hope it gets a signal. I think my solar panels can handle that little drain, and I'll still need supplies."

"You have electricity way up there?"

"Well, I have two small solar panels on the roof. It's enough to run a refrigerator and a couple of lights, but that's about all. The CB signal is so weak most of the time though I don't know how much good it will do. I have a heck of a time getting out to Ross most of the time. Once in a while I can catch a skip from another CB'er, but at least I can try to stay in touch. Will you keep the CB on? Ross and I always used channel fifteen when we could get through."

"Well sure. We always have our set tuned on."

"Good, that way if the prosecution bogs down or there's a delay in the case, you can alert me. And besides, I'll feel better if I know you're doing okay."

"Thank you, but you've already fulfilled your knight in shining armor obligation. The Sheriff can watch over me now."

"Oh, I know I couldn't come running out of the hills in time to help in any emergency, but if anything happens, at least someone would know. And I'll feel better if I know you're okay. I'll try to call you in the evenings about sundown, okay?"

"Okay, I'll listen for your call."

Jolene started clearing the table. Josh said, "Do you have keys? I'll lock up the store."

"Sure. Thank you." She went to the table to look through the effects of her deceased father the deputy had placed there. She paused over the contents of her father's pockets. Josh's heart fell when she tenderly touched each item. He could only guess what was going through her mind. But the look on her face said it all. Josh wanted to go to her, but she had to deal with her loss one thing at a time.

She handed Josh the keys, and said softly, "I hate this place."

Josh grimaced, then nodded, took the keys and went out into the store. Bo rose from his resting spot on a throw rug and trotted after him.

Outside, Bo paused at the first bush while Josh looked around, alert for anything out of the ordinary. They went around the building then back to the front parking lot. Reentering the store, Josh locked and barred the door. He walked the aisles until he found a small bag of dry dog food. He and Bo returned to the living quarters. Josh locked that door behind him. They wandered into the kitchen where Jolene stood washing dishes.

"Do you have another bowl so I can feed Bo?" he asked.

"Right in that cabinet over your head," she turned and pointed.

"Thanks," Josh said, getting a bowl and setting it beside the water dish already on the floor. He filled the bowl with dry food and said, "Eat, Bo."

Bo sniffed the food and looked at Josh as if to say "What's this boss?" He was used to eating table scraps, or more likely equal portions of meat.

"It's food, Bo. Now eat." Josh pointed to the food.

Bo sniffed the dog food again and tentatively picked up one tiny morsel. He crunched the pellet, paused, and then attacked the food with renewed verve.

Josh turned to Jolene. "You wash – I'll dry."

"Thank you." It's universal law, you know." She handed him a towel.

* * * *

The next morning Josh checked his post office box near the front counter in the store. He placed his mail in one of the supply boxes and went outside. From the elevated stoop, Josh gazed around the village. Plenty of time to kill. "Bo," he called, "come." After a moment the big dog barked from behind the closed door. "Sorry boy, I forgot you can't open doors."

Opening the door Josh said, "Let's go check out the town." As they strolled, Josh counted twelve houses scattered along the main road and several farms scattered further out. A gas station sat at the other end of the main road that intersected the highway. Another small road went south about half way between the general store and the gas station. Ross had told him there were more farms and a small church along that road. At a leisurely walk the entire tour took less than half an hour.

When he returned, Jolene told him she had called a realtor in Soda Springs to arrange a meeting to talk about the sale of the general store. And she had also called a funeral director to arrange for the burial of her father as soon as the coroner released the body.

A sheriff's car pulled into the gravel parking area about 10:00am. Josh sat on the elevated porch of the store waiting for him. The double barrel shotgun leaned against the wall next to him.

"Morning," the deputy called as he got out of his squad car.

It was the same deputy that had first responded to their call for help yesterday. "Hi," Josh called back.

The deputy stepped onto the porch and stuck out his hand.

"I didn't really introduce myself yesterday in all the confusion, Mr. Grant. My name is Zimmer, Mark Zimmer."

Josh grasped the deputy's hand. "Glad to know you, Mark. Please, call me Josh."

"Okay, Josh. By the way, the prosecutor wants to know if you can be in his office in Soda Springs on Monday?"

"What time?"

"He said any time before five o'clock. Said he'd fit you in unless he's in court, and court's always over at three."

"Okay," Josh replied. "I can ride in here and catch a lift into town with Jolene, if she's supposed to go as well?"

"Yes sir, he wants her there too."

"Okay, I'll go in and see if that's alright with her."

Josh found Jolene sitting on the couch looking through a photo album. Her eyes were red and swollen. He sat down beside her. "You okay?"

"Yeah, I'm just holding on as long as I can. These are tears of joy for what we had as a family. My mom and dad were good people. This place was so full of love when I was growing up."

"I know, Jo," was all he could muster.

After a pause he said, "The deputy's here. He wants to know if we can come to Soda Springs on Monday."

"Yes. I have nothing else to do. Can you go too?"

"I told him I'd be there, providing I can ride in here and get a lift to town with you. It'd take me forever on horseback."

"Of course you can." She looked into his eyes. "And thanks again for understanding."

He squeezed her shoulder and got up to return to the deputy.

Zimmer stood on the front porch talking on his portable radio. Josh waited until he'd finished then said, "We'll be there, but it won't be until well after noon. It takes a while for me to get in here on horseback."

"Okay, thanks. I'll tell the prosecutor. By the way, you did a hell of a job here last night, Mr. Grant."

"A lotta luck," Josh said with a shrug.

Josh edged closer to the deputy. "Listen, you seem like a peace officer who takes his job seriously. Now I don't mean to insult you, but I know the Outlaws. They are serious shit. They'll try to avenge their dead brother. I don't think they'll do anything stupid until after the trial, but they might. I would really appreciate it if you could check up on the young lady here as often as you can. These guys mean business. And if you would spread the word to the other deputies working this area, it'd be a comfort"

"No problem," Deputy Zimmer said. "I know you big city boys think departments like ours don't know what we're doing, but we do. We work the same way you did only on a smaller scale."

"No. I didn't mean it that way. I've never felt like that. You know what you're doing. I just want to make sure you're aware of what you're dealing with here. I've dealt with the Outlaws before, and they're a bad group." Josh shrugged feeling frustrated that the deputy had misunderstood his intentions.

"Please just try to keep an eye on her, will you?"

"Sure will, this is my beat, and I'll check on her, but just so you understand, this is a big county. It runs about forty-six miles north and south, and sixty-four miles east and west. Soda Springs is about in the middle. We have four road deputies, plus a few state troopers on day shift to cover the entire county, and less on nights."

Josh shook his head. "God, how do you do it? When I was a patrol officer in Detroit, I worked the Eighth Precinct and it was a total of four point eight square miles. We had more than a hundred patrol officers plus supervisors and detectives in that one district."

Zimmer grinned. "Different worlds, huh?"

"Different and the same," Josh said with a shrug. "Please do what you can. I'm worried for the lady."

"You got it," the deputy said, as he opened his cruiser door and sat. "See you next week," he called, when the engine started.

Chapter Eleven

The long slow trip back to his cabin gave Josh ample opportunity to think. Scenarios continually flashed through his mind, all of them bad. Jolene's safety weighed heavier than he'd let her see. Hope the Sheriff's office takes the situation seriously. But even if they do, they've got other problems to deal with. Most departments have manpower issues and an overload of calls for service. They can't be everywhere.

The team plodded the trail with familiarity while Josh scanned the brush for any sign of ripened raspberries. Relaxed in the seat, Josh's thoughts turned again to Jolene, but this time not as a victim. Pictures of her bare breasts played through his mind. He smiled. Having thoughts about a woman that didn't invoke crippling memories of Ellen actually felt good for a change.

He looked at Bo, curled on the tarp near the front seat. "She'll be okay, don't you think, Bo?"

The dog raised his head and cocked it to one side. Josh smiled at him. "She's strong; she'll get a handle on her life."

I'm talking to the dog again, he silently admonished.

She is strong, but she sure doesn't deserve what she's had to endure recently. Hell nobody does. He tried to convince himself his worries for Jolene were no different than he would feel for any other human being in a similar situation.

But he worried about her from a purely selfish point of view as well. She intrigued him, and it felt good. He wanted to get to know her, and to do that she would have to stay alive.

Images of her floated through his mind. He tried to dismiss these personal thoughts, telling himself he was only lonely. Hell, he thought, someone like her wouldn't give me a second look if we had met under different circumstances. She's young and beautiful, and I'm a lot older than her. Still, he couldn't force the reflections out of his head.

Josh drove the team on auto pilot. He vividly recalled how fresh Jolene had looked when she emerged from her room after showering. He lingered on the sight of her radiant smile when she came into the living room. Her shimmering raven hair looked the same wet as it had dry. How could the color black reflect so much light?

Her mood had changed as well. For that moment, at least, the hot shower seemed to have cleansed her spirit as well as her body.

Portions of the conversations they had during dinner replayed pleasantly through his mind. But most of all, he felt the warm comfortableness of having her nestled into his shoulder, and how she smelled. He hadn't experienced the scent of a woman in a long time. Lately his world consisted mainly of animals and manure. He knew he shouldn't be dwelling on lascivious thoughts of Jolene, but he couldn't stop the rush.

The times when she had actually looked into his eyes, he'd been drawn into the incredible depth of her dark, almost black, eyes. Her long shiny black hair formed a soft and natural frame for her tanned face. She had a hint of Asian or Indian look about her. Josh seemed to remember Ross telling him once that his wife had some Shoshoni blood in her lineage. That could account for her look. He hadn't seen her wear any makeup, even after her shower. She had a natural glow that didn't seem to require makeup.

Thinking of her caused his mind to jump around the various scenarios involving the Outlaws; none of them were good. "Damn it!" he cursed, causing the horses to perk their ears and Bo to raise his head. Why is this happening? If they come back I won't be able to help her. I know it.

If they want her, they'll get her. And nothing I can do about it. He tried over and over to force his mind away from Jolene. He couldn't control the machine gun of wildly scattered thoughts and images in his head.

Abruptly his thoughts turned to Ellen. He sagged as he exhaled. Josh felt the guilt invading his body but couldn't stop it. He had never had romantic thoughts about any woman other than Ellen since they'd married.

He looked up as they crested a hill, surprised to see they were almost home. The trip had gone so quickly. He guided the team onto the trail leading into the thick woods that eventually opened into his valley. Clear of the woods, Josh stopped the team and gazed down at his farm.

Taking a deep breath of the sweet tasting mountain air, Josh stood in the wagon and scanned the picturesque scene. A narrow stand of tall straight pines stood off to the right of the lane behind the hay field midway to the cabin and continued all the way to the lake. Most of the logs for his cabin had come from that stand of pines. The clear emerald green lake lay about three hundred yards east of the barn.

On the other side of the lake, the next ridgeline rose majestically. The cabin and barn stood off to the left of the lane. The cornfield and garden paralleled the lane on his left. Sprouts of emerging corn dotted the gentle slope from the garden to the spot where he stopped.

In every direction varying shades of green dotted by brilliant colors of tiny wild flowers greeted his eyes. A smile eased onto his lips. The sloped roof of the chicken coop sat offset behind the cabin. In the distance, the riding horses, milk cow and bull grazed in the pasture behind the barn. This is how it's supposed to be. I take care of the animals and they sustain me.

The base of the mountain to the north closed off the pasture and cornfield. A mountain runoff stream ran parallel to the base of the mountain, hidden by the thick tree line. That stream cut through the far corner of the pasture providing water for the stock. Gazing at his domain, Josh felt comforting warmth ease into his body.

As if he didn't deserve the comfort, his thoughts abruptly jerked back to the frustrations of recent events. He flopped back onto the wagon seat. "Damn." How his life had changed in a blink. He wanted his boring life back. But then, Jolene… Couldn't put her plight out of his mind.

Josh took in a deep breath and exhaled slowly. He shook the reins and clicked the horses into motion again.

Bo jumped from the wagon and ran ahead. When Josh got to the barn, Bo had the chickens and barn cats worked into a frenzy. After unhooking the team Josh hung the harnesses. Then he set about the tasks of feeding stock and milking the overloaded cow. The barn door stood open so the animals were free to graze.

Inside the cabin he started a fire in the old Magic Chef wood-burning stove. The familiar smell of the cedar wood burning offered a pleasant feeling of home.

Drawing water from the reservoir on the back of the stove, Josh set the pot on the stove to heat for coffee, then set about making his supper. He went out to the smokehouse, attached to the barn, for a generous slice of smoked ham from last fall's wild hog kill before returning to the kitchen. From the root cellar he retrieved two potatoes and a small onion. He checked the jars of home-canned goods lining the shelves. Nothing else interested him, so he made do with a limited supper. He fed Bo a chunk of ham, along with some of the dry dog food he'd brought home.

After the dishes were put away, he tried to read, but again couldn't stay focused. What was happening to his well-organized life? Any time he wasn't busy with chores, his thoughts turned to the striking young woman he'd left alone and the uncertainty of her future. On one hand he relived the exciting and comfortable time with Jolene, and the next, horrifying thoughts of what might happen to her invaded his mind. He should have stayed with her – but he couldn't. He was needed here. He was taught at a young age to care for the animals. They needed feeding and milking every day.

Josh turned his mind inward and felt the tension that seemed to be a constant companion lately. He sprang from his chair, assumed a prone position on the floor, and began doing pushups. When he reached one hundred, he flipped to his back and knocked off a hundred crunches. Now the tension was muscular and not emotional. He took a cool shower and went to bed.

Chapter Twelve

Jolene buried her father on Sunday. The finality of the ceremony left her hollow.

The little country church on Range line Road held a scattering of local farmers and store customers. She stood next to the casket, shook hands and accepted hugs from well-wishers, her mind unable to focus on many of their words.

She heard the word closure mentioned. She knew well the rhetoric about closure, but she refused to buy into it. There's no such thing. How do you ever reach closure when someone you loved for a lifetime is just ripped from you, senselessly murdered by a pack of animals? If I could have only said goodbye, she thought.

People she hadn't seen in years filed by in a blur. She had no answers for their questions of what she would do now. She knew they meant well, but none of it helped. Her father was gone. And that was the only closure she would ever get.

She spent the night curled on her bed reliving her life through the eyes of innocent childhood. Helping her mom in the kitchen. Sharing a packed lunch in the woods with her dad. Where had it gone? No father, no mother, no one to love her, no one to love – just memories.

* * * *

On Monday morning Jolene showered and dressed by 9:00am. After a busy and emotional week, she had little to do for the rest of the day except to wait for the mysterious man who had rescued her.

"Josh." She said his name out loud, smiled, and shook her head. She rose from the old rocker and walked into the store for the umpteenth time, only to return a minute later. The wait seemed interminable.

She wondered why she was so apprehensive about his arrival. After all, she only wanted to get this ordeal over with and start a new life; it had nothing to do with him. She did worry about him though. She had tried to raise him on the CB several times but got no answer.

She had hired the young Hannedy boy from the village to watch the store when she wasn't there. Her dad had hired him many times to help stock and unload supplies. Through the week she had spent hours of fruitless thought trying to get a grip on her future. What could she do with her life now? Where would she eventually go?

Her week had been a sad void filled with little other than a blur of emotional thoughts. Thoughts of her failed marriage, the death of her father, and the terror every time she heard a sound that reminded her of motorcycles. Just the thought of the men who attacked her caused her heart to hammer and gave her chills. Living with that constant fear frayed her nerves.

At least this morning she had something to look forward to. The trip to Soda Springs to see the prosecutor would be a welcome break. Any activity not involving fear, sadness, or trauma would be a blessing at this point. As she sat on the porch gazing at the mountains on the horizon, images of the strange man who had rescued her invaded her mind.

"Josh," she said his name aloud again. After such a short time it almost felt like he was a friend. She allowed a smile to break through. What a strange yet comfortable thought. She let her mind dwell on her new friend.

He had seemed so sure of himself without any of the selfish ego she usually found with take-charge men. Normally she didn't like being taken charge of. Of course she had never been in a life or death situation before, and she sure hadn't minded Josh taking charge then.

Her mind turned to the gentleness of his touch when he held her and the softness in his eyes; those incredible light blue eyes.

She had also seen a deep sadness in those eyes. It was confusing, compared to the swift brutality of his attack on those men. The speed and grace with which he had moved amazed her. Yet he seemed like such a gentle man in every way.

The conversations, when not dealing with the crisis, had been pleasant and comfortable. Oh, he did have a tendency to over analyze every detail, but that was understandable. His kindness had helped her cope. She looked forward to seeing him again. He intrigued her.

As she thought of this she scoffed at herself. Only because I owe him my life — and he was Daddy's friend. Sitting in the warm morning sun, Jolene found herself comparing Josh to Bradley, her ex-husband. They were worlds apart. Bradley wasn't overweight by any stretch, but he had a soft look. All features kind of rounded. Polished and good looking sure, but... But what? Well, soft. His idea of casual never involved anything less than a sweater and sport coat. Happiness to Bradley was a rise in the stock market. Josh was more at home in faded jeans and flannel with Bo at his side. Bradley was dark and suave, while Josh was light and weathered... And hard as... whang leather. Jolene giggled remembering her dad's use of that phrase. What the hell is whang leather?

Why am I doing this? What a ridiculous train of thought. She continued the silent conversation with herself, amid mental pictures of Josh. Oh you silly girl, she thought, he wouldn't have the slightest interest in you if he hadn't been forced into the situation. No, I'm not really interested in him like that anyway. I've had it with men in my life. They can't be trusted, and I sure don't need the complication.

But he was interesting. And he did look good. He almost looked undernourished in a marathon-runner way, yet with those shoulders he certainly didn't look skinny, lean maybe, but judging by the way he filled out his jeans in back — not skinny. Jolene felt herself blush slightly and smiled.

His almost white blond hair and faded blue eyes set in weathered tan skin hinted at some age, but that didn't seem to equate when compared to his physical capabilities and fit body. The muscles in his arms were long and sinewy, the way they get from hard work, not from working out with weights. His hands, large, but so gentle.

She recalled how he had moved with such swift but brutal grace when needed, yet returned to a mellowed state almost immediately after the fight. She pondered that. Unusual man.

Chapter Thirteen

Riding Buck, his chestnut quarter horse, would cut Josh's travel time down considerably compared to the cumbersome wagon and team, but it still seemed like an eternity. His mind locked on the worst case scenario no matter how hard he tried to focus on the positive. Was she all right? Had the bikers come back? He shouldn't have left her, damn it. His frustration stemmed from the unknown. He had no way of knowing if anything had happened.

The guilt he felt all week weighed on his mind. He knew he had little choice. He had a responsibility to his animals. The girl had the town and the sheriff. No rationale outweighed the guilt he harbored.

Why hadn't she answered his radio calls? Damned radio! Damned mountains!

For the first time since choosing his present lifestyle, Josh reflected on the negative aspects of it. Living in isolation had helped him cope with his shattered life, but the minute he became involved in the outside world, the same old frustrations surfaced.

Once again he was powerless to protect anyone. He had failed to protect Ellen and Jimmy. And now he had left a defenseless girl at the mercy of the worst group of sub-humans he had ever known.

When he turned Buck from the highway onto the road leading to the general store, he realized he had been galloping his horse to a lather. Grandpa had reamed him once for doing that to the buggy horse. He slowed Buck to a walk and tried to calm himself.

Josh's thoughts turned to his grandfather's sage advice to worry only about the things you can control, and let the rest sort themselves out. This mantra, he had heard and repeated so many times during his life, along with the comforting thoughts of his grandfather, calmed him for a moment.

He stopped Buck at the far end of the parking lot near a grassy area and dismounted. He tethered the horse on a long lead to a low tree branch. Looking at the general store he felt relieved. No yellow crime scene tape.

He strode toward the store with an urgent step. His tension eased even more when saw Jolene step out of the store onto the porch, but that relief wasn't enough to totally eliminate the built up worry that had boiled all week.

She waved, and Josh paused exhaling a deep tense breath.

"You okay?" he asked a little sharply as he arrived at the bottom of the stoop.

"Yes," she answered. Her brows dropped a second before she continued, "I'm fine. How about you?"

"I've been better. I spent most of my time worrying about you. You didn't answer the CB when I called." He couldn't disguise the edge to his voice.

Jolene answered with a bite of her own. "Well I called you too and you didn't answer. And I've been a little busy making arrangements for this place, talking to realtors, and..." Her eyes welled on the verge of tears when she said, "And, I just buried Daddy yesterday."

Josh felt as if he had been punched in the stomach. How could he be so insensitive? Rushing up to her, he pulled her into his chest and patted her back. "I'm so sorry Jo. I had no idea. I was so worried about you, I didn't even consider what you must have been going through. I had no right to take my frustration out on you. I should have known..."

"Oh my God," he exclaimed. "I should have been here for the funeral. I didn't think they would release him this quickly." Josh's eyes pleaded, "Please forgive me, Jo."

After a moment, she stepped back. "Oh, I'm sorry too. The stress is just getting to me. When did you call?"

"It doesn't matter. That damned radio is useless. But I'm here now and you're okay. That's all that counts. I've been so worried about you." He wanted to say more about how sorry he was to have missed the funeral, and what a good friend Ross had been, but he didn't want her to focus on the painful memories of burying her father.

After an awkward silence, Jolene said, "That deputy stopped by a couple of times to check on me. He said you told him to."

Josh nodded. "Good."

"And I talked with the Hannedy's, up the road, about your horse," Jolene said. "They have a small farm and agreed to board him whenever you need it."

"That's great, Jo. I was a little worried about what to do with Buck. I could have hobbled him in your back field, but I would have worried. I really appreciate you thinking of that."

She smiled. "The Hannedy's son, Chad, has been working here at the store while I've been busy, and he may be interested in buying it if we can work out a land contract deal. He's here now. Would you like to meet him?"

"Sure."

Jolene turned and led the way into the store.

"Hey Chad, come here," she called. "I want you to meet someone."

When he appeared, wiping his hands on an apron, she said, "Chad, this is Josh Grant, the man I told you about."

"Josh this is Chad." she suppressed a small laugh. "The man I just told you about."

The two men smiled and shook hands.

Chad could have been a poster boy model for a rural America. He was almost as tall as Josh, but lighter of frame. In his late teens, he had close cut light hair and bright hazel eyes that highlighted his easy smile. He looked like an older version of Opie Taylor, freckles and all.

"Do you know the details of what happened here last week, Chad?" Josh abruptly asked.

"Yes, sir."

"You scared?"

"Well, no. I guess not."

"Well you should be. They'll be back."

"Josh," Jolene said. "Is that really necessary?"

"I just want him to be aware of the possibility."

"Do you know how to use a shotgun, Chad?"

"Sure."

"Well Ross keeps a double barrel in the closet, and I want you to get it and keep it behind the counter and with you at all times. If you hear or see any motorcycles, you call the Sheriff right away, and keep that gun with you all the time. You understand?"

"Yes sir." The boy looked more serious now.

"Josh…" Jolene plead again.

"Damn it, Jolene, I know these guys. They won't let it rest. They'll be back." He looked the boy up and down. Good strapping farm kid. Seems level headed. Didn't hesitate about the shotgun. Good.

"One other thing, Chad — keep that CB radio on. The deputy told me they monitor channel 9, and I'll stay in contact when I'm home, not that it'll do much good."

"Okay, I can handle that."

"We better be going, Josh. Soda Springs is almost an hour's drive," Jolene said.

"Okay, you lead the way to Hannedy's and I'll follow on Buck."

"You get that shotgun, Chad," he called back.

After Josh unsaddled Buck and released him into Hannedy's pasture, he walked back to Jolene's Jeep.

Peering over the top of the Jeep, Josh looked in both directions down the road. In the distance he heard highway traffic. All was peaceful, no motorcycles. Maybe he was wrong. Maybe those bikers had only been passing through. Maybe he worried too much. His team back in Detroit always kidded him about constantly worrying over the minor details. Sometimes they called him Momma, but never to his face.

He took a breath, relaxed, tossed his hat onto the back seat, and entered the car.

Chapter Fourteen

Outlaw headquarters

An old abandoned sawmill near the village of Conda served as the Outlaw's clubhouse. The huge two-story building sat on several acres abutted to wilderness. Between the rear tree line and the mill, a dirt race track had been gouged out of the hills. The ground floor remained as it had been when abandoned. A large open space with rusted pieces of machinery scattered about the scarred timbers and layers of sawdust heaped along the outer walls. Large piles of abandoned cut logs dotted the entrance to the property.

The gang's actual headquarters took up the top floor of the structure. The rear half of that level had been converted into a bunk house of sorts. Several cots lined the walls amid trash, strewn articles of clothing, odd motorcycle parts, and the ubiquitous beer cans. A potbellied stove stood in the middle of the room.

A large room in the center of the top floor served as a communal meeting room, complete with a television and sound system, an old pinball machine, two refrigerators, and a long bar along the outside wall. The large musty room contained haphazardly placed torn couches, stained lounge chairs, and several battered tables. Empty chip bags and beer cans littered the dirty floor.

In the front corner, near the stairway, the old mill office served as Snake's domain. Compared to the squalor in the community room and bunk house, Snake's office was relatively sterile. A phone and laptop computer rested atop a chipped and peeling wooden desk. A bunk behind the desk was actually made. In the corner opposite the door sat a lounge chair, small table and lamp.

Frank and Toad entered the office where Snake sat in the battered Lazy Boy reading an old copy of Biker World. "You wanted to see us Snake?" Frank asked.

"Yeah." Snake looked up, not even attempting to mask the disgust on his face. He had talked several times through the week with attorneys, waiting to hear if bail would be set — no such luck. They were going to hold Jake until the trial. Snake knew he had to do something before that.

"In case you guys haven't gotten the picture yet. Let me explain." Snake got up and paced. "We try not to do stupid shit like this. We make lots of money from protection, and drugs, but only if we fly under the radar. When we do stupid things, it draws attention from the cops. We don't want that, now do we?"

Frank and Toad hung their heads like school boys caught smoking.

"Now we have a problem we have to correct, and the only way to do that is to do something equally stupid. We have to eliminate the witnesses to get Jake off. We have to honor the brotherhood."

"So you guys gotta make this right." He paused considering the foolishness of that statement. This pair had proven their ineptness many times over. But he wasn't about to send another brother into harm's way when these two idiots were available.

"We got a brother in jail," he continued, "and the attorney tells me he'll have to cop a plea just to get life. We can't let that happen. If you two assholes hadn't run off..." Snake glared at them.

"Well, yeah, Snake, we wanna make it right," Frank offered. "You want us to go break him out?"

"Jesus Christ!" Snake screamed. "Do you really think you can just waltz into the county jail and break somebody out? What the fuck's wrong with you Frank?"

"Well, I ah... Jeez Snake, I just want to help Jake."

Snake looked toward the ceiling heavens and sighed. "Look, there's no way we can get to Jake, Okay? We have to eliminate the witnesses so he won't be convicted. Does that make sense to you?"

"Yeah, I guess so." Frank shuffled his feet.

"And don't forget, one of those witnesses killed Pete. I want that guy. You two are a part of this mess and I want you to fix it."

"Oh, yeah, sure. We can do that," Frank said.

Toad stood sullenly silent.

Snake didn't express his doubts.

Snake looked hard at them both for a long moment before speaking. "Tell me Frank," he started, "just how would you go about fixing our little problem?"

Frank paused, rolled his eyes up as if thinking and looked at Toad, who shrugged his shoulders. "Well," Frank began, "we'll just go back to that store and kill that girl." He nodded his head and pasted a satisfied grin on his face.

"Sure you will," Snake said. "And the guy?" He lowered his head, raised his brows, and held his palms up. "What about him?"

"Well, we'll kill him too."

"Just like that, huh?" Snakes eyes narrowed.

"Well, yeah, I guess," Frank stammered. "He probably lives in that little berg somewhere."

Toad picked at something hidden in his nose.

"How you gonna find him?" Snake asked.

"Uh," Frank hung his head. "I don't know."

"Okay," Snake said, shaking his head. "Enough of this shit. Now you two listen. I'll tell you exactly what you're gonna do." He waited to make sure he had their attention. "I want you to go and watch that store." He paused between each sentence. "You stay out of sight and keep your eyes open. And you wait for that guy to show up. And you keep a sharp lookout for any cops to come around. You got that so far?"

"Yeah, Snake," Frank mumbled.

Toad nodded.

"Okay, you watch. If the guy shows, you get them both. If he doesn't show in a couple of days, you get the girl. Now Frank, don't kill her unless the guy is there too. If you can't find him, I want to use the girl to get to him. I want that guy. You understand?"

"Sure, Snake."

"Boys don't fuck this up. I want that prick. And I want them both before Jake's trial. I'm letting you do this so you can redeem yourselves. If I have to get somebody else…" He let it trail off, watching for a sign that they got the message.

"Okay, Snake. Don't worry, we'll handle it," Frank said, then turned to Toad. "Come on Bro, let's go to work."

Toad rolled his eyes at Frank and sighed.

Chapter Fifteen

Josh hadn't been in a car for a while. Telephone poles whizzed by so fast, he felt disoriented. He glanced at the speedometer — only sixty. He tried to relax. As his mind adjusted to the speed, he realized they'd been traveling in complete silence. The only sound being the knobby off-road tires hissing on asphalt. The stillness thickened until, as if on cue, they both started to speak at once.

"What will hap…?"

"Where are you…?"

They laughed. "What were you going to say?" Josh asked.

"Oh, nothing really." Jolene shrugged. "Just making conversation. I wanted to ask if you know what to expect at the prosecutor's office."

"Yeah, I guess. He'll want to get our official statements of whatever we can testify to. It's all in the deputy's report, but he'll need to get it again from us."

"Why?"

"He'll need detailed information that a crime actually happened. Ross's death and your testimony of what they did to you, will establish that. It's known as the elements of the crime. He'll also offer hints about our testimony."

Josh glanced up at a red tail hawk floating motionless on a thermal, before adding, "And, of course he'll need evidence that the scum arrested actually did those crimes. That'll be harder for Ross's death, because there were no eye witnesses. Hopefully they have prints from the knife, and it won't be difficult to match the knife to the wound."

Josh focused on the trial process. "In the assault on you, your testimony along with what I saw, and your cut clothing will be enough. There'll also be an inquest into the death of the one I killed." He paused. "That one should be alright too, with our statements. There's no doubt it'll be self-defense with him having a knife. It all should be fairly routine."

"Maybe routine for you, but not for me," Jolene commented.

"They'll probably bypass the Grand Jury and file on information," Josh rambled on thinking of court procedures. "But the preliminary hearing has probably already taken place. That's just to see if they have enough to hold him for trial and to set bond."

"You mean they'll let him out on bail?" Fear crept into Jolene's voice.

"No, I don't think so. Or if they do, it'll be so high the Outlaws won't be able to raise it. This is a capital murder case, and they'll need a very good reason to grant bail."

"Oh, okay. I hope not," she said. "How long will it be before the trial?"

"Well, it should go a little quicker than most. The evidence in this case is pretty overwhelming, so the prosecutor will push for a quick trial, but it'll still take weeks — maybe months.

They both sat silent for a while. Then Josh asked, "Do you know where you're going after this is all over?"

"No. But I don't want to go back to Spokane. That's for sure, and that's the only other place I've ever lived. There are just too many bad memories there."

"What happened to make it so bad?"

Jolene remained silent.

Josh quickly said, "I'm sorry. I didn't mean to pry again. I guess old police interrogation habits are hard to break."

"No, it's all right," She said. She remained silent apparently thinking. "I probably need to talk about it." She paused, took a breath and plunged forward.

"I told you I was divorced." She grimaced. "I met Bradley in college — that was my husband." She paused. "We got married right after graduation. We were so young and inexperienced. We thought we were in love but..." She trailed off, then continued, "Anyway, short version, I eventually found out he had several affairs. That really hurt, and I just fell apart." She glanced out the window. "I thought that sort of thing only happened in the movies. We even went to counseling for a while. Stuck it out a little longer, but we'd just grown apart. When I found out he continued his latest affair while we were in counseling... Well..." She looked away.

"What an asshole," Josh blurted out, before thinking. He had seen so many of them on domestic violence calls. He reached over and touched her shoulder.

Josh saw an expression flash across her face he hadn't seen before. She looked as if she were in pain, but there was anger there as well. She took another deep breath. "I just couldn't live like that, so I left. There's nothing left in Spokane now except sadness and failure. I'll never go back there."

"I know the feeling," Josh said.

Jolene thought for a moment. "You know, I can't help but feel... well, even though it hurt at the time, a part of me was relieved. Married life didn't turn out to be the fairy tale I'd read in so many books or anything like Mom and Dad had."

Josh wanted to tell her it could be, but held back.

She looked at Josh and gave a resigned shrug. "It's funny how just a few short months at home with Dad made me feel so much more grown up — so whole again." After a pause, she went on. "Anyway," she shook her head as if to clear it. "my degree is in marketing, but there sure isn't much call for that in Platte Junction." Jolene stared at the road ahead. Josh couldn't interpret the distant look on her face.

They drove on in silence for a while as Josh silently chided himself for asking questions that made her dredge up sadness. He tried another tack. "You have any idea what you'll do about the store?"

"I just don't know. I've talked with a realtor, but it's not going to be a hot item on the market, and I can't do anything with it until Dad's estate is settled. Chad and I have had some conversations about it, and he might be interested, but I know neither he, nor his parents, can afford a major real estate purchase. They're just simple farmers." She shrugged and glanced out the side window.

"I don't think I want to keep it," she continued, "the memories are just too painful, but it looks like I'm going to be stuck here for a while. Settling Daddy's estate and it sound like this trial could take forever."

Josh didn't look forward to a long trial, but he found himself hoping she could find a way to stay at the store. Having her around would get him to town more often.

When they exited the highway and started into Soda Springs, Jolene's mood seemed to elevate. She pointed out buildings and stores with idle chit chat about each. Then she brightened even more. "Maybe I can find a job here." She remarked.

"Yeah," Josh said, "it's not a major city, but I'm sure there's some business here that could use your marketing skills. At least you'd still be in the area," he said before thinking.

He felt his face redden. Thankfully, he saw out the corner of his eye, she hadn't noticed or gave no sign if she had.

Jolene smiled as she wound through the streets. "The court house is right over there." She nodded. "Help me find a parking spot."

* * * *

The meeting with the prosecutor went about like Josh had described, and they were finished in less than two hours. The Prosecutor assured them that he would get an easy guilty verdict.

When they left the court house, Josh said, "I still owe you dinner. Are you hungry?"

"I could eat, but you sure don't owe me anything. I'll always owe you."

"Just doing my duty, Ma'am." He tipped his Stetson with a grin.

They found a steak house near the highway entrance and the hostess settled them into a table with a view of the parking lot.

"Tell me Josh," Jolene said, after the waitress left to get water and silverware, "What made you relocate clear out here in the middle of nowhere?"

"I traveled through here some years ago with my family. We were on our way to Yellowstone." Josh stared out the window. "I saw these mountains and thought they were the most beautiful I'd ever seen." He felt the soft smile stretch his lips. "I carried a mental picture, of a valley with a lake I saw early one morning from the highway, in my head for years after that."

"When I decided I had to get out of Detroit, this area seemed about as far away as I could get. The ideal place to start over. I spent a lot of time trying to locate that same spot when I first came out here. If the place where I settled isn't the same, it's awfully close."

"Why'd you have to get out of Detroit? Although I can certainly understand why someone would want to get out of Detroit."

"It's a long story, Jo."

She smiled. "We've got nothing but time, Josh."

A waitress brought water to the table and took their orders.

When the waitress left, Jolene looked at Josh with raised brows, waiting for his reply.

Josh took a breath of resignation. He wanted to tell her his story, but it hurt to dredge it all back up. Oh well, payback time, he thought.

He reluctantly began, "As you know, I was a Detroit cop, detective sergeant actually. Ellen and I married right after I graduated from the police academy. She finished her nursing degree a year later... We had a son, Jimmy..." Josh struggled for the condensed version.

"After I made detective, things started going sour. I was promoted to sergeant and work took more and more of my time." Josh felt his jaw tighten as he remembered. He struggled on, "I always felt as if I were fighting a losing battle. Drugs, crime, and violence were rampant in Detroit, as they are in most major cities, and I didn't make much of a dent in any of it." Josh paused as the waitress set their meals on the table.

They both started to eat; Josh hadn't realized how hungry he was. Jolene ate with gusto as well.

Between bites of steak and baked potatoes, Jolene asked, "So what happened that made you just quit?"

"Well as I said, I had less and less time with my family. It seemed like every time we planned something, I'd get a call out to investigate some crime and have to leave whatever birthday party, Cub Scout function, or soccer game, not to mention the times I was called out of bed in the middle of the night."

Josh forked a bite of salad, drank some water, and gathered his thoughts and courage. His voice took on a more somber tone as he continued.

"About four years ago now, it was Jimmy's tenth birthday. We had planned a big night out ending with a movie. Once again I had to work late because of a bank robbery that turned out to be a homicide of a retired cop, and I missed that special night with my family…"

He paused, trying to stem the emotion building in his chest before continuing, "Ellen and Jimmy went on without me as they usually did." Josh stared at his plate and paused again, taking in several shallow breaths. Jolene reached across the table and touched his hand.

Josh looked up. His face pinched in anguish, eyebrows almost touching and continued, "Later that night, I received word of a drug related drive-by shooting at the mall where Ellen and Jimmy had gone to a movie." Jolene sucked in a breath. Josh lowered his head and his voice. Breathing and talking became difficult. His voice cracking, he blurted out, "They were gunned down in the parking lot."

"Oh, no!" Jolene gasped. "Oh, Josh, I'm so sorry." Tears welled in her eyes.

Josh continued to stare blankly at the table. He wiped at his eyes with his napkin before continuing. "I'm learning to deal with it more each day." After a cleansing breath, he finally said, "But after that I just couldn't handle the stress of the job." His mind flitted to the drinking and the suicide attempt but he didn't want to dredge that up. "I couldn't function in that setting. Hell, I couldn't function in any setting for a while. I even visited the department shrink. He helped somewhat. But I eventually had to get out. So, here I am." He tried a lame smile.

They finished their meal in relative silence. Jolene excused herself to go the restroom while Josh paid the check. When she rejoined him they walked to the Jeep.

"Can you still drive?" Jolene asked.

Josh gave her a quizzical look. "Huh?

"Drive. Can you still drive? It's been a while hasn't it? I'm a little tired."

"Is the Pope still Baptist?" Josh opened his eyes wide and smiled.

Her brows dropped a second before she smiled. "Butt head." She tossed him the keys.

They both sat in silence as Josh familiarized himself with the Jeep's controls. He blankly stared ahead pensively for a moment thinking of the depressing stories they both had recently shared. Josh turned the key and said with a grin, "Hell of a first date, huh?"

She playfully slugged him on his shoulder.

* * * *

By the time they arrived back at the store the sun rested just atop the distant mountain peaks. The sky glowed with a soft peach hue over the greenery. Josh had to decide whether he wanted to make the trip home in the dark or wait until morning. He knew he could make it at night, he had done it before. But he had enjoyed human company lately and didn't want to give it up just yet.

"Isn't that sky gorgeous?" Josh stared out the Jeep windshield.

"It sure is." Jolene said. "Josh..." she paused, a pensive look on her face. "Do you have to go home tonight?" She bit her lower lip.

He looked at her momentarily stunned. She had read his mind. He quickly said, "No... I guess not."

Josh thought Jolene's face flushed. It could have been reflection from the sunset.

She followed up with a stammer, "I mean... Do you think you could stay here tonight? It'll be dark soon... I don't think you should ride at night." She looked at her feet, and then blurted out, "And I don't feel like being alone. Last week was bad enough, but I had things to keep me busy."

"Sure, Jo." Josh's spirit perked. "That would be great. I'm sure the animals will be all right for one night."

She smiled. "You keep referring to the animals. What all do you have out there in the hills?"

They got out of the car and strolled toward the store.

"Oh, not much, just chickens, a cow and bull, two draft horses, some barn cats, and another riding horse. But they all need fed and the cow needs milking almost daily."

"And don't forget Bo," she said with a smile.

"Oh, Bo's not an animal. He's my partner. He's watching the farm."

Jolene hip bumped him and chuckled.

When they entered the apartment, Jolene said, "Make yourself comfortable," as she angled toward the kitchen. Over her shoulder she added, "I'll put on some coffee."

After coffee, and a lackluster game of Scrabble, they settled onto the couch. The radio was tuned to a country station.

Josh laid his head back and sucked in the pleasant atmosphere. He stretched and yawned extending his arms wide. When he realized his left arm came to rest on the back of the couch over Jolene's shoulders, he jerked it back. He didn't want her to think it was a cheap high school stunt to get his arm around her.

Jolene glanced at him and smiled.

He sheepishly smiled back to cover his embarrassment, and said, "Did you know your dad helped me put my place together when I first came out here?"

She turned to face him, tucking her right leg under her. "No. How did he do that? What about the store?"

"Well, that was before your mother died. And he didn't actually help me build the place, I hired some guys to help with some of that, but he sure helped me haul and load furniture, appliances, and equipment up there."

"He even spent the night with me when we put the wind mill and water tank up. That was a job." Josh smiled. "I couldn't have done it without him."

"He was the best dad." Jolene reflected. "He always had time to listen to my troubles. He was never judgmental. I know he didn't like Bradley when I first brought him home, but he never said anything. Never said I told you so when it didn't work out either."

"He was a good man, Jo. I liked him."

That night, snuggled under a quilt in Ross' old room, Josh examined the pictures of Jolene on the wall and reflected on the day. This evening was almost like living a normal life. Almost.

The next morning after breakfast, Josh reminded himself of the Outlaws. A familiar worry settled into his gut. He couldn't think of any way he could protect Jolene and take care of his responsibilities at the farm at the same time. But it had been over a week and nothing had happened. And the Deputy had checked on her. Maybe he was being paranoid. Maybe they were gone.

"Don't forget about the CB," he reminded Jolene. "I'll try to keep mine charged up, but you'll have to notify me if they tell you when we have to go back for the trial. And Jo, be alert for the sound of motorcycles, just in case. And keep that shotgun loaded and nearby at all times."

"Okay, Josh. You're a worry wart. I don't think I have anything to fear now that the Sheriff is involved."

Josh sighed. "Well, call me when they want us to go to Soda Springs. If we don't make contact, I'll come in sometime soon to check."

"Oh, I'll stay in touch if we can get through. I still don't know what I'm going to do after the trial, so I'll be around for a while." She smiled shyly.

Josh looked at her wondering what she meant by that last part. Finally he said, "I hope so, Jo."

"You want a ride to get your horse?" she asked.

"Sure," Josh replied.

Josh saddled Buck and then argued with Ben Hannedy about paying for boarding his horse. He finally wedged a twenty dollar bill in the hinge of the stall while Ben wasn't looking.

He led Buck back to Jolene's Jeep. "Well...," he started, and then faltered, "I guess I'll see you when they call us for the trial. Or," he added, "if you need anything just call on the CB and I can be here in a few hours."

She looked up at him. "I hope you get your CB working so you could call periodically to chat. I've really enjoyed our visit Josh. Thank you for all you've done."

"Yeah, well, even with good power, the reception signal sucks out there. But I'll keep trying. We'll see. I'm usually not in the house much during the day, so if you try, call after dark, and I'll do the same, okay?"

"That sounds good." She smiled.

Josh decided to test the waters. "Maybe I'll come back in for a short visit next week to check on you." He looked at her for a reaction.

"Oh, that'd be great, if you can." She softened her voice. "And Josh, thank you again for everything."

He hesitantly circled her with his arms and looked into her eyes. "You're very welcome. I just wish we'd met under different circumstances. I don't get much human conversation, and despite the bad circumstances, I've really enjoyed your company."

They hugged for a moment and then awkwardly released each other.

Josh mounted Buck and spurred the chestnut gelding off toward home.

Chapter Sixteen

Buck gingerly trod the rut-gouged trail, his hooves naturally finding sure footing. Josh trusted the horse enough to let his own brain go on auto-pilot. His thoughts swam the pleasant currents of yesterday and this morning. Jolene's face hung like the Mona Lisa in every corner of his mind. Flashes of raven hair framing a radiant smile haunted his mind.

Overhead, white cotton candy clouds surfed the azure sky wherever the forest canopy broke. Buck snorted and did a quick dance step to stay in the rut. Josh, jarred alert, felt the stupid smile plastered on his face. "Idiot," he said softly just before he lost the battle with the grin and laughed out loud.

Strange how all of a sudden he missed human interaction, especially with someone like Jolene. Oh, talking with Ross had always been pleasant, but it had never caused him to think something might be missing from his life. Just pleasant conversation. He'd have to think about this new and confusing twist to his life.

As he rode, the recent conversation with Jolene about his previous life darkened his mood. Sure, he had healed over time. This place had helped, but the memories never faded, nor did he want them to. Likewise the pain diminished over time, but it too would never go away. Time doesn't heal all wounds. It just builds up scar tissue to lessen the pain. But it's never gone.

Four years. Had he really managed that long without Ellen and Jimmy? A shiver went up his arms. In a heartbeat he could experience the intimacy they shared. He could feel — physically feel — the sensations of making love with his wife. Those feelings kept him awake some nights.

During rides like this it was easy to allow himself the painful luxury of reliving those precious moments with Ellen and Jimmy. Every memory, every detail etched in his mind like ancient cave drawings. From the time he would walk, little tow-headed Jimmy had run out of the house every day to greet Josh when he came home. He would latch onto a leg until Josh tossed him onto his shoulders for a horsey ride back to the house.

Holding onto those memories brought comfort, but only for a while. Like that time-in-a-jar song, this jar was full, and sealed tight. No new memories of Jimmy and Ellen could ever go into that jar. Sometimes Josh wanted to smash that jar of memories against his mountain. But no, he kept them safe in his mind, revisiting them on these long rides, killing himself with them. It was his penance to punish himself with constant reminders of his failure to protect his family.

Flashes of black hair and full, succulent lips....

Buck came to an abrupt stop at the end of a sharp switch back and skittered back a step. Josh jolted alert. A huge black bear and her cub stood on the trail not thirty feet in front of him. Rays of sunlight cut through the foliage thrusting them all into a surreal Twilight Zone setting. Josh's hand moved to the rifle scabbard under his left leg. She-bears with cubs can be very dangerous. Protecting babies is a trait animals and humans have in common. Can't fault that.

Josh hesitated, eying the bear. Both he and the bear stared for a moment digesting the fight or flight syndrome. As if realizing there was no immediate threat, the bear and her cub ambled off the trail and back into the deep woods.

Josh laughed softly and clucked Buck forward again. How many times had he found himself suddenly exposed to danger as a police officer?

The gentle rock of the saddle lulled him into a false sense of security and he let his mental guard down. Those pleasant memories of his past life turned to that horrible day when it had all ended.

* * * *

The gray detective assembly room was a living, breathing cacophony of sounds that would confuse a linguistics professor, but was easily understood by every detective contributing to it. Suspects, witnesses, and complainants being interviewed amid dictations, constant phone calls, crimes being discussed, stories and jokes told, and asses being chewed out; all at the same time.

It was business as usual.

In his corner of the chaos, Detective Sergeant Josh Grant listened to Bobby Reynolds and Tony Goulette, two of his men, plead their case for an arrest warrant.

"Look Sarge, we got enough on this asshole to get a warrant. A street crew stopped him for a light violation not far from the carry-out within twenty minutes of the robbery. He was driving a light blue van just like the one the clerk described."

"They search him?" Josh asked.

"Yeah, well," Bobby started, "they patted him down."

"They find a weapon?"

"No," Tony broke in, "But they found a wad of cash in his pocket."

"Did the amount match what was taken in the robbery?" Josh already knew they wouldn't have enough probable cause for a warrant, or they would have already arrested the suspect.   They only wanted his approval so he would share the blame if the arrest went bad. But he would listen to their arguments and offer a third opinion as to how they could proceed from here.

"No, it was more," Tony said. "But he could have had some cash of his own before the robbery, and it was a big wad, Sarge."

"Did the officers say how the cash was stored? I mean was it all in the same pocket? Was it in two distinct wads or all together?"

"Yeah, we asked them that." Bobby offered. "They said it was all in the same pocket."

"What about the van?"

"They did a cursory search under the moving vehicle doctrine, but didn't find anything else."

"No gun?"

"No," Bobby said, looking down.

Josh scrutinized the pair. They were good detectives, and they knew he wouldn't authorize going to a judge for a warrant with this little probable cause. They just wanted him to make their day easier so they could get on with their overload of other cases.

"Look," Josh finally said. "You know this won't fly, but he still might be your man. You know the drill. Go talk to some people."

Both detectives had a knowing grin and a sheepish look on their faces. "Come on guys," Josh continued, "you know how this works; try to find out something about his background. Do a records check. Look for possible witnesses. Hell, stake him out for a while, maybe he'll make a mistake. And at least go interview him again. He might slip up and mention something the officers missed."

Bobby's grin broadened into an embarrassed looking smile. "We had to try, Boss."

"I know," Josh said smiling. "Now get to work and stop wasting my time."

Josh had follow-ups to do on his own caseload and wanted to get as much accomplished as possible so he would be free to leave at the end of the day. This was his son Jimmy's birthday and he and Ellen were taking him to Chuck E. Cheese and then to a movie at the mall. Josh had vowed not to miss this one.

By four o'clock, Josh was the only member of the Robbery/Homicide Squad left in the detective assembly room. The rest of his team were either out investigating their backlog of cases or testifying in court. The phone rang, and he didn't want to answer it this close to quitting time.

"Josh, this is Chuck Bell, in dispatch. I got a big one at the downtown First National, and I can't raise any of your guys."

"Shit," Josh muttered.

"I know," Chuck said. "This one's bad though. One of the security officers is down with a gunshot wound. Don't know how bad yet. And Josh, he's one of ours; a retired cop named Paul Ryan. You remember him?"

"Yeah," Josh said. "He's a good man."

"Uniforms are on the way to the bank, but they'll need a detective there before we notify the FBI."

"I know," Josh said reluctantly. "I'll head over there. Keep trying my guys, and send anybody you find, okay?"

"Sure," Chuck said, and hung up.

Josh gathered his equipment case and headed for his car. He might have time to handle the scene until a team of his guys arrived and still make it home in time for his son's birthday celebration.

* * * *

Uniformed crews had the crime scene secured when Josh arrived.

They would take care of the original report which would show up on Josh's desk tomorrow. All customers and bank personnel were still in the bank. As he entered, Josh took one look at the uniformed guard lying in a pool of blood still on the marbled floor and knew he was dead. If not, he would have been removed to the hospital by now. He looked at the uniformed sergeant on the scene, and the sergeant just grimaced and shook his head. Both men shared a mutual moment over the loss of one of their own, feeling emotions they couldn't show in public.

Josh approached the sergeant for a briefing of the crime. After Sergeant Bryant filled him in, Josh went to the teller, who had originally been approached, to get her story.

He identified himself and asked her to tell him what had happened. He noticed the smeared mascara and the fear still on her face.

"I already told the officers," she said. Her face pinched, as if not wanting to relive the moment.

Josh could tell she was still upset over the ordeal. "I know, Ma'am, but I need you to repeat it to me, okay?"

"Well," she began. "These horrible men came right up to my counter and pointed a gun at me.... My God I thought I'd die. And then he said, 'Give us all the money in your drawer.' So I started to do that. Then the next thing I knew, there were some shots... Oh it was horrible... and I ducked down behind the counter."

"Can you give me a description of the men?"

"Not really, I was so scared and they had some kind of sheer masks on their heads."

"Were they white or black?"

"White, I think. But they could have been light complexioned blacks. Both their noses were real wide and flat. But that's all I could tell."

"What about the gun? Can you describe it?"

"No. It was just a gun."

Josh continued, "What about after you got back up from behind the counter?"

"I stayed down there for quite a while. I heard a lot of commotion and screaming, but I didn't see anything."

"And after you got up?" Josh probed.

"Well, they were gone and poor Mr. Ryan was lying on the floor in all that blood." She sucked in a ragged breath as if remembering the gore.

Josh thanked the woman and walked back to the sergeant. "The clerk doesn't have many details." He commented.

"I know," the sergeant said. "I talked to the loan officer, whose office is right over there." He pointed to a glass front office. "He told me he hadn't seen the two who went to the teller, but when the shots rang out, he saw another man with a stocking mask standing over Ryan with a gun in his hand. Then the three men panicked and ran out of the bank without any cash. That's about it, Josh."

"Okay. Have you put out a description yet?"

"Yeah, what little there is."

"Any witnesses notice a vehicle?"

"Nope. Nothing."

"Okay," Josh said. "You continue with the robbery details and interview all the customers and employees, and I'll get started on the homicide. Oh, and notify dispatch, will you? Tell them to call the Fibbies and tell them this is a good one."

"Sure Josh."

Josh took a moment to use a phone in one of the bank offices to call Ellen and give her the bad news.

"Josh…" Ellen drew out his name. "You promised."

"I know El, but…"

"No you don't. You don't know anything." Josh detected the hurt and anger in her voice.

"Ellen," he pled. "I didn't volunteer for this. For Christ's sake a cop was killed."

"And out of thousands of cops it had to be you they called? What? Is everybody else at home with their families?" She spat out.

Josh hung his head. "El, you know how this works. I was the only one they could reach. I had no choice."

"You never have a choice except when it comes to us."

"Aw, geez El, give me a break, Look you and Jimmy go on to Chuck E. Cheese and maybe I can break free in time to meet you at the mall, okay?"

"Josh..." He could feel the coldness in her voice. "More likely we'll see you tomorrow — if you can break away from your precious job by then."

The line went dead.

Josh was mad at the world, and it showed. Other officers at the scene instinctively gave him a wide berth as he conducted his investigation.

It was well after nine o'clock when Josh returned to his office after the stressful visit to Paul Ryan's home to notify his wife of Paul's death. Like all cops, Josh dreaded the task of giving anyone the news of a loved one's death. Giving that information to the wife of another cop is paralyzing. Sitting in his chair drained, Josh's stomach and chest ached equally.

He still had to write up his investigation report while it was fresh in his mind, but he couldn't concentrate. The mixed emotions of heartfelt compassion for the new widow, and the guilt and anger he felt for having missed his son's birthday had rendered him inept at his immediate duties. He sat silently thinking of his guilt when his desk phone rang, jarring him back to reality.

Not wanting to answer it, but knowing he had to in case it was new information on his case, he picked up the receiver and snarled into it, "Grant! What?"

"Sergeant Grant, this is Lieutenant Bailey in dispatch, could you come down here a moment? I need to talk with you."

"Aw, shit, LT, I'm up to my ass in alligators here. Can't it wait?"

"No, I'm afraid not, Josh," his voice had a soft sad quality of finality. Josh wondered if it had anything to do with his case.

"Okay, I'll be down in a minute."

When Josh entered the dispatch center, he felt several pair of eyes follow him to the Lieutenant's office. When he entered, Bailey said, "Please, close the door, Josh."

Now Josh's curiosity was piqued. Had someone from the bank called to complain about him? Why was Bailey being so serious?

"What's up, LT?" Josh tried to affect a casual air.

"Josh," he began. "I'm afraid I have some bad news."

Josh's mind raced along with his heart. Had Ryan's widow had a heart attack after hearing about her husband? What had gone wrong?

The lieutenant arose and came around his desk. "Josh, there was a drive-by shooting earlier tonight.... And..." He stammered, as if unsure of how to proceed.

"And?" Josh asked, annoyed, thinking a case such as that shouldn't fall to his squad since it was a drug related robbery. And why call him down here just to tell him?

"And," Bailey looked at the floor. "Josh... I just found out... I'm afraid your wife and boy were victims in that shooting."

"What?" Josh's brows furrowed, and his mouth dropped open. His brain froze. What did he say? No. He looked Bailey in the eyes and saw the pained expression on his face, Josh's knees buckled.

He caught himself with the edge of Bailey's desk, and quickly flopped back heavily into a chair along the wall, unable to breathe — it felt like his heart stopped beating.

Josh stared at the lieutenant, his eyes squinting and pinched hoping the lieutenant would say it was a mistake. But Bailey's anguished face told him it wasn't. He was afraid to ask their condition. Bailey must have noticed the expression on Josh's face. He filled in the blanks. "I'm sorry, Josh..." He faltered, then forced himself to go on, "They didn't make it."

Josh buried his face in his hands and wept. His entire body racked with aching sobs. Each sob ended with a soft, anguished "No!"

After a very long time sitting in the chair unable to think or act, Josh glanced up and found Bailey seated at his desk.

"You want some coffee, Josh?" the lieutenant asked.

Josh stared at him in confusion, his face blank. Finally he answered, "No." He shook his head then said, "Where are they, Will?"

"Probably at the morgue by now. The homicide boys from that district are still at the scene. They've got a hell of a mess out there. Multiple victims."

"Are they sure it was Ellen and Jimmy?" Josh asked hesitantly.

"Yeah," Bailey looked at the desk top. "Parsons was one of the first uniforms on the scene, and he recognized them. He said he used to work with you in patrol. And Ellen's purse was still on her arm."

Josh started to cry softly again, then suddenly jerked his head up, and said with final resignation, "Thanks, Will. I'm going to the morgue."

"Are you sure you want to do that, Josh?"

"No, I don't want to do that, but I'm going."

* * * *

Josh zombie-plodded to his car. To hell with the office and to hell with the job. His world had fallen apart. His mind flitted in milliseconds, abruptly stopping at each dead end, then rushing to another. Synapses fired at machine gun speed, but nothing made sense — nothing.

In a fog he somehow managed to drive to the morgue. He pressed the buzzer at the door as he held up his ID for the camera. The door clicked and Josh walked in. He didn't recognize the attendant.

"I want to see Ellen and Jimmy Grant," he told the young intern who greeted him.

"They're homicide victims, Detective. Are you on this case?"

"No." Josh said softly. "They're my family."

"What?" the attendant blurted, and then after a pause, "Oh, I'm sorry."

Josh just nodded his head.

The attendant looked around as if someone might help him out of an awkward situation. He stammered a few times to find words. Eventually he said, "I'm afraid you won't be able to see them until the investigating unit and the coroner has a chance to examine them. You know the possibilities of contaminating evidence." He held his hands out palms up trying to show helpless compassion, "I have to follow the rules, Detective."

The tension, guilt, and anger bottled inside Josh broke loose in a rush. His eyes squinted as he looked hard at the attendant. "Look you." He poked a rigid index finger hard into the man's chest. "I want to see my wife and child." He repeated the chest poke as the young man backed up. "And I want to see them right now. You either wheel them out here for me, or I'll empty every damn vault in this God-damned place and it won't be orderly, I guarantee. You got that?"

"Yes, but…"

"No buts. Just do it." Josh fixed him with a dangerous stare. "I know not to contaminate evidence asshole."

"Well, okay, I guess. But I'll have to report this."

"You do that," Josh said. "In fact, you go do that right after you wheel them out here. I want to be alone."

Minutes later two sheet-draped carts were standing in front of Josh. He hesitated, just staring from one cart to the other. Reluctantly he pulled the sheet back from the larger body and sucked in a hard breath.

He gently touched her cheek, and said, "I'm so sorry El. What am I going to do without you?" Tears continued to spill down his cheeks.

When Josh pulled back the other sheet, he burst out crying anew. This time it was the same agonizing wail of despair he had witnessed so many times in others throughout his career. The agonizing wails of those forlorn victims unable to process or cope, always stabbed icicles into his heart. Although he always pined with them, prior to this, he never knew how devastating it felt. Now he did. It felt like all his internal organs had been ripped from his body, leaving a hollow cavity and an empty soul.

Remembering that day caused Josh's stomach to cramp and the familiar empty feelings to return. Those depressing days that followed had flung him into an abyss of despair. How many evenings had he spent curled up in a chair with a bottle of Jack Daniels, contemplating eating his gun.

Buck deftly sidestepped a fallen limb jarring Josh out of his funk. Looking around his surroundings he saw they were nearing home. At the top of a knoll he could see his valley through the trees. He sucked in a deep breath. This place had helped make him almost whole again. A pleasant calm engulfed him. His farm never allowed him to wallow in despair for too long. He had responsibilities here he could handle.

He offered a silent prayer of thanks for Grandma and Grandpa who had taught him he could live like this.

Chapter Seventeen

Outlaws

Well after noon Frank and Toad found a wide spot along the highway just off the road leading to the general store. In an area dense with trees and brush, they carefully wove their bikes among the trees and concealed them behind honeysuckle bushes.

"Ow!" Toad cried, when a tree limb brushed aside by Frank smacked him in the face. "God Damn it Frank, watch what you're doing."

"If you wasn't so damn fat it wouldn't a hit you."

"Do it again and I'll squash your skinny ass."

"Ah hell, Toad, lighten up."

The two made their way through the thick woods until they were near the road. From their vantage point they had a good view of the general store and parking lot. Crouched next to a large tree with scattered brush all around, Frank and Toad watched the store. Their hiding spot was well above the road and they could clearly see the front of the building and surrounding area. They maintained their vigil for hours without seeing much activity. When a car pulled into the parking lot, they both leaped to their feet in anticipation.

An older lady got out of the car and went into the store. Ten minutes later she emerged carrying two bags in her arms. The pair watched her get in her car and drive away.

"That wasn't her." Frank said.

"No shit." Toad replied.

Several other customers visited the store through the day but none came close to looking like the guy they wanted. Toad jumped up smacking himself repeatedly on his legs. "God Damn it," he tried to yell in a whisper.

Frank startled alert. "What the hell? Be quiet Toad."

"Damn ants are eating me up," Toad said, still swatting.

"Well find another spot and be quite."

That evening when they saw the lights go out in the store, they worked their way back to their bikes and rode off to the clubhouse.

They were back to their lookout spot early the next morning. Throughout the early hours they watched several customers enter and leave the store. Later that afternoon Frank saw a tall young man step onto the stoop and begin sweeping it off.

"Look Toad! Is that the guy?"

"Hell I don't know. It could be. You mean he's been in there all this time and we didn't see him?"

"I guess," Frank said. I don't know how the hell we missed him. Let's go get his ass Toad."

"Now hold on a fuckin a minute, Frank. I don't remember what the guy looked like, but I didn't think he worked there. Wasn't he a customer?"

"How the hell should I know? He sure seemed to know the place well. Maybe he was and maybe he just got the job. Who the hell else could it be? He looks about the same size."

"Ah, Frank if we fuck this up again... Are you sure it's him?"

"Fuckin A, it's got to be him. Who the hell else could it be? You saw him sweeping the place. It's gotta be him."

"Well okay, but let's figure out a plan. How we going to do this?"

"Okay, we'll wait, see... and watch, and when we think it's clear, we sneak up to the store and go in. We shoot the fuckin guy and the girl. No witnesses, and Jake gets off."

"Shouldn't we wait 'til it's dark, Frank?"

"Hell no. If he works there, he could leave soon, and they won't be together. We got to get 'em both."

"Okay, but this better work, Frank."

"Quit worrying asshole. We got guns this time. What could go wrong?"

Chapter Eighteen

Frank and Toad waited until all highway traffic disappeared and no customers could be seen at the store before leaving the woods. They sprinted across the road and headed for the general store. Skirting the parking lot, the pair dashed through the open field and eased along the back side of the building. Reaching the stoop at the far end, the pair hid below the concrete porch. Frank climbed over the metal railing and motioned for Toad to follow. After several tries Toad hefted his mass over the railing. The pair inched their way along the rough-cut cedar siding toward the front door. At the entrance Frank shouldered the door and both burst in with guns drawn.

A tall young guy stood behind the counter. His body went stiff. Eyes wide open, he stared at two gun barrels. Frank followed the dude's shifting eyes to a shotgun leaning against the wall. When the bastard made a frenzied lunge for the double barrel, Frank pulled the trigger. The kid fell to the floor.

"Shit Frank," Toad yelled. "That's not the guy. That's a kid. Now what the hell are we going to do?"

"Get the girl," Frank said.

They turned and headed back toward the apartment door. They burst into the room. Empty. Three doors on the right. "She's gotta be here, Frank whispered. "We watched all morning. She didn't leave."

Then he motioned for Toad to take the second door and he would take the first. They split up and went to the rooms. No girl. Two more rooms. Frank ran to the kitchen motioning for Toad to search the last room.

As soon as he entered the kitchen Frank noticed the open rear door. "Fuck!" he yelled.

Toad waddled to his side. "She ain't here, Frank."

"No shit, Batman." He pointed to the open door.

"I didn't remember this place even had a back door." Toad said, then twisted his head toward the front. "Listen... That's a car. We better get the hell out of here, Frank."

"Yeah, this way." He tugged Toad's arm toward the rear exit.

They ran out the back door to avoid anyone coming in the front. As they rounded the building headed for their bikes, they saw a black jeep spin gravel coming out of the garage and onto the road.

"Damn!" Frank called out, pointing to the road. "That's gotta be her." They sprinted across the open field toward the woods where their bikes were.

Just before reaching the road, two shotgun blasts rang out. Both Outlaws flopped to the ground. Frank dove and rolled, and came up with his gun pointed back at the building. He saw the son-of-a-bitch from the store trying to reload the shotgun one handed. Too far for either him or the shotgun to be effective, but Frank fired off two quick shots anyway before he scrambled to his feet.

Up and running again, Toad huffed, "Thought... you... shot him, Frank."

"Fuck you!" Frank shouted between sucking breaths. "Come on damn it, she's gettin away.""

The bikers scrambled across the road. Just before entering the woods where the cycles were hidden, Frank pointed at the escaping vehicle turning left onto the highway. "Come on Toad."

The outlaws got to their bikes winded and dripping sweat. They gradually worked them out of the brush and onto the berm alongside the highway. The car was out of sight. They started the choppers and sped off in the same direction the Jeep had gone.

After a few miles running wide open, Frank spotted the jeep, just before it disappeared again. His chopper wound tight, gaining on the four-wheeler. No way she can outrun us.

When the bikes crested the hill, Frank could see a long distance ahead — no Jeep. What the hell? Where'd she go? The bikes sped past a side road off to their left. Frank held up his hand and skidded to a screeching a stop. The smell of burning rubber and blue-gray smoke filled the air. Frank swiveled his head several times trying to spot her. Circling his arm over his head, Frank motioned for Toad to go back to the road they had just passed.

"She had to take that road," he screamed over the noise of the motorcycles.

The Outlaws sped onto Long Run Road and accelerated. But the twisting, hilly road slowed them. The dense forest made it difficult to see far ahead. Just when Frank was about to give up, he spotted a black vehicle as it made an abrupt right turn into thicker brush.

"We got her now," he shouted above the roar of the bikes.

When Frank got to the point the Jeep had disappeared, he saw only a dense rutted trail.

The cycles raced well behind the bouncing jeep up and down steep hills and sharp switch backs. The jeep disappeared at every curve and hill. Tree and bush limbs clawed at the bikers as they sped by. Ruts in the trail forced both them and the Jeep to slow down. But little by little they gained on her.

Going up a steep grade Frank on the lead bike was able to accelerate and gain ground. Near the top, he decided he was close enough. He sprayed several rapid shots toward the Jeep. The bike jerked over ruts and debris, but Frank figured one shot might have hit something. Suddenly the Jeep lurched to the left off the trail and disappeared. "I got her!" he yelled.

The outlaws stopped. They could still hear the Jeep crashing through brush and small trees. Leaning his bike against a nearby tree, Frank eased himself to the edge where the Jeep had gone over. The Jeep bounced to a stop upright. The roof was caved in and smoke poured from under the hood. Frank saw no movement. He smiled.

"Well, that had to kill her," he said.

"Shouldn't you go down and check, Frank?"

"Hell no. I'd never get back up. No way she could've survived that fall. And I probably shot her anyway."

"I don't know, Frank."

"Let's go tell Snake. He'll be buying the beer tonight."

Chapter Nineteen

The afternoon sun beat down with a vengeance on Josh and his team as they circled the hayfield for the first cutting of the year.

Although he had started shortly after daybreak, the task would take until dusk to finish. After the last pass with the cutter, he unhooked the mower and hooked up the rake to form the hay into rows to sun dry.

At the end of the row, Josh called, "Whoa, boys," wiped his brow on his sleeve, and inhaled the aroma of the hay. The sun rested high enough over the ridge line to assure Josh enough time to finish this job.

Something in the distance drew his attention. He jerked his head to the left. What was that? It sounded like faint cracking noise from deep in the woods, like tree limbs breaking during an ice storm. But no ice, no wind. It couldn't have been that.

Not at all sure he'd heard anything over the squeak of the hay rake, he concentrated. He noticed the draft horses' heads turned and ears perked. They too had sensed something. He strained his ears. Something sounding like an avalanche crashing down the mountain echoed through the forest. Nothing natural out here would make a noise like that.

Too far back to the barn to get Buck. Josh quickly unhitched the team and led Dan to the hay mower so he could climb up on his massive back. Scooping up the loose leather harness and straps, Josh wrapped all except the lead straps around a yoke horn.

Anxious heels to Dan's ribs coaxed him into a canter. The big horse loped up the lane and onto the logging road. Josh scanned the woods right and left as he rode. At the top of the second hill Josh slowed Dan so he could listen and have a better view of the woods. Further on, near the top of the next grade, he could see freshly broken brush and small trees leading off the side of the trail. He urged Dan on. When he arrived, he saw a deep ravine off to the right of the rutted trail. He slid off the big horse and looked over into the crevice to see what had caused the destruction.

At the bottom of the ravine he saw a black Jeep angled against rocks at the bottom. His heart hammered in his chest. It had to be Jolene's Jeep. Steam rose from the hood. Panic engulfed Josh as his heart continued to race. "Jolene!" he called. Josh scrambled down the jagged path made by the vehicle. Grabbing limbs and brush as he went, he fell twice.

The Jeep appeared to be empty until Josh was abreast of the driver's door. Then he saw her slumped over into the passenger seat. His heart sank. Scrambling around the Jeep, he managed to open the passenger door after several jerks. Blood covered Jolene's face and pooled under her. Josh put his fingers on her carotid artery and felt a weak but steady pulse. No way to get medical help out here. No way to notify anyone. "Shit!"

How to get her back up that hill? He couldn't carry her. The grade was too steep and rough. He would need his hands free to hold on to trees and brush just to get himself back up. He couldn't build a travois. That wouldn't work anyway. She'd slide off. Remembering the heavy rope he kept on Dan's yoke to drag hay, he clawed his way back up to the road.

He snatched the coil of rope looped over the yoke and tied one end to the yoke horn. He turned the giant horse down the trail and turned the rope around the base of a tree that had a low limb to keep the rope from riding up. With the rope looped over his shoulder and around his waist, he said, "Whoa, Dan." Josh slowly descended into the ravine again, playing out rope as he went, while talking softly to the horse.

As gently as possible he extracted Jolene from the Jeep and laid her on the ground to examine her more closely. Blood soaked one leg of her jeans where they were torn. Josh found a box of tissues in the Jeep and stuffed a handful into the hole in her jeans over the wound. The gash on her head had almost stopped bleeding, but he held another gob of tissues to that wound as well. Her right eye showed swelling and the first tinges of blue. None of her limbs looked twisted at strange angles. She was unconscious but breathing. Should he move her? He had to move her.

Josh tied the rope around his body and picked Jolene up. Cradling her securely in his arms he started for the steep incline. "Dan, hi on!" He called out.

When he saw the rope was about to become taught, he called, "Whoaaa, Dan." Then again, "Easy, Dan, hi on."

The giant horse started moving forward slowly. Each time Josh slipped on the treacherous terrain, he called out for Dan to whoa, and then started him up again. Finally, he reached the logging road and laid Jolene down again. He re-coiled the rope and looped it over the yoke.

How could he get her back to the cabin? She's light but that's a long way to walk, and it would take a while. He had just about resigned himself to the task of walking back while carrying her. Then on the other side of the trail, deeper in the woods, he spotted a downed giant oak tree. It leaned at an angle and the trunk rested several feet above ground.

Josh carried Jolene to the tree and laid her gently on the highest portion of the large trunk he could reach. He led Dan alongside the tree and using a lower limb, climbed onto the tree trunk. From there he slipped onto Dan's back and inched him alongside Jolene. Josh eased her into his arms, and using his knees, urged Dan back on the trail. "Barn, Dan, barn." The big horse lumbered back toward the farm. Their progress was painfully slow, but the possibility of dropping Jolene outweighed the need for speed.

Josh guided the big Belgian up next to the porch where he could slide off easily with Jolene in his arms. Bo stood on the porch with a quizzical look on his face and his tail still.

Josh carried Jolene to his bedroom where there was an electric reading light and laid her on the bed.

Josh rushed off to the pantry for his medical kit. On the way he stopped at the stove to fill a pan with water from the stove reservoir and put it on to heat more.

Before Josh left Detroit he had gone to his best friend, Dr. Sam Adkins, and asked for some emergency medical supplies in case he found himself in dire need with no way to get to a doctor or hospital in a hurry.

Years before, while Josh was still in uniform working night shift, he had brought a prisoner to the St. Regis emergency room for treatment. Sam, a new intern, had just started his hospital residency period. The prisoner, a strung-out doper who'd either fallen down or been beaten up needed attention before he could be booked for possession for sale. The junkie, obnoxious during the trip to the hospital, became even more so when he had an audience. His screaming obscenities had the emergency room staff on edge.

Josh stood tethered to a land line phoning in his report while a young nurse attended to the doper. He heard the Junkie yell, "You stupid cunt, suck my dick!" The nurse gasped, Josh dropped the phone and leapt up. A young doctor standing near the gurney where the prisoner sat took one quick step and threw a powerful straight right into the crack-head's nose. Blood splattered the wall and gurney. The junkie flopped half-on and half-off the gurney.

Josh had wanted to cheer. He could tell several others did as well. He went back to the phone and told the complaint clerk he would call back. After hanging up, he approached the doctor and said with a grin, "Well now doctor, was that an assault I just witnessed?"

"Hell no," the doctor said. "That was the latest triage technology I learned in Doctor School. You see, the patient was bleeding profusely from that head wound, and I had to slow it down before I could stitch him up," The doctor continued to instruct, "By causing a lesser wound I have diverted the blood flow from the major wound to a lesser, allowing me to address the more serious problem." He stuck out his chin and looked at Josh. "Now would you call that an assault, Officer?"

Josh said, "No sir. I'd call that advanced medical science, and I think I want you to be my family doctor when you finish your residency."

* * * *

Over the years of Sam's Emergency Room tenure, there had been many times when Josh was right beside him as Sam sewed up victims and suspects. Sam was a natural teacher. He often instructed Josh in the fine art of suturing a wound or setting a bone, as they swapped callous jokes.

On the day Josh prepared to leave Detroit for good, he had lunch with Sam. His friend ceremoniously presented him with a large zip-up duffle bag full of professional medical supplies.

"These should cover about any medical emergency you might have. Everything is sterilized and hermetically sealed. Keep the meds cold if you can," Sam said, then added, "but above all else, be aware of an old medical saying – a doctor who treats himself has an idiot for a patient."

"Isn't that supposed to be about lawyers and clients?" Josh asked with a grin.

"Yeah," Sam acknowledged, "but I thought it sounded good here. Look," he went on, "This case has just about everything you might need, and I included some instructions to remind you of some techniques and information. I know you've had advanced first aid, and an innate affinity to medical treatment, and of course you've had my brilliant guidance… but, you've got to promise me you'll get to a hospital if you get really sick or have any symptoms for a long time."

"I will," Josh promised.

"And remember it's not going to be easy giving yourself stitches or shots. It's different when it's someone else, okay?"

Josh snatched the large med kit from the cabinet and whispered, "Thanks, Sam." A smile crept onto his face. But I sure wish you could be here now.

He carried the supplies to the kitchen. From the back lower shelf of the refrigerator he retrieved the heavy plastic pouch containing the meds. At the sink he scrubbed his hands with lye soap. He retrieved the pot of hot water he had put on the stove and returned to the bedroom.

Using a flashlight Josh lifted each eyelid and examined Jolene's pupils. They both constricted when hit with the light. The head wound had stopped bleeding. He cut the leg of her jeans to reveal the gash there. It was long but probably not deep enough to require stitches. The bleeding had practically stopped. That was a good sign. But that head injury….

Bo whimpered from the bedroom door. "I know, Bo. She'll be okay, boy. You go lie down now." The dog went back to the kitchen and flopped onto his rug.

Josh applied layers of gauze pads to the open wounds and held pressure to her head and leg to further stem the bleeding. "God I hope she's not in a coma, he whispered." Should he wake her with ammonia inhalants? Better not. She'll shake her head at the first whiff. Can't have that, not with a head injury. Crap, I can't treat coma. She'll be in dire need of liquids and I have no way to force fluids. If she doesn't awaken on her own…

Josh unfastened her jeans so she could breathe better. He felt his face flush when he saw the top of her powder blue cotton panties. He tapped her cheek with extended fingers several times calling, "Jolene." She had to wake up so she could help him assess her injuries.

Her eyes fluttered. He tapped again, a little sharper. "Jolene."

Her eyes opened and closed. She blinked several times. She looked at him through glazed eyes but gave no recognition.

"Come on Jolene, I need you awake."

"Huh?" she finally responded, her voice weak and hoarse. Then her eyes widened. "Josh!"

"What...? Where...?" She closed her eyes again and moaned.

"It's alright. I'm here. You're okay."

Eyes still closed, she said, "What happened?"

"Here, drink this."

She opened her eyes and stared at the glass of water he held. Her face held a confused look.

Josh lifted her shoulders cradling her head with his elbow so she could drink. "Just drink this if you can."

She sipped from the glass he held to her lips, then sagged against his supporting arm. He eased her back into the pillow.

"What happened?" she repeated.

"I was hoping you could tell me. You had an accident. You went over the edge..."

"Accident!" Jolene started to sit up, then sank back into the pillow. "Oh, God, my head hurts." She sucked in a deep breath and exhaled slowly. "No accident, Josh, they shot at me."

"What...? Who...? Ah shit, you mean the Outlaws. How'd they find you?" Josh felt his blood pressure rising.

"They came to the store...." Her voice and face softened with concern. "Oh God, Josh, I think they shot Chad."

"What...?" Damn, knew I shouldn't have left them at the store. Got to stop worrying about animals. They're not as important as a human life.

"Chad was tending the store while I was in the house. I heard a shot, and just ran out the back door. Oh Josh, I panicked." Her face scrunched up. "I didn't have time to get a gun, or even my cell phone. I just ran for the Jeep."

"My God, Jolene." He caressed her cheek. "Why did you come here and not to town?"

"I knew they could catch me if I tried to take the highway to Soda Springs. I thought I could lose them in the woods, but they must have seen me turn onto Long Run Road. They caught up to me on top of that curve. When they shot at me, I jerked the wheel and went over that embankment. That's all I remember."

She paused to catch her breath. "I was so scared.... And then the crash.... How did you find me?"

"I heard a loud noise. Didn't know what it could be, but when I saw the Jeep I knew it was you. But I thought you just ran off the road."

Josh thought for a moment. The shots must have been what I first heard. "How many guys chased you, Jo?"

"Only two that I saw."

"I wonder why they just went away?" Josh rolled his eyes up and to his left, thinking out loud, "They probably thought you were dead. It didn't take me long to get there and I didn't see any sign of them."

"Or maybe they just didn't want to waste the energy to go down and check on you, thinking you would surely die. Either way we might be lucky. If they think you're dead, that could be the end of it, at least until you surface again at the trial."

"Oh, Josh, I'm so worried about poor Chad. I know I heard a shot in the store. Do you think they killed him?"

"Don't know, maybe. I sure hope not." He paused. "Maybe it was him shooting at the Outlaws."

"No it didn't sound like a shotgun. She paused and thought. "Wait a minute, I think I heard two more shots while driving away. At the time I thought those jerks were firing at me, but it did sound different — more of a boom than a crack."

"That sounds like a shotgun, Josh said. "I hope it was Chad. That might indicate he's alright. I'll try to raise him and the Sheriff on the CB."

Jolene sank back into the pillow. Her face showed more of a worried look than a painful one.

"How are you feeling, by the way? You had me really worried."

Jolene paused. "I hurt all over, especially my head."

"Just relax. You've got a lot of cuts and bruises. I was about to patch you up when you came to."

Her body tensed. "What do you mean patch me up?"

"Well you've lost some blood and have some open wounds, and probably a concussion I need to attend to, then we'll see about getting you to a doctor. Here, drink some more."

"Doctor? I'm not going anywhere near a town or anywhere they can find me. I feel safe here."

Josh helped her sit partially up so she could drink.

"We'll see about that," Josh said as he pulled on a pair of latex gloves. "But first let me clean your wounds and see how bad they are."

Josh set the pan of hot water on the bedside table. He placed a cake pan under the side of her head and flushed the head wound with water. He gently swabbed the gash with the washcloth soaked in water and PHisoHex antibacterial soap, then flushed it again.

He watched Jolene clinch the bed cover and grit her teeth. "Sorry, but this has to be done."

"I know but it hurts like hell. Couldn't you just chant an incantation over me or something? You are a witch doctor aren't you?"

"No, I'm a sensitive man and you've hurt my feelings. Now lie still and behave."

The cut seeped new blood from the washing, so Josh applied a clean four inch compress and held pressure for a couple of minutes. When the bleeding again stopped, he swabbed it with Betadine, then another compress. It wasn't a gaping wound but should have stitches. Without shaving the entire side of her head he couldn't butterfly bandage it to keep it closed.

He moved on to the leg wound. This too he flushed, cleaned, applied Betadine, and a compress. When the bleeding stopped, he carefully dried the surrounding skin. He pinched the wound tightly together and with one hand and applied antibiotic cream with a Q-tip then pulled a large adhesive butterfly bandage tight over the cut to keep the edges together. He'd wrap it later.

Josh gently rolled Jolene onto her right side.

She sucked in a sharp breath. "Aaah!"

"What?" Josh winced.

"My ankle. Oh, boy."

Josh eased her back down and went to her feet. The left ankle was definitely swollen. Jolene gritted her teeth while Josh carefully removed her sneakers and socks. "Can you move your foot?"

She moved her foot in small increments.

"How bad does it hurt when you move it?"

"It aches, but not a sharp pain."

"Try sideways."

"That's about the same, maybe a little worse," she pronounced after moving.

"Wiggle your toes."

She did so with little pain reaction.

"Okay. Probably just sprained, not broken. But no way to know without X-rays. I'll wrap it later, but I saw more blood on your right side when I rolled you over, so let me look at that first."

Blood had soaked through her shirt. "I'll have to remove your shirt so I can see where the blood came from."

Jolene's face reddened as she made a move with her right hand to unbutton her blouse. She grimaced with new pain.

"Here, let me do that," Josh said, and began unbuttoning her shirt. "Raise your arm if you can."

She raised her arm enough for Josh to get her sleeve off. The bra fastening strap was soaked with blood and there was a small cut in the material at the base of the cup. It had to come off.

Oh shit, now what? No time for modesty. "I'm sorry Jolene but you're bleeding underneath your bra strap so we have to take it off."

Her eyes widened for a second before her face relaxed. "Okay, I guess. It's not as if you haven't seen my… uh…" she gave a little embarrassed shrug. "You know, before."

"I averted my eyes." Josh grinned, trying to ease the tension.

"Sure you did."

He reached around her and unhooked her bra and lifted the back strap, but left the remainder in place. A small but deep laceration at the back side of her right breast still oozed blood. Jolene tried to turn her head to see but couldn't. "What is it?" she asked.

Josh suppressed his inner Leslie Nielsen urge to say, 'It's a device designed to support your boobs, but that's not important now'. But he did smile.

"It's another cut. Not too big but it needs attention." He held a compress to the gash long enough to slow the bleeding. "Stay in that position while I clean it." As he worked, he thought aloud, "I think I can pull this one together with a butterfly bandage too. But I'm afraid I'll have to stitch that head."

"What?" Jolene's eyes widened. Josh felt her body tense. "What do you mean stitch it? She said."

Josh had the wound cleaned and most of the bleeding stopped. "Wait a minute," he said, while applying ointment and a tight butterfly bandage.

He stepped back from the bed so she could see him. Pulling up his left pant leg, he pointed to a barely visible three inch scar on his left calf just above his boot top. "I ripped this pretty good last year on a roll of barbed wire and put five stitches in. Not bad huh?"

"You did that to yourself?"

"Yep, and I've stitched up a couple of the animals too."

"But how…?"

"Trust me Jo; I know what I'm doing. Our only problem could be infection. We'll have to keep all your wounds very clean until I can get you to a doctor."

She closed her eyes a moment then opened them and responded, "I told you I'm not going back there. Now you just do what you have to do.

"Okay. I've got some strong antibiotics for later. Do you want me to numb the cut before I stitch it?"

"You can do that?"

"Yes, I have the medicine and equipment."

"Are you really some kind of doctor? I don't understand, Josh. I thought you were a cop."

Josh could see the concern on her face. All this at once must be overwhelming. "It's another long story Jo. For now just trust me, and I'll explain it all. Now, do you want me to numb it before I suture?"

"I think so, do I need it?"

"I did mine without numbing it. The needles are very sharp and there's not much pain, and the scalp is probably the least painful to stitch. But, your choice."

"Is it dangerous? The numbing I mean."

"Well, No. Infection is the big worry, but not for the numbing. I have sterilized syringes and sealed vials of Lidocaine."

"How'd you get all that?"

"Same long story, my best friend back in Detroit is a doctor."

"Okay, okay," she squeezed her eyes closed. "Numb me."

Josh filled the syringe and injected lidocaine at several places in the wound. We'll give that a few minutes to work. Meanwhile I'll get some ice packs for your ankle and eye."

"My eye? What's wrong with my eye?" She hesitantly touched her face. She winced when she touched her right eye. "Wow, it's all puffy, and it does hurt a little."

"It's swollen and already starting to turn black and blue. I'll get ice."

He returned and applied the ice packs to the injuries. "Okay, now you won't feel much except maybe a little pulling, but try to hold still."

After Josh finished stitching the head cut he cleaned and bandaged it.

He checked her blood pressure. It read 130 over 85, a little high for her age and condition, but under the stressful circumstances, not bad. He handed Jolene a sleeping pill and the glass of water. "Take this."

"What is it?"

"A sedative. You need to rest."

"I don't need to rest," she protested.

"Yes you do. The more you move the more you'll hurt, and you've lost blood. Your body needs rest. Now drink that whole class of water. I'll be right here."

She sagged into the pillow. "Yes, sir."

Chapter Twenty

"One-Bravo-three," the Caribou county dispatcher blared over Deputy Zimmer's radio.

Mark snatched the mic from its holder. "One-B-three, go ahead."

"One-B-three, report of a shooting at Folkereth's General store in Platte Junction. Ambulance on the way."

"Damn." Zimmer slammed his palm against the dash board. "Clear, dispatch." He made a skidding U-turn and stomped on the accelerator.

Sliding to a stop in front of the store, Zimmer saw two men on the elevated porch. One man held a blood soaked towel to the shoulder of the other. "What happened?" he said, as he approached the men.

"My son's been shot," the older man said.

"An ambulance is on the way. Let me have a look at the wound. Chad's father lifted the towel from the boy's shoulder to reveal a small entrance wound on Chad's upper arm near the shoulder. The back of his arm had a larger hole, torn around the edges, where the bullet exited. "Keep pressure on that," Zimmer said. "And you are?"

Mr. Hannedy introduced himself and Chad. "Chad's been working here since Ross was killed."

"Those motorcycle guys came back just like Mr. Grant said they would." Chad offered.

"Where's the girl who lives here?"

"Jolene? Don't know," Chad said. "She must have heard the shot." He looked to his arm. "I think she ran out the back, cause I saw her drive off in her Jeep."

"Okay," Zimmer exhaled a sigh and took out his note pad. "Now tell me everything from the beginning."

Chad gave the details of the biker's entrance and subsequent escape into the woods, as well as Jolene's escape. "I saw them running towards the woods, over there," he pointed. I shot at them with the shotgun, but they were too far away."

"Which way did Ms. Braxton go?"

Chad pointed toward the highway.

"Can you give me any physical description of the men?"

"Well," Chad squinted his eyes. "I didn't get much warning before they shot me. But one was short and fat with a full beard, and the other one, the one who shot me, was thinner and he wasn't too tall either – maybe five ten or so. Both of them were dirty looking and wore motorcycle type clothes."

"Anything else you remember, Chad?"

"Not that I can think of now."

An ambulance skidded to a stop next to Zimmer's cruiser. While Two EMTs Went to the back of the van, Chad said, "I think they went after Jolene. I heard the roar of the bikes from out on the highway." He nodded in the direction the Jeep had gone. "Didn't see them though."

"Okay," Zimmer said. "You go to the hospital and get patched up. I'll finish up here and come to Soda Springs to talk some more."

While the paramedics attended to Chad's shoulder, Zimmer turned to Mr. Hannedy, "How did you learn about the shooting?"

"Chad called me right after he called 911. I just live up the road a piece." He pointed toward his house. "I came a runnin. Scared the crap outta me."

"Do you know what kind of Jeep Ms. Braxton drives?

"One of them smaller ones. I think it's called a Wrangler. It's a black rag top with a roll bar."

"Wouldn't happen to know the license plate number, would you?"

"Nope."

Mark wrote in his notebook. "Does she have any relatives in this area?"

"Not that I know of. Since her mother died Ross was the only one."

"Any idea where she might go?"

Hannedy scratched his head. "No sir, unless she tried to go to Grant's."

The ambulance doors slammed shut. "Thank you Mr. Hannedy. I'm going to the hospital to talk more with Chad. You might want to drive there too, just in case they release him after treatment."

"Don't worry, I'm on my way."

On the way to the hospital Mark checked BMV records and found the license plate number of the vehicle registered to Jolene Braxton. Where the hell could she be? Maybe she made it to Grant's. I should have checked on her more. A cold dread crept into Zimmer's stomach. I should have listened to Grant.

From the hospital, Zimmer relayed the information to the dispatcher, who broadcast a BOLO alert for the Jeep. He gave a description of the bikers and the dispatcher broadcast an APB for them.

In the recovery room the deputy took an official statement from Chad. The doctor told him the bullet had gone through the triceps muscle and didn't hit a bone. Some blood vessel repair and twelve stitches took care of the wound. He wrote Chad a prescription for antibiotics to fight any infection and told him he could go home in a few hours.

After filing the shooting complaint, Zimmer went to the county prosecutor to file for a John Doe arrest warrant for the two bikers. He listed the charges as Felonious Assault and Attempted Murder.

Chapter Twenty-one

Sitting at the kitchen table hands gripping a cup of coffee, Josh felt mental exhaustion creeping up. Had he done everything he could? Knowledge of internal injuries eluded him. But other than general soreness she hadn't complained of anything else, except the headache. That head still worried him. Concussion could be a problem. The anxiety weighed on him and he knew it. He rested his head in his hands.

Josh's head jerked up when he remembered his horses. Shit! Dick was still harnessed to the hay mower in the field. How could he have forgotten? He sprang to his feet and ran outside. Dan was also gone.

"Bo," he called. When the dog ran onto the porch, Josh pointed to the house and said, "Stay with Jolene."

Josh leapt off the porch and sprinted up the lane to the hay field. Dick stood close to the same spot Josh had left him, peacefully munching fresh cut hay. Nuzzling the large horse, Josh cooed, "Good boy." Relief flooded his body. Josh unhooked the horse from the mower, gathered the harness, and turned Dick sideways to the mower, where he climbed up and onto the wide back and heeled the horse toward the barn.

In the large open section of the barn, Dan stood calmly outside his stall. His big head over the half door nibbling at bits of oats left in his feed box from this morning. Josh experienced the jubilance of a mother finding her missing children. He unharnessed both horses, put them in their stalls, and gave them a fresh ration of oats and filled their water buckets.

Before returning to the house, Josh took a moment to open the riding horses' stalls so they would be free to graze.

Josh went to the bedroom to check on Jolene again, and found her sleeping peacefully. Standing over her, his mind filled with doubts. Would she be alright? Everything seemed to check out, but he had no way to be sure. He was no expert. She seemed to react normally so maybe nothing major… But damn, this is different. No problem treating himself, but this is somebody else's life. She could be in real danger, but a trip in the wagon might do further damage. Shit, no answers. What the hell had they gotten themselves into? No, they didn't get themselves into it – the outlaws did. Damn them! Damn his inability to fix any of it. Josh looked around for something to punch.

* * * *

Throughout the night Josh continued to check Jolene's eyes for signs of concussion. She flinched when he raised her eyelids, but eased back to sleep. Each time the pupils constricted equally. Still he worried. Tomorrow might tell him more. Might have to load her in the wagon and head for civilization no matter how she felt about it.

He tried the CB off and on as she rested. A trucker had responded once, but the transmissions were so static-filled and broken, neither could understand. The new battery was charged to capacity, but his location didn't provide adequate reception even with a good battery.

Josh napped in an easy chair he had dragged from the living area next to the bedroom door where he could look in. Before daybreak he awoke and checked on Jolene again. No signs of discomfort. He returned to the kitchen to stoke the fire in the stove and put a kettle of water to boil for coffee. He'd forgotten to make a thermos of coffee the night before.

While Josh busied himself making coffee in the kitchen, Foghorn, the farm's alpha rooster began his raucous crowing outside the bedroom window. In the middle of his first screeching welcome to the new day, Josh heard a piercing shriek. He jerked his head toward the bedroom in time to see Jolene sitting straight up in bed, eyes wide with horror, screaming. Just as abruptly, when the blood rushed from her head, she flopped back down, unconscious again.

Josh rushed to her side just about the time Foghorn let loose with his second piercing wake-up call. Jolene's eyes popped open, and she started to spring up again, then as if remembering the last time, she eased herself back onto the pillow.

Her eyes fluttered a few times in Josh's direction then popped wide again.

"Josh... What... Where am I?"

"Just take it easy Jo, you're safe now."

She sighed and visibly relaxed. "Oh yeah, I remember."

Her face became alert again. "What the hell was that God awful noise?" she croaked through parched lips.

"That was only Foghorn." Josh handed her the glass of water from the night stand.

"What?" her upper lip curled. "Why do you have a fog horn?" She sipped the water.

"No, it's not that kind. Foghorn is one of my roosters."

Bo stood in the doorway anxiously wagging his tail and looking at Josh. He woofed softly.

Josh turned to him. "Okay Bo, go on."

The dog bolted to the rear door and through his dog opening.

Jolene had an even more confused look on her face. "What's going on, Josh?" Her brows angled and mouth open before she added, "I can't make any sense out of anything."

Josh had to smile. "It's kind of a morning ritual around here. Foghorn crows and Bo goes to chase him. He never catches him because Foghorn can fly. His wings aren't clipped like the hens. Sometimes that old rooster even dive-bombs Bo. It's great fun and exercise for them, and it keeps me entertained."

Josh turned to the door. "Just a minute. I'll get some more ice for that ankle and eye." He returned with two plastic bags of ice and gently applied it to the ace bandage around her foot and over a dry towel on her eye.

"Ow," Jolene said when the cold struck her aches. "That hurts worse."

"It'll get better in a minute."

"Oh Josh." she suddenly blurted, fear showing on her face. "They tried to kill me."

"I know, Jo. But you're safe for now. Just try to relax."

Jolene sank back into the pillow.

"How're you feeling, by the way? You've had me really worried."

Jolene paused for a moment. "I still hurt all over. It feels like all my muscles have been ground into hamburger, and I have a pounding headache. But you're right; the ice is helping."

She reached for her head and felt the gauze surrounding her head. "Why is my whole head covered?" her voice inched toward panic.

"It's not that bad, relax. I had to cover that wound, and a full wrap does it best. I'll unwrap it later and check for infection. Right now I need some coffee, how about you?"

"Yes, that would be nice."

Josh poured the hot water into the drip-o-later and waited. A few minutes later he poured them each a cup of coffee and returned to the bedroom.

Setting the cups on the night stand, he gently helped Jolene prop herself up onto a pile of pillows so she could drink. She groaned with the effort and winced when new aches throbbed through her body. As she sat up, the covers fell away from her upper body. Her face registered shock when she noticed she had neither a blouse nor bra on. She sucked in a breath and snatched the covers back over her bare breasts. For a moment Josh thought she was going to scream again. He turned away.

"What happened to my clothes?" she finally asked, in the voice of a mother asking her child, who ate the cookies.

"Uh... well... I had to remove them. They were blood soaked and you needed to be comfortable. You were asleep and I didn't want to wake you..." Josh hung his head.

Josh went to the dresser and pulled out a sweat shirt and handed it to Jolene, then turned his back.

"Oh, okay. I guess," she said, while slipping the large sweat shirt over her head. "You seem to have developed a habit of coming up with ways to see me half naked," she teased.

Josh tried to look innocent. "I never looked either time. I even stitched you with my eyes closed."

"Sure you did," she scoffed.

"I have a robe you can wear. Might be a tad large, but it'll cover you," Josh said, walking to his closet.

"Thanks," she said when he returned with the robe and laid it across her lap.

"Let me have a look at that ankle," Josh said, lifting the covers from her feet.

"So now you have a foot fetish, huh?"

Josh felt his face flush, but he smiled.

After probing the ankle he asked her if she could move her foot. She cautiously moved the foot in each direction. Josh watched for a reaction. He saw her grimace, but no sign of sharp pain.

"It's a little better than yesterday," she said.

"I think it's going to be okay," Josh pronounced. "I have to do morning chores. But I'll get another ice pack and some books for you to read if you like." He turned to go then turned back. "I don't have any Chick Lit," he grinned. "Anything else you like?"

"You got any Louis L'Amour? Her face and tone dripping sarcasm. Then she grinned a wide fake smile of her own.

"No, Ross took them all back."

Josh went to the book shelf and picked out London, Irving, and Pratchett to give her a variety to choose from. She picked the books up one at a time.

"I've read White Fang, but I don't know these others. They'll do. How long will you be gone?"

"Not long. Rest if you can. It'll help, and drink that water.

* * * *

Josh took his stainless steel milking pail and along with Bo, walked the worn path along the pasture fence toward the barn. The steel gray sky yawned to the new day.

Barn odors of sweet hay, worn leather and manure invaded his nostrils the instant he entered the side door. He breathed in through his nose. The aroma, both strangely repulsive and comforting at the same time. He smiled.

He set the pail on a table and lit a lantern to brighten the dim barn. Four aluminum pie pans nailed to the wall behind the lantern shelf acted as reflectors that spread light throughout this section of the barn. Josh opened the sliding door to the pasture and went to the ladder to the hay loft. As he climbed, Josh called out, "Bo, fetch Lucy."

Bo ran off for his morning chore while Josh forked hay from the mow to the floor below. Tiny shards of hay chaff floated in the air; sparkling in the lantern light like snowflakes on a full moon night. Josh climbed down the ladder, got another pitch fork from its hook and delivered a fork load of hay to each of the horses' stalls and one to the feed manger for Lucy. He then put a scoop of oats in each of the horse's feed bins as well.

Lucy ambled into the barn, seemingly oblivious to Bo's herding efforts at her heels. She walked deliberately to the milking stall, put her head through the neck restraint and began munching hay.

Josh levered the neck restraint closed and positioned his milking stool and the bucket. He pulled a sanitary wipe from the dispenser on the wall and wiped each teat. Sitting on the short stool, he tucked his head into the fold of Lucy's left flank, and started relieving her swollen udder.

Each squeeze and pull of a teat soon resulted in a calming, pfffst, pfffst, as the milk hit the bucket. The sound of milk squirting into the pail brought Tom and Jerri, the two barn cats, running to his side as they did every morning. Josh aimed a teat at them and squeezed. They each lapped the milk out of the air and licked their whiskers between squirts. Bo sat off to the side with his head cocked in awe of this ritual.

For a while Josh was back in his calm world and all was well. When he finished milking he released Lucy and opened each stall so the horses could go out to pasture and graze at their will.

He extinguished the lantern and headed for the house with the pail of fresh milk. Bo strolled beside him.

"You doing alright?" he called to Jolene as he set the pail on the stove and suspended a thermometer in the milk. He would check the temperature until it rose to 165 degrees and then keep it there for fifteen minutes. This was his home style of pasteurization. It worked for his grandmother. It probably wasn't necessary, but it didn't hurt anything either.

"I'm fine," Jo said. "Are you done already?"

"No, I still have to gather eggs and feed the chickens, then I'll be done for a while."

Josh knew how long it would take the milk to heat up so he grabbed the soft woven basket and headed for the chicken coop, telling Bo on the way out to stay in the cabin. The chickens did not like Bo in their compound.

Josh scattered cracked corn around the coop yard and chickens noisily followed him around. In the hen house, he went about gathering the eggs from each nest except for number three. That one he left for the hen to hatch so he would always have a new supply of chickens. He rotated the nests each time a new batch of chicks hatched.

Back in the cabin, Josh checked the temperature of the milk, looked at the wall clock, and set the pail off the stove to cool. He would filter it later.

He washed the eggs he had gathered and then retrieved his jar of bacon grease from the refrigerator. "Are you hungry?" he called to Jo.

"I don't know. I guess so."

"How do you like your eggs?"

"Scrambled, I guess."

Josh set about frying scrambled eggs and making gravy from the bacon grease. He had biscuits left over from yesterday. That little would suffice for now. When he finished making breakfast, he took a tray into the bedroom.

As they ate, Josh said, "I've been thinking, Jo. I think those guys will be back. The others won't just accept that you might be dead. They'll want to be sure, and then there's still me.   I'm sure they want me dead even worse than they want you. They may not know I live out here yet, but if they come back they'll figure it out. It won't be hard for the motorcycles to negotiate the trails. Sooner or later they'll happen on the farm. So I'm going to make some preparations."

"Can't we just call the Sheriff on the CB?"

"I tried that several times last night; so much for them monitoring channel 9, and so much for my CB. I'll keep trying though. I think I'll try moving the antenna. That might help."

"Josh, you're scaring me. What can we do against men like those?"

"Well, in a way I want to scare you. You need to understand..." He absently scrunched the blanket between thumb and fingers. "This time if they come back, there will be killing, and I want it to be them and not us."

"Jo," he continued. "It's really hard to just shoot someone, but we'll have to do that if they come back in numbers. Can you handle a gun if necessary?"

"Uh, yeah, I guess so. Daddy used to take me hunting and target practicing." She looked up at the ceiling a moment then turned back with a cold stare. "And don't worry; I won't have any trouble shooting any of those animals,"

"Good. When you can get up and around, we'll do some more practicing, if they give us enough time. In the meantime you rest and get well."

Josh mentally took stock of his weaponry. He had two shotguns, a .308 deer rifle, a .222 varmint rifle, his duty weapon – a Glock 9mm, his uniform weapon – a S&W .357 magnum, and a snub nosed S&W .38. He also had a Ruger Single Six in 44 caliber, but he only had birdshot ammo for that gun because he carried it with him in the fields to shoot snakes and rats. He remembered he had a few sticks of dynamite left over from the original clearing of his home site. He'd have to find those. He had an ample supply of ammunition for each weapon under normal circumstances. But things could get abnormal real fast if they came back.

Chapter Twenty-two

Jolene twitched and shifted position several times. She sighed, picked up a book, read a sentence or two and put it down, craned her neck to see out the window. Nothing but mountain tops. Three days confined to this miserable bed. This must be what it's like being in prison. Enough to drive a woman stir crazy. More stir crazy. She looked forward to hearing that damn rooster.

A door closed and something rattled in the kitchen.

"Josh?"

"Yeah, it's me."

"Josh, my ankle feels a lot better now," she mewed. "Can't I get up and move around?" she called in the sweetest voice she could muster.

When Jolene looked up, Josh stood in the doorway looking down at her with his head cocked and lips pursed. His bare arms glistened with perspiration.

"Oh..." She hadn't expected him so quickly. "Really, Josh, I'm feeling fine, but I'm bored out of my mind."

He didn't respond, but walked to the end of the bed and probed her ankle. Jolene willed herself not to wince.

He stared at her a while longer, then said, "The swelling's down some. Let me re-wrap it and we'll see."

She watched him turn and re-entered the kitchen. He returned and began wrapping her ankle with a fresh Ace bandage. Jolene felt the tightness of the wrap yet marveled at the soft touch of his large calloused hands. How can hands so toughened by farm work be so gentle and comforting? His hand slipped up her bare calf as he held her leg to examine the wrap. She felt a shiver flutter up her spine.

"Don't move," he commanded. "I'll be right back."

When he returned he held her jeans in his hands. He handed them to her. "One leg was shredded and bloody so I cut them off. They'll be easier to get into this way too. Here see if you can pull these on."

She looked at him a moment and when he failed to get the message, she said. "Well, turn around."

"Oh, yeah," Josh chuckled, turning his back to her. "Although I must say, since I've been carrying you to the bathroom for three days, it's a little late for modesty, don't you think?"

"It's never too late, and besides I had the blanket."

She struggled into the jeans. "You can turn around now."

Strong gentle hands pulled her upright then practically lifted her from the bed and helped her to stand. Josh pulled her left arm over his shoulder. With his right arm around her back, they walked a few steps alongside the bed. She gingerly put more and more weight on the foot. She felt weak. Was it because of lying in bed so long or because his right hand was so close to the base of her breast?

"It feels okay,"

"Let me know if it hurts. I can carry you just as easily."

"I know, but I want to walk. It feels good to move."

Josh helped her hobble to the front door. She tried to look around but her vision to the left was blocked by Josh. To her right she noted the symmetry of the shiny log walls. The heavy front door stood open. A screen door, held closed by an old fashioned coil spring, led out onto the porch.

Josh eased her into a rocking chair. She closed her eyes a moment to enjoy the fresh air of open space. "Ah, the sun feels so good."

She opened her eyes and gazed right then left, pausing at the lake. "It's beautiful out here, Josh. I had no idea."

"Home sweet home." Josh said, turning his head to the lake.

"And you built this place," she nodded back toward the cabin, "all by yourself?"

"No, I had a lot of help from the horses and a few chain saws, not to mention the volumes of Foxfire books. Without them I'd have been lost." Josh seated himself on the porch his back against the log wall, his legs crossed at the ankles. Bo flopped down beside him and rested his head on Josh's leg.

Jolene gazed at the rugged man, casually caressing his dog's ears. Those long legs, and big raw boned hands – so gentle. A man and his dog. Now there's a post card picture. With a slight flick of her head, Jolene tried to focus on what he was saying. Why did her thoughts wander? Was the warmth she felt from the sun?

"Bo and I lived in a tent most of that first summer." Josh ruffled Bo's head as he continued, "Actually I had some temporary help from a couple of guys I hired from a bulletin board at Home Depot in Bennington. And your dad helped me move most of the furnishing and equipment up here. It's still a work in progress though."

While Josh talked, Jolene's eyes swallowed the panoramic view from mountain tops to the crop fields, the barn, and to the lake. A blue heron fished just beyond the small dock where the cattails began. She panned right to view the gentle slopping plateau, bordered on the left by lush forested hills and to the right a more rugged mountain that seemed to rise straight up from the valley. She saw the edge of the logging road running across the saddle between the two mountains. No vegetation, only rocks visible along that section of the road. It appeared to abruptly stop where it reached the steep jagged slope.

"Where does that road go?" she asked, pointing.

"Nowhere. It just stops at the bottom of those rocks. No more forest beyond that. I've been up there a few times. It's a rough climb. I found a crumbling rock foundation just past where the road ends. I think it might have been the old logging office." He pointed, "See off to the right at the base of those rocks."

"Yeah, I think, but I can't see too well from here." Jolene turned back to the lake, basking in the quiet.

The ambient silence disturbed only occasionally by a distant songbird was spell binding. The air tasted crisp and clean.

"It's just so peaceful and serene, Josh."

"I know. The whole of it invades my being every day."

"Can we swim in the lake?" she asked. Her face lit up at the prospect.

"Sure. I do all the time. I think we had better wait until your wounds heal up a bit though."

"Oh, yeah, I didn't think about that."

After a moment, Jo asked, "Don't you get a little bored way out here?"

"Not really. I guess I don't have time to get bored. This place keeps me pretty busy, and when I do have time, I go fishing, hunting, or just explore the hills." Josh tugged the top of one sock up out of his boot.

"I do have an old guitar I plunk around on once in a while, and a whole lot of books. So no, I never get bored. I've had enough excitement in my life anyway. Smiling, he waved his arm in an arc. "This is all I need."

Jolene sat silent, miffed she'd let that statement bother her. Of course he's content here. What else would he damn well need? So why did it get under her skin? And what place did she have questioning his choice of lifestyle. Men.

"You okay?" Josh asked, jarring her out of her reverie.

"Yes, of course. I was just thinking about poor Chad. I hope he's alright."

"Me too," Josh echoed. "When you're able to take care of yourself better, maybe I'll ride in and check on him."

They sat quietly, soaking up the afternoon sun.

* * * *

Josh sat thinking about riding into town to check on Chad, but he knew he wouldn't leave Jolene alone. Not again. Surely the Sheriff knew about the shooting and would be investigating. Nothing he could do to help. Just have to wait until she can travel, or until he could talk her into it, before going back.

"How about a cup of coffee?" Josh said after a while.

"Sure, that sounds great."

Josh walked into the cabin, poured two cups of coffee from the thermos and returned to the porch.

When he arrived he saw that Bo had taken up a new position sitting next to the rocker with his big head in Jolene's lap. She had a distant smile on her face. Josh shook his head, smiled and handed Jolene a cup of coffee. "Disloyal cur." He said to the dog.

Bo cocked his head. "He likes me best." Jolene's head twisted to match Bo's. She had a superior grin pasted on her lips.

Josh sat back down on the porch. Bo stayed where he was. After a moment, Josh said, "Yesterday while you were napping, I went up the trail to check on your Jeep. There wasn't sign of anyone else being around it. I don't think we'll be able to get it back up that hill though. It's trashed anyway."

"What are we going to do now, Josh?"

Josh's mind refocused back to their survival. "Jo, you said you used to go hunting. Have you ever fired a handgun?"

"Daddy had a twenty-two pistol when I was little. I shot tin cans once."

"I'll be right back," he said.

Josh went into the cabin and up to the loft. There he opened the large trunk and rooted around until he found his off duty 38 snub nosed revolver. In his ammo canister he found a box of wad cutter ammunition. He always kept the holstered Ruger hanging by the rear door, and since the incident at the store, his Glock by his bedside, but the other weapons were stored away.

Back on the porch, he opened the cylinder of the weapon and showed Jolene it was empty. He closed the cylinder and handed the gun to her. He showed her how to grip it in both hands, and to expect sharp recoil and loud noise when it fired. Josh noted a sharp focus in her eyes and a look of determination. Good, she's taking this seriously. If they come in numbers we'll be in big trouble.

"For now," he said, "I just want you to grip it tightly and squeeze the trigger. You don't need to cock it. The hammer will automatically cock and fire. Try it."

She pulled the trigger through and the hammer fell. "That was hard to pull."

"It'll get easier with practice. Now hold it straight out a minute, and hold tight." Josh positioned his left hand under the weapon. "When it fires it'll feel like this." He smacked the bottom of the gun with his hand sending it up. She held on. "Good."

"Look." Josh held up a hand spreading his first two fingers in a V. The index finger of his other hand went between the first two. "This is what the sight should look like." Just align that front sight post between the V in the rear sight and aim that at the middle of whatever you're shooting at." She held the gun with both hands and gazed down the short barrel. "Now point it at a tree or something and try to hold that sight picture while you squeeze the trigger."

She did that a few times, then said, "It shakes all the time."

"I know, but don't pay any attention to that. Just concentrate on keeping the sight aligned on the target. The shaking won't have much effect on the shot."

Jolene practiced a few more times. Josh noticed the trigger pull was easier for her and the weapon shook less. "Let's try a couple of shots," he urged.

He loaded the revolver and handed it back to her. "Now hold it real tight, aim, and squeeze," he said. "Remember it'll jump and make a lot of noise so be ready."

She pointed the weapon and fired smoothly.

"What were you aiming at?" Josh asked.

"I don't know," she replied. "I had my eyes closed."

Josh laughed. "That's okay for the first time, but try not to make a habit of it."

Jolene pointed the gun at a Black Cottonwood tree just on the other side of the lane. Josh focused on her eyes. They stayed open as she fired. He saw a fresh chip in the tree bark where the bullet struck. "Very good," he said.

He went out to the tree and pulled one of the large leaves from a low hanging branch and wedged the stem into the bark to give her a more exact target. After a few more rounds she was grouping most of her shots close to the leaf.

"You're a good student," he said.

"Thank you."

By the time the wad cutter ammo was nearly gone, she had hit the leaf several times.

"We'll work on shooting a rifle too." Josh said.

"Oh, I know I can shoot a rifle, I shot my first deer when I was fourteen."

"Good, but we'll get in some practice anyway. In the meantime, I want you to keep that little gun with you at all times." Josh lowered his head and looked directly into her eyes. "I've got a holster for it and a belt if you want. You'll have trouble getting it into the pocket of those jeans, but the sweat shirt will hide the holster."

"Now, how about some lunch?" Josh said.

"That sounds good,"

Josh held out his arm. Jolene used it to pull herself up and clung to it as she limped alongside.

When they reentered the cabin, Jolene paused looking around the room. "Wow, now that's a fireplace."

The huge stone structure stood in the middle of the back wall. Passage ways on both sides of the massive stone hearth led to the kitchen.

Josh followed her gaze around the small room. Her head lifted. "What's up there?" She pointed.

"That's the loft. I've got another bed up there and a large storage area. That's where I've been sleeping lately."

She hopped to the back side of the chocolate brown leather couch and touched it. "I can't believe you and Daddy hauled all this stuff way up here."

"Well back then I had most of the delivery trucks meet me at the store, then Ross and I would lead them to the end of Long Run road and we'd load up and make as many trips as needed. Sometimes I was able to hire the drivers to help too."

Jolene's eyes opened wide. "In that wagon you brought to the store?"

"No. When I first came out here I had a custom four wheel drive pickup truck. It could handle the trail with loads of lumber, shingles, and things like that big old stove and sections of the water tank."

"What happened to the pickup?"

"Ross sold it for me after I bought the horses and wagon. I wanted to live like Grandma and Grandpa, so no cars."

She gave a weak smile and nodded her head.

"We came out that way Josh?" she said, looking toward the stairway that angled up and over the left passage. Then pointing to the right passage, "but where does that go?"

"To the kitchen, the same as the other one."

Josh helped her through the right hall and into the kitchen. They passed a counter top with a double sink. Pointing to the faucets, Jolene asked, "You have running water way out here?"

"Only cold," Josh said. "The windmill fills a holding tank and I get gravity pressure. I do have warm water, and I do mean only warm, for the shower. It's another small thermal tank on the roof." Josh ran his hand through his hair. "When it's dreary out I take some fairly cold showers, in summer though, it's hot." He smiled at her.

"I saw the shower in the bathroom. I wondered how it worked," Jolene said. "Can I try it today?"

"Sure, with all the sun we've had, it'll even be hot."

They continued across the kitchen toward the other side passing the rear door that led to a small sheltered back entrance. The refrigerator was against the back wall next to the door. And next to that sat an old fashioned washing machine with a bicycle frame attached.

"What on earth is that contraption?" she said, pointing to the machine.

"That's my washing machine, slash, exercise equipment. I peddle, and it turns the washing paddle. Then I hand crank them through the wringer and hang them out to dry."

Jolene shook her head.

A table stood in the middle of the kitchen, and the small bedroom and bathroom occupied the other half of the area. The kitchen side of the stone fireplace and chimney had another opening for a grill. The wood burning cook stove was adjacent to the grill and also vented into the back of the chimney. A huge hood hung over the stove with a duct pipe running from the top of the hood through the bedroom wall.

"What's that, Josh?" she asked, pointing to the vent pipe.

He smiled. "That's my heat duct, sort of. It channels some heat into the bedroom in the winter. I rigged up a little system made from the gears of a cuckoo clock to run a fan inside the duct. It blows warm air from the stove into the bedroom." He puffed up with a little pride, as he smiled at her.

"Well that's the tour." he said. "When you're getting around a little better I'll take you around the rest of the farm.

Sitting at the small table, Jolene asked, "What's for lunch?"

"How about a chicken salad sandwich? There's some chicken left over from last night."

"Sounds good."

Josh cut four slices of bread and lay them aside.

Jolene eyed the loaf of bread. "You bake your own bread?" She said her voice incredulous.

"Yep, I've still got my Grandma's sourdough starter. It's been alive for over a hundred years. I hope you like sourdough bread."

"You'd make someone a good wife someday."

"Aw shucks ma'am."

After the sandwiches and a glass of milk, Josh noticed Jolene staring intently at him. "What?" he said with raised brows.

She smiled "Getting kind of scruffy aren't you. Couldn't you invent a shaving device to run off that bicycle?"

Josh rubbed his fingers over the growth on his chin. "Oh, this, usually not much reason to shave out here. I often let it grow until it itches, or I have to go to town where there's a pretty girl." He did his best to leer at her. "Besides it doesn't seem to bother Bo much. Does it bother you?" He smiled. His eyes bore into hers.

"No, not really. But it's... so... white."

"Oh, that. Hell I've been graying since I was in my mid-twenties. My dad was the same way. The first time I grew a beard I was shocked and shaved it off as soon as I saw that it came in white. Actually, I'm letting it grow now so I might not be as recognizable in case those goons come back. It might buy me a few seconds."

"Back in Detroit," He ran his fingers over the new growth. "I was always the guy chosen to be the homeless street guy for stakeouts. With a beard I looked the part."

"Should I grow one too?" she smiled.

"Please don't." He smiled back. "But we'll try to keep you out of sight as much as possible."

"Want me to hide under the bed? Or maybe get a cow costume."

After a short pause, Josh said, "Seriously Jo, I know I harp on this subject, but we have to stay tight." He put both hands on her shoulders and looked into her eyes. "We have to assume those assholes will be back, and maybe a lot more of them. We just don't know when. The longer it goes, the more complacent we'll get. So try to stay alert. Think about survival and escape routes. I kind of want to keep you alive." He smiled.

"I'll try to, Josh. But I'm just not used to this, and it's nerve wracking."

"I know it is." He put his hand on hers. "But if we're not alert, they'll sweep in here, take us by surprise, and it'll all be over in a heartbeat."

He paused again, thinking of things he could do in preparation. Josh knew one of his strongest and maybe his most irritating trait was his pragmatism. It had made him such a thorough detective, and at the same time such a pain in the ass to his squad. His mind focused on ways to disguise Jolene.

"Can you sew?" he asked.

"Sure, a little. Why?"

"Well, we've got to get you out of those tight cut-off jeans. I have an old treadle sewing machine and I have some things that you might be able to alter. My cotton robe for example. If you can take in the back and put some buttons on the front it could be a dress of sorts."

She had a doubtful scow on her face.

"I know," Josh said. "It'll be frumpy, but that's a look we want to go for if they spot you."

"Okay, Josh. I can see what you mean. Do you have a hat I could wear? That might hide my hair."

"Sure, I'll find you one later."

The bikers will be out of their element out here and I have some ideas to give us even more of an advantage."

"Okay, I'll do whatever you tell me to. I can see that I wasn't too well off at the store. I trust your judgment."

"Tomorrow," Josh began, "you get started on some clothing. I have work to do around here. The first thing I have to do is to get that hay into the barn. And Jo, while I'm gone, would you periodically try the CB. You might catch a skip from a trucker.

Chapter Twenty-three

Outlaw Headquarters

"Hey Snake," the triumphant voice of Frank called, as he and Toad rushed into the chapter headquarters. "We took care of the girl. She won't be at no trial to testify."

Snake appeared from his office. He displayed a rare smile. "What happened? Were there any witnesses this time?"

"Well no, not really. We got her way out in the woods. They won't find her for years. There was a kid at the store when we went for her. We had to do him too. The girl ran off and we chased her way out in the boonies. But we got her."

"Oh, shit!" Snake yelled. "You offed a kid now?"

"Well, not really a kid," Frank said. "More like a teenager. We had to Snake. I thought he was the guy. He was in the store, and the son-of-a-bitch was going for a shotgun."

"Well," Toad interrupted. "You didn't really kill him Frank. Remember when he shot at us."

"Aw fuck! Another witness?" Snake screamed.

Frank glared at Toad, who concentrated on the cracks in the wood floor. After a pause, Frank offered, "He went down so he probably bled out eventually."

Snake sat down and rested his head in both hands, sighed, looked up at Frank and said, "Okay. What about the other guy, and tell me the details about the girl."

"Well, uuh... we don't know about the guy. He wasn't nowhere around, and we looked all over that little berg for him. Anyway, the girl got in a Jeep and took off before we could get her. Lucky we spotted her. She went out the back door. We grabbed our bikes and went after her. Chased her way the hell up in the mountains. Stupid bitch, don't know what the hell she was thinking. Nothing out there but dead-end trails. A rough ride, but we finally caught her and ran the bitch over a cliff. She ain't never coming back." Frank smiled while Toad looked on sullenly

"You sure she's dead?" Snake asked.

"Oh, sure. She has to be. Nobody could have survived that. The Jeep rolled and everything. She never moved or nothing."

Toad said, "It weren't no cliff, Frank."

Snake turned to Toad and said, "It wasn't a cliff? Then what the hell was it?"

Toad glanced at Frank who stared menacingly at him.

"It was a pretty steep hill." Toad shrugged.

Snake's voice tightened. "And did you go down that 'pretty steep' hill and check her?"

"No," Toad said. "I told Frank he should go down, him being the smallest and all, but he said he knew she was dead."

Frank again glared at Toad as if to say, 'shut the fuck up'. To Snake, "I think I shot her," he offered, weakly.

"You think you shot her?" Snake put both hands to his head. Blood rushed to his face. Suddenly he grabbed a coffee cup from a table and flung it against the far wall barely missing the two bikers.

"I told you fuckers not to kill the girl unless you got the guy too. Now how the hell are we going to find him? You just keep messing this up more and more."

The two inept Outlaws looked at Snake with mouths agape.

Snake rubbed his temples trying to think. "Okay," he finally said. "Lay low for a while; that berg will be crawling with cops. Then get your asses back out in the boonies," Snake slowly enunciated each word. "and check that girl. If she's dead get rid of any evidence including the body. If not, find her and bring her back here. And stay the hell away from that store."

Chapter Twenty-four

Josh guided Dick and Dan in a circle trailing a heavy rope to drag the dried rows of hay into larger piles so he could fork them onto the wagon to be taken to the hay mow. When they completed the circle and stopped, Josh once again saw the horses' ears perk up. He tensed, focusing his ears. An unmistakable rumble of chopper mufflers echoed. Only Harleys sounded like that. Josh froze.

Damn! Why hadn't he thought to carry a weapon other than his snake gun? Didn't think they would be back this soon. How'd they find this place? Could he make it back to the cabin? No. They'd see him and shoot before questions. Could he shout a warning to Jolene? No, that might also alert them, and she probably couldn't hear him anyway.

The exhaust rumble grew closer. Should he hide? Where? What good would that do? They'd just go to the cabin — Jolene's there. How many of them? Not many from the sound.

His brain in overload felt like mush. Inhaling a deep breath and exhaling through his mouth brought calm. He simply had to play this out and deal with it as it came. Shifting the holstered Ruger around to the back of his bib overalls with the grip angled to his right, he pulled the brim of his straw work hat down to hide his face. Josh worked the horses closer to the cabin lane. He had to intercept them before they just roared down to the cabin and Jolene.

Two motorcycles cleared the woods and coasted to a stop when the bikers spotted the cabin. They turned right and eased forward toward the cabin.

When the Outlaws noticed Josh and the team in the hay field, they coasted to a stop. Josh waved his arms and shouted, "Hey, you boys lost?"

The bikers stared, confusion on their faces. One of them yelled, "Who the hell are you?"

Josh put his hand to his ear, as if he hadn't heard, and said, "Huh?" continuing to walk toward them. As he drew closer, he recognized they were the same two Outlaws who had fled from the store. He couldn't believe it. He thought they would have been long gone from this area. They must be really stupid.

The pair shut the bikes down and one of them shouted, "Where's the girl from the Jeep?"

"Sheep? I ain't got no sheep." Josh replied, working his way closer with his left hand to his ear.

"The girl, you old deaf asshole!" the man shouted again.

"Girl? What girl?" Josh continued to play dumb, moving closer.

"The one from the wrecked Jeep down the hill; she has to be here. There's no place else she could go," he said, his gravelly voice resonating frustration and anger. "We want that fuckin' girl."

Josh said, "Look boys, I don't know what the hell you're talking about. The only girl around here is my old lady, and you can't have her. I've grown kind of fond of her." He smiled.

By the time Josh was within twenty feet of them, they had dismounted their bikes and looked ready for action. Although he recognized them, they showed no sign of identifying him.

The smaller biker, with a menacing growl, said, "Look, old man, you're not gettin the picture here. We're not here to play games. We want that fuckin' girl, and we want her now. If you know what's good for you, you'll hand her over. If not – then you're in our way, and you die." The biker opened his Jacket to reveal the butt of a pistol sticking out of his pants.

Josh forced a look of fear and disbelief on his face as he inched forward fixated on the gun. Leaning in for a closer look, he said,"That's a gun!"

"No shit," the man said.

By then Josh had advanced to within arm's length of the man while staring down at the weapon in the biker's belt. In a flash, Josh drew and placed the barrel of his Ruger 44 precisely on the tip of the man's nose. The hoodlum's body jerked stiff, his eyes frozen wide. Josh knew the barrel of a 44 caliber must look huge up that close. The biker couldn't know it was only loaded with bird shot, and even bird shot this close would be deadly.

"But yours is still in your belt," Josh said with a cold stare.

He quickly reached with his left hand and smoothly extracted the Colt 45 from the man's belt while he was still frozen. The confused look on his face fought for a hint of recognition, but apparently fell short.

Josh backed up a step and pointed the Ruger at the bigger man. "You!" he commanded. "Open your Jacket."

The man reluctantly did as he was told. Sure enough the grip of a revolver showed above his belt. "With your thumb and index finger only, take that gun by the grip and toss it my way."

The man just looked at Josh with a glare and then glanced at his partner who still looked dumbfounded. Josh hardened his voice and took a step closer. "Boy, you've trespassed on my property and threatened me with guns, now I can plant you right there in that corn field," Josh lifted his chin to point. "and go about my business. Or you can toss me that gun right now and go about yours. Your choice."

The outlaw gingerly grasped the weapon and tossed it toward Josh.

"That's better," Josh said, holstering his gun and quickly working the slide action of the biker's Colt to feed a round into the chamber. "Now, what am I going to do with you boys?" he mused.

"You're not going to do nothing with us," the second biker said trying to affect enough bravado to intimidate Josh. "Our brothers will come out here and butcher you slowly and burn this place to the ground."

"I think you're right," Josh said flatly. "I know your kind, and I believe they'd do that. So I guess I don't have much of a choice."

A confident grin started at the corner of the man's mouth. Josh continued talking while taking a more deliberate aim at the man's eyes, "I'll just have to shoot you boys with your own gun and bury you and those bikes somewhere you'll never be found." Josh closed one eye as if to improve his aim.

"Now wait a minute!" the fat one said, his grin quickly turned to fear. "Don't do that… Ah… Please," he added.

For a moment, Josh seriously considered the option of killing them. It was the only way to ensure his and Jolene's safety, but he quickly dismissed that thought. He knew he couldn't just shoot someone in cold blood, no matter how much they deserved it.

"I don't know what else to do. You boys scare me, and I got my misses to protect. You come in here with some wild story about some girl and the next thing I know you're talking about taking my woman and killing me. What else can I do?"

"No, mister. You don't understand." The smaller one found his voice. "We made a mistake, you see. We thought you was somebody else. We was wrong about the girl. We don't want your wife. We was just looking for... ah... our sister, who had a wreck back down the road."

"Oh, so this is all a big mistake, huh?" Josh lowered the weapon.

"Yeah," the smaller man said. "Our bad. No hard feelings?"

Josh paused as if thinking it over. "None on my part, if you boys are truly sorry."

"Oh, we really are," they said, almost in unison. "Can we just go now?" The small one added.

"Well, just let me check those saddlebags and make sure you boys don't have any more weapons, and we'll see."

He went to the bikes, keeping his eyes on the men. The saddle bags contained only a large hunting knife, some clothing, and a dime bag of marijuana. "Hope you don't mind, but I'll just keep this for a while," he said, holding up the knife.

"No, that's all right. You can have it."

"Would you boys like to stay for supper? I can have Dora rustle something up in a hurry. We don't get much company out here."

"No, thanks," Frank stammered. "We oughtta be going. If it's all right with you?" he added.

"Well, okay, but I have to tell you I'm still a little suspicious. This here's private property, and those motorcycles scare my animals. If I hear or see them again I think I'll just shoot first and save myself the hassle. You boys getting this picture?" he said, looking hard at them.

"Yeah, I guess we are," Frank said, and then added, "I don't guess you're going to give us back our guns, are you?"

Josh just shook his head and motioned with the pistol for them to head out. When they turned from his lane and headed down the logging road, he breathed heavily and his shoulders sagged.

He felt physically drained. They'd be back. This was the second time he had humiliated them and they wouldn't let it lie.

He couldn't kill them, No way to hold them, or get them to the Sheriff, so he had no choice.

Thinking the situation over, Josh brightened. Two bikers had escaped from the store — these two. Only two had run Jolene off the road. These same two came here. Hell, maybe there wasn't a gang after all. Maybe these two idiots were all alone.

Josh finished dragging the hay and hitched the Belgians back to the rake and led them to the barn to get the wagon. When he had completed the swap, he went in the cabin to tell Jolene what happened.

Her mouth hung open throughout his story. When he finished, she said, "Holy cow. I didn't hear a thing. I was plunking on your guitar," she pointed to the living room. "and singing like I was a country star." She hung her head. Josh grinned as he filled a glass with water.

"Bo Barked up a storm," Jolene continued, "but I thought he was complaining about my playing. So I told him to hush and lie down."

Josh gave a breathy chuckle. "It's okay. You couldn't have heard much anyway. The bikes were idling and it's a ways off."

"You were right about them," Jolene said. "They won't give up will they?"

"No." Josh said, "But the good news is they may be the only ones left in this so called gang."

"What? Why do you think that?"

He explained his theory. Then held up the two guns he had confiscated. "But at least now we have two more weapons."

Chapter Twenty-five

That evening, near the end of supper, Jolene said, "What's wrong Josh? You look a million miles away."

Josh set his coffee mug on the table. "Sorry, I've been going over some things in my head."

"What kind of things?"

"Well plans, or possible plans. Mostly worries. I'm pretty sure the gang will come back and try again. And we can't count on those two morons being the only ones." Josh dabbed his mouth with a napkin. "They won't buy my story after they've had time to think about it. And when they do come back they'll be all business. No threats — just action. So we have to be ready to act ourselves."

Jolene stopped her fork half way to her mouth and set it back on the plate. The intense concentration on her face told Josh she was as committed as he. He continued, "I figure burning us out of here will be their top strategy. And I sure don't want that to happen — here or at the barn. So we have to make a stand someplace else."

"But where can we go, Josh?"

"I've been thinking. That old rock foundation up where the logging road ends might be perfect. It's nestled right against a cliff and the only thing left is a shallow pit and some rubble. If we can get to it in time, it might make a good fort."

"Okay, but we can't just stay there until they come back, can we?"

"No, they'll have to know where we are, or they'll just come in, thinking we're here, and burn this place down. Can't have that."

"So how are we going to pull that off?" Jolene sipped her water.

"Well, I think I'll take some of our weapons and ammunition and store them in a tarpaulin until we can get there. Then we can somehow lead them away from the cabin and barn."

"How're we going to do that?"

"Don't know yet, but I'll think of something."

"What if that doesn't work, Josh?"

"I don't know that either. I guess we just run and let it all burn." Josh turned away wincing at that painful thought.

After a moment of silence, Jolene said, "Josh, I think I can travel now. Should we go to town and call the Sheriff?"

"That's an option I guess, but they'll come back here anyway and burn me out. I can't let that happen. I just can't leave, Jo." Josh looked down at Jolene, and shook his head. "Just can't." Looking directly into her eyes, he said, "But that's a good idea. I think you should ride in and get Hannedy or someone to take you to the Sheriff."

"No way. I'm not going anywhere without you."

"But…"

"No. I'm not going. That's final."

The glare in her eyes told him not to push it. "Okay then. But we keep the horses saddled so we can get away fast, we can go places on horseback they can't."

Jolene's face twisted, "I feel so horrible. God, if they destroy everything you have here…"

"We won't let that happen. We'll be okay Jo." Josh hoped he sounded more confident than he felt.

"I'm really sorry for putting you in the middle of this." Her eyes softened.

"You didn't put me in the middle of anything – I did." Josh reached across the table and touched her hand. "As they say— shit happens."

Bo's low throated growl awakened Josh instantly. He sat up, eyes wide trying to find light. Only moonlight filtered into the loft. He felt for the flashlight next to the bed, but didn't turn it on. Snatching his Glock with the other hand, he eased out of bed and headed for the stairs. Bo's growl intensified. Josh touched the dog and he quieted.

Silently, Josh tread the stairs, pausing on the landing. Moonlight through the windows showed nothing in the living room. Through the hall and into the kitchen. Bo growled again. Josh held the flashlight alongside the Glock and turned it on, swiping his arms right and left across the room.

A pair of beady eyes glowed in the diffused light at floor level. Josh jerked and pointed the light at the eyes. Bo barked. A fat raccoon waddled toward the rear door, then scampered out the dog opening. Josh sighed and lowered his head and weapon, as his heart rate started back to normal.

It wasn't the first time critters had come through the doggie door looking for a morsel of food, but they usually didn't set off Josh's survival alarms like this one had.

On his way back to the loft, Josh held his hand over the flashlight lens and shined it into the bedroom. Jolene lay peacefully asleep. He watched for a minute. Hmmm, no snoring.

The next morning during breakfast, Josh told Jolene about their visitor last night. At first her eyes wide in horror as he drew the story out, then she laughed when he told her it was only a raccoon.

"Not funny at the time, Josh said. "You feel up to coming to the barn with me? You should be familiar with the entire place, and I have to do chores."

"I'd love to."

Josh put the dishes in the sink and held his hands out for Jolene. She grabbed both hands and stood. Josh walked slowly as Jolene hobbled alongside to the barn. Bo raced ahead.

When they entered, Josh pulled a bench near the milking station, and motioned for her to sit, while he attended to his feeding chores. He sent Bo for Lucy.

Jolene twitched her nose adjusting to the barn odors while watching him milk the cow. "How in the world did you learn that, you being a city boy and all?" she asked.

"I was raised on a small farm in Ohio. After my dad died we went to live with my grandparents. I think I told you they were Amish. Well, I didn't think so then, but it was a great life."

The cats skirted warily around Jolene and took their usual position next to Josh.

He aimed a teat and gave the cats a squirt. "That's one of the reasons I choose to live this way. There's peace in being self-sufficient."

A joyous laugh burst from Jolene. Josh looked up as she giggled. He hadn't heard her laugh until now. It sounded musical.

"What?"

She pointed at the cats. "That was wonderful, Josh. Do it again."

Josh aimed and squirted. Tom and Jeri lapped the milk from the air. Jolene laughed again, slapping her leg with joy.

Josh returned to his milking, chuckling himself.

"But you mean you learned all this farming stuff as a kid? I saw the canned goods, the garden, and these old tools." She nodded to the hay rake and mower. "You built the cabin and barn, and living like this... Well it's beyond my comprehension."

"Well, what I didn't learn from my grandparents, I found in the Foxfire books. I have the entire collection."

"Foxfire books? You mentioned those one other time. What are they?"

"It's a series of books put together by an English teacher in Georgia, back in the sixties. He had his students interview old hill people about how they lived and survived without modern conveniences. The books cover every conceivable topic known to human survival."

"Well I'm still amazed at how you live like this. Before seeing it, I would have said it was impossible, but now that I've seen it, it seems to run pretty smoothly. Things need done around here and you do them, but nothing is hectic or stressful." She paused. "Well, some things are lately."

Josh smiled, happy that she had seen the beauty of his new life.

"Still," she continued, "as wonderful as all this is," she waved her arms in a circle. "Don't you yearn for people to talk to?"

"Oh sure. Sometimes. But at the same time people have caused me a lot more heartache and trouble than animals," Josh said, continuing to milk.

He looked up at Jolene. Her face had a distant sad look. Uh oh. "Actually," he added, "these past weeks have given me a little different perspective. Having you around has helped me see what I've been missing.

"Yeah, having me around has sure made your life simpler."

Josh noted her jaw clinch when she ground out the words. "Look Jo, our situation has been hectic yes, but there's been stretches when things felt... well, normal and I haven't had that in quite a while. I kinda like it."

Chapter Twenty-six

Outlaw Headquarters

"Well?" Snake eyed the two hesitant fools sheepishly standing in his office looking at their boots. "You'd better have some good news for a change. Is the girl dead?"

Frank winced, "We don't know, Snake."

"You don't know!" Snake yelled. "What the hell do you mean, you don't know?"

"Well, damn it; she wasn't in the Jeep when we got back there, and we looked all around, but couldn't find the bitch."

Toad mumbled, "Tell him about that old man, Frank."

Frank gave Toad a quick warning glance.

"What old man?" Snake asked, working himself into another rage.

"Did you idiots have to off somebody else?"

"Oh, no," Frank said quickly. "He was just some farmer that lived up in those mountains. We thought the girl might be there, but he said the only woman there was his wife."

"And you believed him, huh?"

"Well, no, not really but he kind of got the drop on us and made us leave."

"He made you leave! He made you leave! Weren't you two armed?"

"Well sure, Snake."

"Well?" Snake said, eyes wide, mouth incredulously agape.

"Well," Frank stammered, "He, ah, well... He kinda took our guns, and... well, we were lucky to escape."

"He took your guns! Just like that, huh?" Snake snapped his fingers and shook his head. "How in the hell did he take your guns?"

"Well, you see, he had this real big pistol, and he pulled it out before we saw it."

Snake stared at the pair in disbelief. Frank rushed on, "Hell, Snake, that old man was going to shoot us in cold blood. He really thought hard about it. He said he'd just bury us and our bikes in the woods, cause he was afraid we'd come back. He'd a done it too, I seen it in his eyes, but we talked him out of it."

Snake glared at them for a long time. Finally he spoke.

"I should just take you two assholes to the Sheriff and turn you in myself and be done with it. It would sure make life easier."

"You, and what army?" Toad challenged, his face reddening with anger.

Snake reached to his belt and drew a Colt Python. "Me and this army," He said, patting his gun with his free hand. "By the way Toad, where's your gun?"

"Oh, yeah," was all Toad could say as he hung his head.

"Now Snake," Frank interjected. "We can still make this right."

Snake was capable of just shooting them both, and Frank knew it. He rushed on, trying to calm things down. "Let's just go out there and kill all the sons-a-bitches. We can do it. We take all the boys and just wipe them out." Frank moved closer. "Listen, Snake, I think that old guy might be the same guy who busted up Jake and Pete at that store, or he could be that guy's dad. I couldn't really tell cause he looked a lot older."

"What?" Snake said, shaking his head as if to clear it.

"Yeah, he looked a lot older with that beard and all, but Snake, he was fast and hard for an old man. And we didn't get a real good look at him at that store, but this dude was real fast with that gun." Frank squinted his eyes in thought. "Yeah, it all makes sense, he's the same guy, or if he is the dad, then the asshole's probably there too. What do you say we just go out there and get him and the girl all at once?"

Snake looked hard at both men, "You two could have done that a long time ago if you weren't so fucking stupid. Now I have to do it."

"But Snake, we want to do it. We owe him," Toad started.

"Oh, don't worry. You'll get your chance. We're going out there alright, but this time I'll make sure it happens." He thumped his chest with a clinched fist. "In the meantime you two get outta my sight. I've got some planning to do."

Chapter Twenty-seven

Josh hauled wagon loads of hay to the barn where he forked it onto a canvas sling attached to a twofold pulley system on the barn hood. Each load forked onto the sling then pulled up to the loft and tied off. Josh climbed to the loft each time and moved the sling of hay along the roof rail and unloaded it in the back of the mow.

That job finished and other chores attended to, Josh headed for the cabin. Pausing at the gate, his arm resting on a fence post, he gazed at the distant horizon. A deep breath, exhaled from the bottom of his diaphragm, punctuated the view. The afternoon sun setting atop the western mountain range, cast a warm golden hue over his entire valley. He couldn't stop the soft smile.

After supper he and Jolene settled on the couch in front of a small fire. Josh produced a jug of peach wine from last fall's harvest and poured two glasses.

"You are something else," Jolene commented, sipping the wine.

"Why?"

I just can't get over how you live like this, and it all seems so… civilized."

"Oh, you think I should be more like a caveman, huh?"

"Yeah sure." She raised her glass. "A caveman who serves wine to the damsel in distress."

Josh turned to her and raised his glass. "To the best looking damsel in this caveman's domain."

"Thank you sir." She nodded, tilting her glass to his. "And to my fuzzy caveman savior."

They shared a smile with their wine.

* * * *

The next day after morning chores, Josh gathered all his weapons and sorted out which ones to keep in the cabin and which ones to stash in the old foundation. The ammunition for each weapon stored with each stash. He oiled and wrapped the guns in a canvas tarp and sealed it with duct tape. In a tote bag he stowed two quart canning jars of water, a bag of dried deer jerky, and some dried apples.

Supplies ready to go, Josh called to Jolene, "Hey Jo, will you come and help me?"

"Be right there," she answered.

When she arrived on the front porch, he said, "I'm going to haul this stuff up to the foundation I told you about. You want to come along?"

"You bet I do."

"How's the leg feel?"

"Much better. I hardly notice it."

Josh returned from the barn leading Buck and the other horse.

"You've already met Buck; this one's name is Red. He's a Tennessee Walker. You ride Buck. He's gentler and smaller than Red."

Walking around to the left side of Red, Josh said, "When I get up could you hand me that bundle?"

Jolene picked up the load as Josh mounted the big horse. "This is heavy," she said.

"Full of guns and ammo. You can take that other tote bag. It's got water and some jerky, just in case."

As she bent for the bag, he said, "Oh, I forgot to ask if you can ride?"

"Hah! Of course I can. I used to have a pony when I was little, and a boy I dated from Mason had horses. We used to ride all the time."

"Okay then, mount up and follow me."

Josh walked the horses up the quarter mile lane struggling to balance the load on his lap and saddle. He managed to nudge the reins enough to turn Red up the logging trail. Bo romped along with the caravan. When they'd gone as far as they could on horseback, Josh threw his right leg over the saddle horn and slid off with his load. Bo happily chased after a flitting butterfly.

Josh led Jolene another fifty yards or so up the steep hill through rocks and rubble to the foundation nestled into a jagged cliff. Setting his bundle down, he looked back to the logging road. A clear view of most of the road. Good. No cover.

The sloping valley to his left led down to his fenced cornfield. To his right the road ended against a rock wall on one side and a sheer drop on the other. No way for them to sneak up on the foundation.

Perfect, he thought. Now if only we can convince them to chase us up here.

He and Jolene set about clearing the rubble out of the foundation to make a place for themselves where they wouldn't be too exposed. Satisfied he had done all he could to ensure their safety, Josh said, "Well, let's get back."

At the end of the lane to the cabin, Josh pulled Red to a halt. Buck eased alongside. "Jolene, we're going to have to run these horses hard if it comes to it. Can you handle that?"

"I think so. It's been a while."

"Okay," Josh said. "Let the reins slack and nudge Buck in the flanks with your heels. He'll respond. And Jo, he starts off really fast, so grab the saddle horn before you kick him. Let's race back to the cabin."

With that, Jo leaned forward in the saddle and kicked Buck's flanks yelling, "Hah!"

She had a two horse lead before Josh could urge Red into a gallop. Buck would be a sure winner anyway. Red didn't stand a chance against the quarter horse in a short race. The Walker was bred more for running endurance.

When they skidded to a stop at the barn, Jolene eased off the saddle, squealing, "I won, I won." She hopped up and down like cheer leader after a touchdown.

"You did good," Josh said dismounting.

"That was so much fun."

Aside from laughing at the cats, this reaction of pure joy was the first Josh had seen since they'd met. He smiled. She wears joy well.

After unsaddling and wiping down the horses, he turned them out to pasture. Leading Jolene back to the cabin he filled her in on the rest of his plan.

They set about gathering small boulders and placing them in a circle in front of the cabin at the edge of the lane. Josh explained they were making a large fire pit so the Outlaws would be lit up if they came at night. "If it's dark when they come, and that's when I'd do it, they'll have headlights to see and blind us. So I want to light them up if we can."

The fire ring completed, they gathered a large stack of downed tree limbs of all sizes from the woods across the lane. These they stacked near the pit.

Josh scurried to the back of the cabin and retrieved some of the old newspapers Ross always saved for him, to use as a fire starter. He returned to the front and placed the paper in the pit. He broke up smaller twigs and stacked them on top of the paper. Larger pieces of wood were added until he had enough for a good bonfire.

Josh returned to the pit a little later with a cup of melted bacon grease, and doused the wood in the pit with the grease.

That should ensure a rapid ignition, he thought. He covered the fire pit with another tarp to protect it in case it rained.

"Well, that should do it," he declared. "I sure hope this works."

Chapter Twenty-eight

After supper Josh went to the barn with Bo to get the horses in. He saddled both and put them in their stalls. "Sorry boys, but you have to keep these on for a while." The Belgians, he released from their stalls and turned out to pasture with the cow and bull. He didn't want them trapped in the barn if it were set on fire.

That evening Josh and Jolene sat at the kitchen table playing Scrabble.

"I'm glad you shaved that awful beard, Josh."

"But you said you liked it, when I first started."

"No, I said I didn't mind, but I lied to salve your ego."

"I don't have an ego."

"Then why'd you shave?"

"It itched." He jutted his chin. "And besides, I don't think I'll need a disguise anymore."

"What… ever." She gave a flick to her head flinging her hair back, Valley Girl style.

They laughed easily.

"By the way," Josh perked up as he remembered he hadn't told Jo yet. "I put the CB antenna up higher on the water tower. I tried to get through to the store, but no one answered. I did get through to the Sheriff though." Jolene's eyes widened. "Well, almost," he continued. "One of the road crews monitoring channel nine, answered when I called. I told him who I was and to have Deputy Zimmer call us when he came on duty. I think he got most of that, but then it started breaking up."

"But… Will they…" Jolene stammered. Excitement lit her face.

"I tried to tell him what happened, Jo, but it crackled and broke up a lot. I'm not sure he got much of my transmission. I did get through to a trucker, and that was pretty clear. So the damn thing is working better."

"That's great, Josh. Did you tell them about the shooting at the store?"

"I tried," Josh spread his hands showing frustration. "Like I said, he didn't get much of my transmission, and there's way too much to tell. Mark was off duty and I wanted to make sure the deputy understood to have Mark call me when he came in. I can explain it all to him later." Josh sipped the last of his coffee. "Other deputies or even the dispatcher might not know anything about our situation. All they could do would be to dispatch another crew, and we know they couldn't get to us. It'll be better when I can explain it all to Mark."

Josh drew another letter, forming a measly two letter word. He concentrated, but not on the game. Might just be paranoid about the Outlaws. Maybe this whole club chapter is as inept as the two he'd dealt with. Maybe they weren't as vengeful as the ones back east. Maybe there were only the two idiots. Maybe his warnings had worked. Maybe.

Jolene formed a word using a z on a double word score. She giggled and clapped with glee. Josh sat stoically with a scowl on his face.

Bo's head jerked up from his nap, ears searching the night. Josh's peripheral vision caught Bo's reaction. Josh immediately tensed, his eyes squinted in concentration. He raised his hand to quiet Jo. Wide eyed fear registered on her face. Josh rushed to the front porch. The faint sound of motorcycle exhaust rumbled in the far distance. So much for paranoia. Bo growled at his side. "Hush Bo."

The distant sounds gradually diminished as bikes shut down, one or two at a time. The night became deathly still. Josh had expected them to come roaring up to the cabin in reckless abandon. So far they weren't following his plan.

In a rush he yelled, "Jo, go get the horses and hitch them to the pasture gate out back." She stood behind him in the doorway, eyes narrowed. Resolve, not fear, hardened her expression.

Josh lowered his voice, "I'll set the fire and get our weapons ready. Do it quickly, Jo. I don't want you exposed if they come down quick."

"What about Bo?"

"Take him with you and tell him to stay in the barn. He'll listen. Leave the door cracked so he and the cats can get out if there's a fire. And Jo, be careful."

She nodded, turned and dashed for the back door.

Inside Josh extinguished the hurricane lamp and headed for the fire pit. He wanted the bikers lit up when they came in. The fire would light up the cabin, but the Outlaws would stay on the outside. No cover on the cabin side. Josh also wanted them to see him and Jolene when they ran.

Standing near the fire ring, he strained his eyes and ears up the lane trying to see or hear movement. Seeing none, he quickly lit the fire and went back into the house.

He heard Jolene talking on the CB. Hysteria rose in her voice as she tried to make someone on the other end understand their situation. After repeatedly giving directions, she finally yelled, "Just tell Deputy Zimmer that Josh and Jolene need help at the cabin."

"You got through?" Josh said.

"Not that it'll do much good," her voice tense with frustration. "That woman wasn't getting the picture."

"Well we'll just stick to our plan and hope for the best," Josh said. He offered a silent prayer.

Directing her to one front window, Josh settled below the other, keeping a vigil on the lane. He had armed her with the twenty gauge shotgun and the snub nosed revolver. Josh had the scoped .222 rifle, the 12 gauge shotgun and his Glock .9mm. They waited.

Josh saw movement from the trees on the other side of the lane. Branches bent and swayed. A lone figure emerged from the darkness and snuck toward the fire.

"Stay down," he whispered.

He spotted some other movements from the brush on the far side of the lane as well. The figure approaching the fire had something in his hand. When the man arrived close to the fire, Josh saw he carried a Molotov cocktail. "Shit," he whispered. A gasoline soaked rag fuse dangled near the flames. In the firelight Josh noted an evil smile on the biker's face.

Josh eased the scoped rifle out the opened window and sighted on the bottle, took a breath and held it. The fuse dipped nearer the flames. The crack of the high powered weapon resulted in a loud "WOOOSH!" when the bottle shattered and sprayed gasoline on the raging bonfire and all over the exposed body of the would-be arsonist. The man screamed and ran engulfed in flames, arms flailing.

The woods and brush exploded with a barrage of gunfire. Bullets smacked into the cabin logs and broke the glass in the upper panes of both raised windows.

When the rain of bullets slowed, Josh told Jo, "Okay, don't expose yourself, but fire five rounds from the shotgun then head for the back door and wait for me."

She positioned herself to the left of the window and did as instructed. When Josh saw her reach the rear door, he called out, "Don't go out yet."

Josh spaced five of his 12 gauge rounds fanning the brush behind the fire and immediately rushed to join Jo. He quietly opened the rear door a crack and peeked out to see if any of them had snuck around the house. The horses stood jittery from the gunfire, but not keyed to an intruder. Josh eased out the door and motioned Jolene to follow. Incoming gunfire peppered the front of the cabin to no avail.

"Come on," he whispered. They sprinted the few steps to the horses. Once mounted, Josh held up his hand waiting for a lull in the gunfire. When it slowed, he yelled, "Go!" and kicked Red into action. They angled from the back of the cabin around the chicken coop and hit the lane at a full gallop just past the corner of the garden. Josh whooped loudly to urge the horses on, and to alert the Outlaws.

Someone yelled, "They're getting away!"

More shots rang out. The last thing Josh heard among all the cursing and shouting was, "Get the bikes."

Buck surged ahead as Josh knew he would. He wanted to keep himself between Jolene and the gunfire.

Well, some of the plan seemed to be working in their favor, Josh thought, as they galloped up the lane.

Shots rang out behind them. When they reached the end of the lane, Josh saw a muzzle flash in front of them, and heard a shot, then two more. He hadn't anticipated some bikers staying back. Turning up the logging road, he shouted to Jolene, "Stay low." When he glanced, he saw her slumped over the saddle horn. "Shit!"

Josh turned in the saddle and emptied the magazine from his Glock in the direction of muzzle blasts. Approaching the end of the road, Josh heard the roar of Harley's starting. Jolene still bent forward. Damn! Damn! Damn!

Buck slowed as they neared the dead end, allowing Josh to catch up. Jerking the reins brought Red to a skidding halt at the road end. Buck instinctively pulled up at the same time. Josh grabbed the halter. Jolene sat up straight.

"God, I thought you were shot, Jo," he yelled.

Jumping from the horse, she said, "No just scared."

Josh turned the horses along the fence line down toward the pasture, slapped them hard on their rumps, and yelled, "Hah!" The horses cut across country down the hill along the back of the cornfield, stirrups flapping.

Scrambling up the incline, head lights illuminated them just before they managed to jump into the foundation pit.

Unable to go any further, motorcycles veered off the road and into the bush. Immediately a barrage of indiscriminate shots peppered the bluff behind the foundation. The second string of blasts came from a fully automatic weapon. Bullets pinged off rocks.

Josh returned fire with the last two shells in his shotgun driving the bikers to ground. One headlight shattered, soon followed by the others being turned off. "When we get return fire," he told Jo. "Wait until it stops, and then fire the last two rounds from your shotgun. Stay down and just put the barrel over the rocks and shoot in their direction. Stay low, then empty your pistol in their direction. I'll reload and get our other weapons."

He quickly retrieved his cache of weapons and ammo and reloaded his shotgun. He had already slammed a fresh magazine in the Glock. After he heard two shots from Jo's shotgun he grabbed her weapon and quickly fed seven more shells in the tube. A strong metallic sulfur odor filled the air. The barrage of wild gunfire continued for a few minutes with little effect.

The Outlaws couldn't sneak up on them. No cover, and the widespread shotgun blasts blanketed a large area. So Josh told Jolene to ease off and save ammunition unless she saw movement.

"Got ya," she called, scanning the area.

What a girl, he thought. She's holding up like a trooper.

Abruptly the shooting slowed as both sides tried to acquire actual targets. Sporadic gunfire and quiet periods continued. During each lull Josh fed shells into the empty Glock magazine. He heard someone barking orders below. There seemed to be more than he had anticipated. This is not looking good, he thought.

The Outlaws had taken cover behind their bikes and the few boulders along the logging road. The forty yards or so between them and the old foundation, stood open, except for scattered high weeds, scrub brush, and loose shale. "You doing alright, Jo?"

"I'm good." He heard the focus in her voice.

Every time Josh saw a muzzle flash, he returned fire. He heard yelps of pain mixed with cursing. No doubt he and Jolene were causing more damage than they received, but he didn't know how many there were. If we can hold out until daybreak, he thought, the Outlaws would be more exposed. Hope we have enough ammo. If not…

The gun battle raged on with periodic calms. Neither side able to gain an advantage. The bikers were pinned down behind boulders and motorcycles, and every time one of them tried to sneak up, Josh and Jolene drove them back or stopped them cold with gunfire. At the same time, Josh and Jolene were effectively trapped in their makeshift fort.

The moon rose three quarters full with a mountain clear sky. Josh saw a wave of movement in the tall weeds on the hillside in front of the foundation. Three quick blasts from the twelve gauge and the movement stopped.

When return fire continued to come, Josh said,"Jo, there's just too many of them. We may not have enough ammunition to hold them off. If I see we're getting low, I want you to sneak out the side and feel your way down that cliffside until you come to a creek. It leads to the lake. You can stay hidden in that thick underbrush for a long time. I'll hold them off until you're out of here."

"I'm not going anywhere without you."

"Yes you are. I'll follow you when I can." No need for both of us to die, he cringed at the thought.

Shots continued to be exchanged through the night. Josh took stock of their ammo supply. It was running low. A motorcycle headlight came on and turned in their direction. Using the last .222 round, Josh shot out the headlight. Damn, we're not going to make it.

The night turned still again. Josh risked lifting his head above the foundation. He saw a bright glare from the logging road. Concentrating on the spot, he discerned it was the moon reflecting from a chrome gas tank of one of the motorcycle. He heard someone shout, "Turn all the headlights on and point em' up there!"

Josh picked up the .308 deer rifle and took careful aim on the shiny reflection. Two motorcycle headlights lit the trail, but before they were turned toward the foundation, Josh squeezed off a shot.

The bullet punctured through the gas tank and spewed gasoline onto the hot exhaust. His second shot struck a header pipe, and the bike burst into flames followed by the gas tank explosion. The night sparkled and the flames exposed several bikers. Josh and Jolene opened up on them with what little ammo they had left. Several went down amid screams of pain. None of the bikers had turned the headlights on.

He reached for one of the few sticks of dynamite. Needed to save some ammo for their escape. "When this explodes, slip out the side like I said."

"No."

"Do it, Jo. I'll use the other sticks and follow." He pushed his last full magazine into the Glock, and tucked it into the holster.

Josh jerked his head up in response to a strange sound echoing through the night air. A distinct "Whoomp, whoomp, whoomp of helicopter blades confused and then thrilled him. The logging road suddenly lit up like a Friday night football field. Rotor blades washed the air clear of gun smoke.

A loud speaker blared, "Put down your weapons. This is the Caribou County Sheriff's office." A burst of automatic weapon fire sprayed the area just short of the fully exposed bikers. The few bikers standing hesitantly dropped their weapons and placed hands on top of their heads.

Josh and Jolene were as stunned as the bikers at this turn of events. Like deflated balloons, both slumped back on the rock rubble as if it were a feather bed and sighed in relief. With no gunfire and the helicopter shut down, the night seemed eerily still. Josh heard Sheriff's Deputies barking orders from the chopper, but little else. Jolene suddenly rolled over to Josh and kissed him on the lips. It was a warm kiss that lingered a moment. Josh instinctively started to press into her in response to the kiss. Just as abruptly, she pulled away, jumped to her feet and headed for the deputies.

Stunned, Josh struggled to figure out what had just happened.

* * * *

Snake lay behind a large boulder near the downhill end of the string of motorcycles when the sky lit up, and the loudspeaker blared. He had taken a hit in the back just before diving behind the rock. It stung, but he couldn't tell how bad it was. He could move freely, so it couldn't be too bad. He slunk farther downhill out of the light. As the chopper landed, amid the increasing noise of the blades and the diminishing light to the rear of the helicopter, Snake saw his chance to escape.

He grabbed the nearest bike and pushed it further down the hill. When he was well past the cabin lane, he mounted the bike and coasted on downhill. When he thought he was out of hearing range, he started the motorcycle and cautiously rode up the trail they had come in on. The further he went, the madder he became.

How could an old man and a girl have thwarted his plan and practically wiped out his entire gang? Well, he'd make them pay. Before he was finished with them, they'd wish they had died a fast, merciful death.

Chapter Twenty-nine

Josh didn't think it could be done, but the chopper pilot had managed to put the bird down on the narrow trail. Several deputies scurried to round up the bikers. Josh trudged toward the helicopter. He saw Jolene waving arms and talking non-stop to a nearby deputy.

Zimmer stood with a huge grin plastered on his face. "See, I told you not to worry," he said when Josh approached. "I knew we'd get these bastards. Didn't I tell you?" They both laughed.

Josh shook his head in wonder and said, "Yeah, you did, Mark, you sure did."

Jolene approached, bouncing around like a child at a birthday party. "How'd you get here? How did you find us? Did any get away? Maybe they're hiding in the woods," she babbled.

"Whoa, little lady. One at a time," Zimmer said, holding up both hands.

"It's just the adrenalin," Josh said to Zimmer, and then turned to Jolene. "Take some breaths. It takes time for the adrenalin rush to fade, but you'll be okay in a few minutes."

"Damn, Josh, you're bleeding," the deputy said, abruptly.

"Yeah, I took one in the arm, just before you showed up."

"Oh, Josh!" Jolene almost screamed. "I didn't know."

"It's all right, Jo, it didn't hit a bone and the bleeding has slowed. It burns like hell, but I'll be okay."

He turned back to Zimmer. "How did you find us?"

"Well, I had a fairly good idea before, and after talking with Deputy Beldon, the guy you talked to on the CB," he explained, "I had a better fix on the vicinity. Miss Braxton here," he nodded at Jolene, "gave some pretty good directions to the dispatcher. I listened to the tape, and then went to meet the chopper pilot." Zimmer took off his hat and wiped his brow on his sleeve. "We still would have had a hard time finding you if it hadn't been for the explosion and fire."

Looking around at the destruction and mass of wounded and dead bikers, Zimmer commented, "It doesn't look like you needed our help anyway, Josh."

"The hell you say. We were almost out of ammo. Our butts would have been fried in no time. Those guys must have been ready for a war. They wasted a lot more ammunition than we did. They shot up the cabin and this whole mountainside."

"Come over to the chopper, Josh, we've got a first aid kit. I'll put a compress on that wound before you bleed to death."

"I can't believe your department has a helicopter, Mark." Josh shook his head.

"No," Mark said. "I borrowed it from the state boys. He pointed to the trooper in the pilot seat, "Steve, is a friend, and he met us in that big field behind the general store. We've used them before for mountain searches."

"Well I'm sure glad. You saved our butts."

Josh took his shirt off and saw a two inch long groove cut out of his left shoulder. "Not too bad," Mark said, reaching for a compress.

The bullet, or maybe a rock chip, had only grazed Josh. A lot of blood but little damage. Mark applied a four inch compress and some tape to the wound.

Mark finished the bandage and something caught his eye. He laughed, pointing to Jolene, who had another deputy cornered, peppering him with questions. "Look at her. She's still hyped."

"She'll crash soon enough," Josh said slipping the bandaged arm into a sleeve.

They stood silent for a moment surveying the battle field. Apparently deep in thought, Deputy Zimmer said, "What a mess. I'm going to have to get some four wheel drive vehicles up here, the coroner, a medevac unit," he unfolded a finger with each point. "And then figure some way to haul all these bikes out of here." He paused looking at Josh. "You folks sure have caused me a lot of work. Could you please stop killing people, Josh?"

"They started it," Josh quipped.

Zimmer lowered his head and gave a mock scowl. "Sooner or later we'll be able to get you to a hospital to patch that arm, but it'll probably be later."

"Don't worry about my arm," Josh said. "I can handle that.

Standing next to them, Jolene said, "Oh no, Josh." A wicked smile lit up her eyes. "I get to do that. I owe you."

"Huh?" Zimmer said, looking from one to the other.

"Never mind," Josh said.

After a moment of thought, Zimmer said, "Josh, do you think I can get a flatbed truck up here to haul these bikes out?"

"Could be," Josh paused, thinking. "The loggers probably came up this high when they cut the trail. It'll have to be four-wheel-drive though."

The other deputies had rounded up and handcuffed the remaining able bodied outlaws and had them sitting in a group near the chopper. Zimmer rattled off information on his radio, calling for medevac for the wounded. After giving instructions to the dispatcher, he handed the mic to the pilot who gave the coordinates for the medevac pilot.

Zimmer stepped out of the chopper and looked down toward the cabin. "Is that your place on fire down there, Josh?"

"No. I built a bonfire."

"A bonfire? Why?"

"We were going to have a pep rally and weenie roast, until they crashed the party." He nodded toward the Outlaws, then flashed a smile at Mark.

Mark shook his head. Another deputy approached. "I need the first aid kit." Mark reached into the bird and handed the kit to the deputy. He turned back to Josh and Jolene. "Looks like I'm going to be here the rest of the night; can you guys make it back to your cabin all right?"

"The rest of the night is almost here." Josh said, looking to the east. "Yeah, we can walk back. Let us know if you need anything."

"Okay, I'll come down when I get this mess cleaned up. I'll need statements as to what all happened here."

"Okay." Josh nodded. By the way," Josh said, turning back, "There's at least one more body down by the cabin someplace. He kinda caught himself on fire. There might be some others there as well. There was a lot of shooting going on."

"Oh shit, Josh. We've got enough here. Bodies seem to follow you around. I'm going to have to charge you with something."

"Like Highway Mopery with intent to creep?" Josh asked with a grin.

Looking at him quizzically, Zimmer said, "Huh?"

"Josh smiled. "Oh never mind, that's only a term we used back home. I thought it might be universal."

"Get the hell out of here before you remember any more bodies."

Josh put his arm around Jolene's shoulders. She leaned into him and they started walking down the trail.

"Is it really over, Josh?"

"Yeah, I think so. With that many out of order or in jail, there can't be enough to rally another attack, unless another chapter gets involved. And as dumb as these yahoos have been, I don't think that'll happen. The Outlaws I know wouldn't let these guys wash their bikes."

When they got to the cabin lane, Josh put two fingers to his lips and whistled loudly. Before they had gone another 500 feet, Bo charged up wagging his tail. They both knelt down to greet him. Bo jubilantly sprayed then with wet kisses.

* * * *

After making coffee and settling Jolene on the couch, Josh and Bo rounded up the horses, put them in their stalls, and fed them a ration of oats. A little after daylight Josh heard someone step onto the front porch. He turned and saw the uniform through the window. The hackles on Bo's back stood up and he growled menacingly. "Stand down, Bo. It's okay." He patted the dog, and called. "Come on in, Mark."

"Well that's about it, except for the one down here. Where is he?" Mark said, approaching the couch.

"I don't know exactly. It was dark and he was running hell bent for leather toward the lake the last I saw of him."

"Okay, the boys are searching the woods. They'll find him sooner or later." Mark paused, then continued. "There were only four dead up top; some of the others were in pretty bad shape though. Most of them had a lot of little holes in them. What the hell were you guys shooting?"

"Well," Josh started, "I didn't have any double-ought buckshot, so I had to use my duck loads – mostly two's and four's. They don't do much damage at a distance. The Glock and the rifles probably did the most."

"Yeah, we'll know a lot more after the autopsies and med reports from the hospital."

"Mark, do you know about what went on at the general store before Jo came out here?" Josh asked.

"Yeah, you were right when you said they'd be back. They shot that Hannedy boy, but he's going to be all right. They left him for dead, but the bullet didn't hit any vital organs. He's a gutsy kid, got off a shot at them even with a bullet hole in his arm. He's back on his feet already."

Jolene's eyelids had been drooping, but when she heard Mark talking about Chad, she focused. "Oh, that's such good news," she said. "I've been so worried about Chad." She sank back into the couch.

The deputy continued, "When we couldn't find Ms. Braxton, I alerted the dispatcher to monitor the CB. And we've been searching. Had some volunteer ATVs out, but they mistakenly searched that other ridge over there." He pointed to his left. "Most of the trails they covered went nowhere. I tried to contact you on the CB several times after the shooting, but didn't get an answer."

"I know," Josh said, "it wouldn't have been possible anyway until I thought to move the antenna up on the water tank. Even then, it didn't work well until after dark. Before that I couldn't get anybody."

As Josh and Mark talked, Josh saw Jolene drifting deeper and deeper into an adrenalin crash. In a few minutes she fell asleep. Josh motioned for Mark to follow him to the kitchen.

Josh poured coffee, and Mark asked, "What are you guys going to do now? I can still offer you a ride back to town."

"No, not necessary. I'll bring Jolene down after she's rested. She'll be at her place so you can tell her when we're needed for the trial or whatever."

Mark took out his notebook and asked Josh to give his statement of what led to the shootout. Mark wrote as Josh rattled off the facts, as he knew them, since the original store incident. When he finished he stretched his arms wide and stifled a yawn.

"Boy," Mark glanced up grinning. "It's nice to have a victim who can give a statement I can write down verbatim. I don't have to ask all those questions to establish the elements of the crime or time line, or anything. You provided the who, what, when, where, why, and how. Finally you make my job easier." He grinned, pocketed his notebook and got up.

"Give me a call when you get to the store," Mark said, "and I'll arrange for a flatbed truck to come up here and get those bikes. We'll need you to guide us up here though."

"No problem," Josh said, rubbing the grit from his eyes.

"You look like you could use some sleep, Josh." Mark said. "How's the arm?"

"It's okay," Josh assured him. "I washed it up and decided it doesn't need stitches. I used some Second Skin and a tight bandage."

Draining the last of his coffee, Mark set the cup down, and said, "Well, okay then, I'm going to go help the boys look for a crispy critter and then get the hell out of here. See you." He waved as he turned toward the front door.

Josh went back to the couch, gently picked Jolene up and carried her to the bed. Too tired to trudge the stairs to the loft, he eased himself down beside her. Sleep enveloped him almost immediately.

Chapter Thirty

Josh awoke a few hours later and gingerly crawled out of bed so as not to wake Jolene. He left the cabin and set about his daily chores with the animals. When he returned with a pail of milk, he found Jolene at the stove, trying to fry potatoes. "How do you adjust the heat on this thing?" she asked.

"You don't." Josh grinned. "You have to move the skillet around. If you need a lot more heat, you can remove one of the lids and get directly over the flames. You'll get used to it." He chuckled.

"Oh, no I won't," she said in mock defiance.

Josh put his hand to his heart, acting as if his feelings were hurt. "But I was hoping you would stay on. I need a cook."

"That's the worst proposal I ever heard."

They both laughed. Probably from the hangover stress they'd recently endured. That, and Josh didn't want to venture too far into that vein for fear of outright rejection.

Jolene moved the skillet, went to him and hugged his waist. "Is it really over, Josh?"

"I think so," he replied, smiling down at her.

* * * *

Jolene rested her head on his chest. Does he even want me to hug him? Other than jokes he doesn't give me any signals. After a brief moment of uncertain comfort, Jolene said, "How burnt do you like your potatoes?"

"Just about like that," he said. "I still have to get the eggs and feed the chickens, so if you want, you can start burning some eggs; there's some in the frige, and I'll be back in a minute."

As they ate breakfast, Jolene asked, "What are we going to do now, Josh? What's going to happen to us?"

Looking up, he thought for a moment and then said, "Well, we have to go back to town tomorrow and meet Mark so I can bring him back here with a flatbed truck to haul those bikes out. After that, I don't know," he trailed off.

Jolene rose, went to the stove and filled her coffee cup, so he wouldn't see her face. I meant with us you idiot. She scowled. Why does he have to be so dense? Why did I cut that wonderful kiss short? Doesn't he care? Doesn't he have any feelings? How can he be so distant after what we've been through together?

She sat down and looked at him. "We'll still have to go through a trial, won't we?"

* * * *

"Oh yeah, more than one. But that'll be a while yet." Josh looked away. What's wrong with me? Why can't I tell her how I feel? I want her to stay on the farm with me. The fear of rejection – that's why. She's so young, and beautiful. She's only grateful. That's the only reason she kissed me. That kiss meant nothing to her. She was just pumped up on adrenalin. But his mind couldn't block out the memories of each embrace they had shared during the past weeks.

* * * *

Jolene stared at her coffee. What do I have to do, to get this man to make a move? Am I not attractive to him? Have I done or said something he didn't like? Is he still hung up over his wife? I know it's different with men. They hang on to love much longer. What can I do to ease his pain and make him notice me?

"So you'll be back in to town once in a while?" she said.

* * * *

"Oh, sure," Josh stuffed a fork of potatoes in his mouth. God I'm stupid. Why can't I just tell her what I'm really thinking? I want her to burn eggs every morning. I want to get lost in those beautiful eyes. I want to kiss her again… Because she would laugh at me – that's why.

As they finished eating the atmosphere became awkward with neither knowing what to say.

While doing the breakfast dishes, Josh asked, "How's your ankle doing, Jo?"

"It's good. I don't have any more pain."

"Good. I think I can take your stitches out now, if you want."

"Okay," Jolene wrinkled her brow. "I guess that would be good."

Folding the dish towel, Josh said, "You go lie down on the bed and I'll get my med kit."

"You smooth talker you. I knew it would come to this. That's all you men think about." She gave him a shy grin.

Josh flushed and said, "No... I mean... I just want to take out the stitches." But when he saw the smile on her face, he too laughed a nervous laugh. If my mind wasn't always in the gutter, he thought, I wouldn't react like that.

When he returned with his kit, Jolene was under the covers. "Will it hurt?" she asked. "I've never had stitches before." She pulled the sheet and blanket to over her arms.

"You haven't? Wow. No, you might feel the pressure and maybe a little itching, but it won't hurt."

"Let me check that ankle first." Josh lifted the cover from her legs and noticed she had taken off the baggy pants she had altered. His mind lurched to pictures he didn't want to dwell on.

He shook his head, then gently probed her ankle and calf just to make sure it was okay. No pain reaction. He removed the bandage from her leg and examined the cut. It had sealed and showed no sign of infection. A coat of Second Skin went over the wound to further protect it.

"What is that stuff?" Jolene asked in response to the coolness she felt.

"It's like superglue. It seals the wound until it heals more. It'll peel off in a couple of days." He recovered her feet.

Moving to her head wound, he gently pulled the bandage tape from her hair. With the area exposed, he snipped each stitch and carefully pulled the thread with tweezers. He swabbed the area with alcohol and blew it dry. He applied a coat of Second Skin to complete the job.

"I need to look at that other cut too, Jo." He looked down.

"Okay." After a second her eyes widened. "Oh, yeah. Well, I guess you have to." She rolled onto her left side and raised her right arm, slipping it out of the sweat shirt. She pulled the back of the shirt up, keeping her breast covered.

Josh peeled the bandage away and examined the cut. No sign of infection and it too had sealed. "Looks good," he pronounced. "I think you'll live."

"Thank you doctor."

More Second Skin applied while Josh fixated on the curvature of her breast. He hurriedly tossed supplies and equipment into his kit. "I have some work to do," he abruptly said.

Out of the corner of his eye he saw the confused look on her face but he couldn't help it. He had to get away for a while. Manual labor might take his mind off of Jolene. His fantasies were driving him crazy. The hoe and garden would give him refuge.

* * * *

Jolene sat in the rocker on the porch relaxing in the afternoon warmth when Josh came out with a glass of iced tea. He glistened with sweat from hoeing weeds in the hot sun. "I had to take a break," he said. "I thought you might be thirsty."

"This is great; just what I needed, thanks."

Josh sat down on the steps and turned toward her. She had discarded the sweatshirt in favor of one of his T shirts. That sight did not dissuade his fantasies. Their eyes locked, but neither could think of anything to say. When the moment became awkward, Jolene said, "Josh, you promised we could go swimming when my stitches were out. What about today?"

Josh smiled. "Sure, why not? But you'll have to swim in your clothes. I don't have a suit for you."

"I know, but at least I can get wet and cool off."

"I'll be right back." He rose and rushed into the cabin. He returned a few minutes later with a couple of bath towels and wearing only swimming trunks.

* * * *

Jolene appraised him in the sunlight. He had dark farmer tan lines on his neck and arms, his legs and torso tanned a lighter shade. The moisture on his upper body highlighted a rippling stomach and a chiseled chest. "We're not quite even in the voyeur category, but I'm getting there," she said, giving him a look she hoped came off as a leer.

He laughed easily. "I told you I never looked."

Getting up, she grasped his hand, and said, "Sure, sure." and led him off the porch toward the lake.

They waded into the lake to test the temperature and found it cool but welcoming in the hot sun. Bo walked the shoreline looking intently into the water, then pounced when he apparently saw a fish or crawdad. Jolene laughed.

Josh shook his head. "He never catches anything, but he loves the water."

Josh dove into the lake and swam a few strokes. He turned and stood in water to his arm pits, and beckoned for Jolene to join him. She waded to her waist then eased her upper body into the water and breast stroked toward him. She stopped short, where she could still touch bottom with only her head out of the water.

"Aaah, this is wonderful." She closed her eyes.

Josh pointed, "I usually swim out to, and around that island. It's less than a mile round trip, you want to come?"

Jolene turned to the island. "Sure," she said, "But wait just a minute. I can't swim well in these heavy pants of yours."

In a flurry of contortions she shed the wet trousers, tossed them to the shore, and announced, "Okay, let's go."

Josh had to turn and immediately start swimming for fear she would notice the blush on his face. The mere thought of her shedding her clothes brought a rush of blood to his groin.

When she caught up, they swam side by side toward the island. Their strokes slow and easy, while Bo paddled in circles each time he pulled ahead. Approaching the island shallows, Jo said, "You go on, Josh. I'm a little tired. I'll wait here for you."

"Okay," Josh said, and started swimming strong crawl strokes that frothed the water. Bo stayed with Jolene. He explored the island while Jolene sat in shallow water. When Josh returned he saw Jolene sitting amid some large rocks, her upper body out of the water. The white T shirt she wore turned opaque with wetness. He couldn't help but stare at the puckered breasts so plainly visible, then diverting his eyes said, "You ready?"

* * * *

She stood and dove into the water and started for shore. He followed. Jolene walked from the water and flopped onto the towels on the beach. This was the first time in weeks she felt whole. This place — this time, she thought. Despite all that had happened, she was happy and contented.

When Josh emerged from the water, Jolene continued her appraising look at his body. She couldn't avoid staring at the bulge in his shorts, unable to stop herself from saying the old line, "Is that a gun in your pocket or are you glad to see me cowboy?" she also couldn't stop the blush it brought to her cheeks. She looked away.

* * * *

Josh looked down and immediately flushed with embarrassment, but quipped back. "It's not my fault. You started it."

"Me! What did I do?"

Josh pointed to her hips where a dark patch showed plainly through her wet panties, then to the erect nipples showing through the wet T shirt.

"But I didn't do it on purpose," she said, tilting her head and putting her index finger to her chin demurely.

They both laughed.

Grasping her hand, Josh pulled her up and said, "Come on, we better get out of these wet clothes."

* * * *

"And into a warm bed?" she said, looking into his eyes, and then quickly clasped her hand over her mouth, shocked at what she had so brazenly said.

* * * *

Josh stood momentarily stunned. Until now their banter and innuendoes had been disguised as humor. Was that a slip of the tongue, or a true Freudian slip? He looked at her for a long moment trying to decide. Is this an open and clear invitation? Was their relationship about to take a turn? What the hell. Time to quit acting like a teenager.

Josh pulled her gently to him, pressing her wet T shirt to his bare chest. She melted into his arms. Instead of feeling the coldness of the wet shirt, he felt hot lava pouring over his body and settling in his loin. She tilted her head up to him expectantly, and they kissed a soft lingering kiss that progressed to burning passion in a few seconds. They continued to explore each other's mouths before finally breaking away.

Josh leaned back and said, "Are you sure about this? I don't want to take advantage of your situation."

She gazed into his eyes. Her right hand brushed a strand of hair from his forehead. "You take advantage of me?" she said. "I've been trying to get you to notice that I'm a real woman ever since we met. You're a slow learner, Josh." She smiled. "How about you?"

"Josh's mind flitted to Ellen. "I feel a little guilty." He hadn't been with anyone since she died.

"Don't."

Leaving the towels on the beach, they swayed, locked together, for the cabin. At the porch, Josh picked her up and carried her through the door. "Tradition." She giggled.

He put her down and they kissed again. The need and urgency built rapidly as they twisted and waltzed as one unit toward the bedroom. More kisses. Josh pulled the wet shirt over her head and outstretched arms and hungrily drank in the view for the first time with a lover's look.

Finally able to enjoy looking at her nakedness without feeling guilty of lechery, his mind soaked up the image and burned it into his memory. He slid out of his swim suit as she slipped off her damp panties. They climbed into bed and pulled covers over themselves. They lay there cuddling and kissing for a long time while their bodies warmed.

* * * *

Gradually their passion grew more fevered. Both pair of hands explored every inch of skin on the other. Jolene discovered that Josh was fully aroused almost instantly and took great pleasure when she felt him shudder as she touched him.

* * * *

They lay on their sides facing. Josh nestled his head into her neck. Soft kisses and gentle nibbles. He lightly traced his fingertips the length of her underarm and teasingly brushed against the side of her breast. Her soft moans thrilled and encouraged Josh.

He continued caressing down her side and over her hip bone. He stroked as far down her leg as he could reach then started back up on the inside of her thigh. Feather soft strokes carefully avoided the triangle, but gently brushed the edge as he went by. A gasp escaped her lips as she arched her hips. Josh continued to trail light skimming strokes over her flat belly then to the inside of the breast he had touched on the way down. As one finger flicked lightly over the nipple, she sucked in a breath and moaned again.

Scooting himself down a little further in the bed, Josh lightly skimmed that same nipple with his warm tongue. Taking cues from her physical reaction to his touches and her moans of pleasure, he finally engulfed the entire nipple in his mouth and flicked it with his tongue.

* * * *

Jolene pressed her entire body against Josh's as if trying to merge into him. She pulled his head away from her breast and drew his mouth to hers. Her tongue probed hungrily as the kiss became harder and more urgent. She found his erection again and slowly stroked. He moaned his approval and need.

* * * *

Josh returned his mouth to the erect nipple while his left hand again slid along her flat belly until it was at the triangle. She spread her legs enough for his hand to gently massage the area.

* * * *

She gave in to the pleasure that swept through her body like a wild fire.

As the passion built, they made love with an urgency born out of frustrations, as well as their need to consummate this new turn before they had time to change their minds. Two bodies blended together in ecstasy as they experimented and encouraged each other. When it was finally, finally over, they lay spent. Neither could move. Nothing in the Universe could move. They commanded it.

* * * *

That evening after supper, Josh built a small fire in the fireplace. The couple snuggled on the couch and sipped Josh's homemade wine. Neither wanted to lose the rapture they felt.

"I feel so good, Josh. I can't believe how comfortable this all is." Jolene started. "You have no modern conveniences out here, and yet you have everything. I never would have believed it possible to live like you do."

"I don't miss many of those so called modern conveniences."

"Wouldn't real hot water be nice?"

"Yeah, I stand corrected." He smiled in the flickering firelight. "But that's all."

"What? No TV?" she said in mock horror.

"No way. That's one of the main reasons I chose this lifestyle."

After a pause, Josh said, "I could get hot water and a few more lights, if I installed another solar panel. I've considered doing that."

"Hmmmm, that would be nice. But the shower today was good and warm."

"It always is on sunny days, but you sure wouldn't like it in the winter."

She nestled further into his arm and nuzzled his neck. "I can't believe how happy I am," she said.

Josh tilted her head and kissed her. "And you can't know how happy I am to hear that."

When he pulled away, she pressed further into him and urgently sought his lips again. Tomorrow they had to go back to her world and she didn't want this night to end. They continued to kiss until the passion once again built beyond their control.

As if by some unknown signal, they arose simultaneously and headed hand in hand for the bedroom. Despite their passion, they were in no hurry this time. They made love agonizingly slowly, exploring each other for every bit of sensual pleasure they could elicit. When they were both spent and completely satisfied, they slept more soundly than either had in recent times.

Chapter Thirty-one

Josh and Jolene sat comfortably rocking in their saddles as the horses plodded the paved road into Platte Junction. The general store and parking lot came into view. Jolene's eyes widened and her jaw dropped, "What the…" she started.

Josh saw the reason for her reaction. "Looks like somebody's opened your store."

They hitched the horses then crunched over the gravel parking lot to the store entrance. When they entered, Chad stood behind the counter waiting on a customer. He smiled and gave a little wave with his good arm.

After the customer left, Chad said, "I hope you don't mind, I couldn't stand sitting around the house anymore."

"No, it's great. I'm just surprised to see you. How are you doing?" She pointed to his left arm in a sling. "And how's the arm?" Jolene rounded the counter.

"Oh, I'm good. The doctor says the arm's healing real well. Get the stitches out next week."

"God, I'm so sorry you had to go through that, Chad." Jolene hugged the teen, careful not to squeeze his wounded arm.

"It's alright," Chad said. "It was mostly my fault. Mr. Grant told me to keep the shotgun ready. I should have, might've prevented some of your problems."

"No," Josh interjected. "That would have happened anyway. I'm just glad we all survived."

"Me too," Chad said. He lowered his head and looked around furtively. "It's really been kind of cool. Two girls from school came to see me. It was in the paper. "

Jolene smiled and Josh gave him a wink.

Josh said, "Deputy Zimmer told me you did real good that day."

"Well I don't know about that, but when he came by yesterday he told me you guys pretty much wiped out that whole gang," Chad commented. "He said there won't be any more problems from them."

"Yeah, I think so too," Josh said.

"I'm going to call the Sheriff's office and tell them we're back." Jolene said, then added, "Anybody want coffee?"

Both men responded, "Yes."

* * * *

An hour later Deputy Zimmer's cruiser, followed by two flatbed trucks, pulled into the parking lot. Josh went out to meet him. "You all want some coffee before we go?" he asked.

"No thanks," Mark said, "Just had some. I think we'd better get started, if we're going to get this done today."

"Right," Josh said. "I'll just tell Jolene we're leaving."

Josh climbed into the lead truck and directed the driver toward Long Run Road. Mark followed in the other truck. At the end of Long Run Josh directed the driver onto the logging trail that led to his range. The going was tough and slow up and down the rutted trails, but the four wheel drive vehicles eventually made it.

When they arrived at the top of the mountain, and exited the trucks, Mark said, "Man, you were right. I never would have found this place by myself. Now I'm amazed that we found it in the chopper the other night."

"Yeah, me too," Josh said. "But I'm real glad you did."

The four men set about the task of gathering all of the motorcycles and loading them onto the flatbeds. When they finished strapping them down, Mark asked, "Are you going back with us Josh?"

"Yep, I have to get my horses. I'll probably spend the night there. It'll be late by the time we get back."

"I forgot about your horses. You need to get a truck." Mark grinned.

"You may be right, Mark. I've actually given that some thought lately."

"You ready to go, Josh?"

"I'll need just a little more time. I have to go down and feed the other animals."

"No problem. Need any help?"

"No, but you're welcome to come along."

Mark trailed along with Josh down to the barn. While they walked, Zimmer said, "I interrogated several of the bikers, but didn't get much, except I want my attorney."

"Figures," Josh commented.

"I tried to get them to identify the leader, but none of them would cop to it. But some of them smiled when I asked."

"That's a little strange. You'd think they'd be anxious to lay the blame off on someone."

"Yeah, I thought so too."

They entered the barn and Mark strolled around examining the old farm implements while Josh fed the cows and horses. "This must be a daily grind," Mark commented.

"Daily, yeah, but not a grind. They depend on me – I depend on them."

"But you can't even go on a vacation," Mark's voice incredulous.

Josh grinned, looking at Mark. "This is a vacation."

"Some vacation." Mark shook his head. "A huge garden to tend, corn, hay, and animals to care for."

Josh stood with a scoop of oats in his hand and stared at Mark. Finally he responded. "This place is paid for. My twenty year pension is only fifty percent. Not much. It's direct deposited in the bank." He emptied the scoop in Dan's bin. "Almost all of it stays right there. My only expenses are a few monthly supplies and some supplemental feed for the animals." He waived his arm in an ark. "What else could I need?"

Mark shook his head. "Don't know, but I'd get lonely out here."

Josh's thoughts turned to the previous week with Jolene. "Yeah, sometimes." He put the scoop in the barrel.

I can see where it might limit your social life," Mark said with a wink.

"Yeah, in a way. But it's uncomplicated and peaceful – usually," Josh added with a sideways glance at Mark.

After a pause, "Anything else you have to do?" Mark asked, as Josh put the lid on the oat barrel.

"Have to feed the chickens and get eggs, if there are any. I milked Lucy this morning," Josh added, "so she'll be okay until I get back tomorrow."

When the chores were finished, Josh and Mark trudged back up the lane to the flatbeds.

"Okay boys," Mark called, "let's mount up."

The trucks slowly rocked and rolled over the trail, inching up and down the trails. Throughout the long trip, Josh sat in a semi-funk thinking of all the new developments in his life. One of the few times the flora of his mountains couldn't quell his negative thoughts.

His peaceful existence had been disrupted by the Outlaws. But that's over now. So why did it still seem so complicated? Jolene. His feelings for her brought a whole set of new worries. Is it fair to her? Is it right for him? He couldn't stop his feelings, but he also couldn't discount the negatives.

He didn't want to leave this place — she didn't want to stay.

He was too old for her – she too young.

He had responsibilities to his farm – she had responsibilities to get on with her life.

Were their feelings real – or the result of circumstances?

Had he taken advantage of her? Their activities of yesterday burned through his mind. Every nuance branded on nerve ends.

Josh felt hopelessly frustrated by questions he couldn't answer. The longer he thought, the more unsure he became.

* * * *

It was well after dark when Mark dropped him off at the store. With a wave, he said, "Thanks Josh. I'll be in touch about the trial."

"Just let Jolene know, and we'll be there."

Josh went into the store and back to the living quarters. "Hey you, I'm…" She flung her arms around his neck. "back," he finished as their lips met.

They gazed into each other's eyes. Josh's mind vacillated as he gathered his courage. Calling on internal strength, he held her at arm's length. With resolve he uttered the dreaded phrase, "Jolene, we have to talk."

Her brows pinched in a look of dismay. "What's wrong, Josh?"

"Nothing... well, I just don't know." He tried to organize his thoughts. "I've been thinking — a lot, and I we have to... sort this all out." His hand flicked a strand of hair back. He looked down absently rubbing an eyebrow. "I mean... if we don't get a hold on this situation now, it'll get beyond our control, and I don't know where it can go." Eyes flitting around, Josh tugged at his belt. "I'm trying to think of what's best for you." he added lamely.

"What are you talking about?"

"Us."

"Us?" She bristled, holding his gaze. "Control it? I don't want to control it." Then her eyes welled. "What the hell's wrong with you?"

Josh put his arms around her, then eased back to look into her eyes. "Look," he finally said softening, "I'm not bringing any of this up to hurt you, but I just don't want us to confuse our feelings. I want to make sure they're real." He paused, thinking.

She gazed at him, brows squished together. "Why wouldn't it be real?"

Josh sighed. "Jo, there's a thing called the Stockholm syndrome..."

"What..." she practically screamed, cutting him off.

Josh saw the futility of going into a long explanation. His shoulders sagged. "People under emotional stress sometimes develop feelings for the wrong reasons."

"What? You're not making any sense." Jolene looked up at him, confusion on her face.

"I know Jo, but trust me. You've been under a lot of stress lately and..."

"And you haven't?" Anger rose in her voice.

"Not like you."

"So I'm just the poor little girl who has no control over her emotions, huh?"

"That's not what I mean."

"Then what the hell do you mean? And what in the hell does any of this have to do with us?" The twisted confusion on her face turned to anger.

Josh tried to explain. "I've seen it before, Jo. People in fear for their lives can attach feelings to someone they don't even know."

Jolene's mouth hung open for a moment, her head moved in tiny back and forth motions. She pushed away from him. "You can be such an ass!" she exclaimed, storming off toward her room.

Josh caught her at the door. "Wait a minute, Jo."

She turned, with angry tears in her eyes. "All that psycho-babble bullshit, and you don't know nothing." Then her face softened, and she added, "I thought you had feelings for me."

"I do," he quickly said. "But where can it lead? I'm a lot older than you, and you have a full life to live. I'm a hermit, and you want the action of a city. There are so many differences..." He let it hang.

"How do you know what I want?" she demanded. "I don't have any idea how old you are and I don't care."

"Well, I thought... ah... when we first met you told me you wanted to get away from here as fast as possible."

"That was a lifetime ago, Josh. In all your years of experience, you sure haven't learned much about women, have you?"

"What do you mean?"

"Women can adjust to changes much quicker than men. We may be more emotional, but we don't just give in to them. Don't you know it's not the place that matters?" She turned away, paused then twisted back, teeth clinched. "And we're obviously a hell of a lot smarter than men." She stomped off toward the kitchen.

Josh quickly caught up to her again and turned her around to face him. "How the hell could I ever expect you to want to hook up with a hermit farmer like me? "

"Try asking!" This time she ran to her room and slammed the door.

Josh sagged, his strength sapped by his own foolishness and her actions. He felt like a fool. He thought he was doing the right thing. He'd tried to protect her from herself, and didn't want to see her hurt. Didn't want to be hurt. Just wanted her to be sure. What in the hell just happened? Instead of better, he'd made it worse.

He called out, "Jolene." No answer. He turned away from the door, then turned back, only to turn away again. His shoulders felt heavy. If his brain were confused before, it was catatonic now. What should he do? Give her time? That's the only thing he could do. Shit, he'd messed everything up again. He wanted to pound his head against a wall. If he pursued it now he'd probably make it even worse.

Josh trudged outside and leaned on the stoop rail, staring at the heavens. Gradually a resolve came over him. He would let her think things over, and then they would talk and work it all out.

Buck and Red were still hobbled in the field where he'd left them. The saddles and blankets lay on the end of the stoop. When he glanced at them he made his decision. He would go back to his place, let her cool off, and come back in a few days. He saddled the horses and rode off in the waning sunlight.

Chapter Thirty-two

Jolene lay on her bed, face and pillow wet from tears. She no longer cried, but her mind flooded by a tsunami of confusion. She felt hollow. What had happened? It seemed like a lifetime ago, yet it had only been a few weeks since her life crumbled. Tears flowed anew as her thoughts turned to the deaths of her father and mother. Oh, Mom. If she were here, she would hold and soothe her, and make it all better.

Josh had done that somewhat. But why was he being such an ass now? God, she'd never understand men. Bradley had cheated, now Josh as much as admitted he didn't love her, even after she had thrown herself at him. Was it just a fling for him? He didn't seem the type…

Abruptly her thoughts turned to their love making. That was real. That had not been simple lust. The time she spent at his farm, the conversations, and the kisses. So, did he care? He said he did. Maybe he does. Why does he have to analyze everything?

Could he be as insecure as she? Was he only trying to make sure she loved him? Maybe they should talk it out.

Jolene got up and went to the bathroom. She splashed water on her face and patted it dry. She eased the bedroom door open and looked out. No Josh. She called softly, "Josh." No answer. She walked through the store and looked outside. No Josh. She perused the field where the horses had been. Gone.

Her heart sank. Now what?

Like a zombie Jolene plodded back into the apartment and flopped onto the couch. She wallowed in self-pity for a time then resolve slowly settled. Well to hell with him. Tomorrow she'd go see that realtor in Soda Springs and try to hurry up the sale of this place. And as soon as the trials were over, she'd be out of here.

Chapter Thirty-three

Caribou County Sheriff's Department

Sheriff Larry 'Bud' Spitler called Deputy Zimmer to his office. When he entered the office Spitler said, "Mark, something's wrong with your report on this biker mess."

"Anything other than the identifications, Sheriff?"

"No, that's exactly what I'm referring to. You've ID'd all the bikers and matched the motorcycle registrations to all but one. If I put this together right, you've got one Outlaw left without a bike in his name, and one cycle registered to," he picked up the report and read, "a Eugene Woosman."

"I know, Bud. Nobody's talking. Could be Fields, that's the one without a bike in his name, borrowed the bike registered to Woosman."

"Well where in the hell is Woosman? And why wasn't he with the rest of them?"

Mark scrunched his mouth and shrugged. "Don't know."

The Sheriff sighed. "Okay, do we know anything about this gang? Where they came from? Where they're staying? Anything?"

"Not much. I've put the word out to the other road crews, but so far nothing." He held his palms out. "I think some of the boys would have noticed them before now if they were located in Caribou. That's a big gang of bikers, and they'd stand out."

"I agree," the Sheriff said. "Have you put the word out to other county departments?"

"Just did that this morning."

"Okay. Go talk to Grant, see if he has any ideas about this mess."

Mark smiled. "I'll have to go to Bledlow's and see if I can borrow one of their ATV's. He lives way up in the hills. And we don't have any four-wheelers."

"They'll give you one. You want me to call first?"

"No. I've used their stuff before."

Chapter Thirty-four

Outlaws Club House

Snake lay on his cot plotting revenge. That son-of-a-bitch would pay for this. He wouldn't just kill him. Too easy. The prick had to suffer. The smell of alcohol assaulted his nostrils as a reminder of his wounds, and his quest.

Snake had read about some of the tactics used by the Vietnamese to get information from American soldiers. Fingernails ripped off, nuts crushed. Each thought sent waves of pleasure through his body. He didn't need any information. A smile spread across his face. Just want the bastard to suffer for what he did.

Possibilities darted through his mind. Go back out to that hillbilly's farm? No. That could be another standoff. The girl was there with him though. How could he get her? Maybe they'd go back to that store.

"Hey Willy!" Snake yelled out his open door. "Come in here."

Willy and Moss Man had missed the shootout. They had gone to Boise that night for a shipment of cocaine. When they arrived at the clubhouse the next day, Snake had filled them in on the action and his intention of revenge.

"Yeah Snake?" Willy quarried, when he reached the doorway.

"I want you to take Moss Man and run in to that berg where the general store is, and scout around. See if you can spot a girl at that store."

"Okay, Boss. How will we know her?"

"She's the only female at that dump. She runs it. Frank said she was gorgeous with long black hair."

"Should be easy to spot," Willy said.

"Listen, don't ride your bikes, take the van. That place might be crawling with cops." Snake paused to run things through his head. "And no colors," he added. "Find some civvies, shave, and try to look normal."

Willy gave him a quizzical look.

"Just do like I said. I want that girl. And I don't want anybody suspicious. If there's a guy, an old dude, with her, all the better, but don't approach him. Get back to me as soon as you find out anything."

"Gotcha," Willy said as he turned to leave.

* * * *

Moss Man and Willy walked into the store and bought a pack of cigarettes from the kid behind the counter. "Heard you all had some problems here," Willy said, with a friendly smile.

"Yeah," the kid said, "but that's all over now."

"I see by the sign out front that this place is for sale. You the owner?"

"No." Chad smiled. "The owner's in Soda Springs. She won't be back until tonight. Want me to have her call you?"

"Oh, no. Maybe we'll drop by tomorrow and talk to her."

"Okay," Chad said, giving the man his change.

Walking to the van, Moss Man elbowed Willy. "Never seen you in a tie before, Willy. You look like a cop."

Willy didn't look at him. He'd be tempted to knock the smile off his face. "Feel like a fucking trained monkey."

* * * *

That night, three Outlaws rode in the van back to Platte Junction. Willy pulled off the side road, and parked under the dark canopy of trees where they could watch the back of the store. Lights were on in the apartment. The front of the store was dark. They watched until the lights in the apartment went out, then waited another hour.

Snake didn't know if the guy was there or not. He wanted complete surprise. "We'll sneak up to that back door and kick it in. When we get inside, we have to be quick. Don't know where they'll be, so we have to hit every room fast."

"She shouldn't be much of a problem, Snake, Willy said.

"No, but if that prick's there, he could be. From what Frank and Toad told me, he's pretty fast. Also might be a dog with them, so be careful."

Moss Man hefted a cut off baseball bat. "This should handle any dog." He grinned.

Snake handed each man a Maglite and said, "Let's go."

Willy eased the screen door open and held it back. The door sat atop two steps making it difficult for Snake to kick. Instead he backed up a few steps and decided to ram it with his shoulder. The elevation would put the lock at about shoulder height. Snake crashed his two hundred-forty pounds into the door and it splintered. The three Outlaws rushed into the kitchen with flashlights on.

They split up and rushed into other rooms. After a moment, Moss Man called, "Got her in here."

The girl screamed as Moss Man jumped on the bed and pinned her beneath him. Snake and Willy came to the bedroom after making sure no one else was in the house. Moss Man had the girl wrapped in a blanket with both arms secured around her. She screeched and kicked to no avail.

Snake casually went to a dresser drawer and drew out a folded pair of white socks. He towered over Jolene even though Moss Man had her feet off the floor. Snake open handed her face, hard. "Shut up, bitch!"

Tears rolled from her eyes. Shake held her chin down and stuffed the socks into her mouth. "Keep her in that blanket till we get to the van, then tie her ass up.

They were back in the van in less than five minutes.

"Look at those tits." Moss Man giggled after binding Jolene's arms and legs. Her bare breasts were too much of a temptation. He pinched and twisted one nipple.

Jolene's tried to cry out through the sock. Her eyes widened with fear and pain.

"This is going to be fun." Willy crowed.

"Nobody touches her, until I get that guy." Snake warned.

"Aw shit, Snake. You're going to kill them anyway."

"Yeah but I'm going to butt fuck her in front of the asshole. I want him to hear her scream. We'll all play with her after I get done with the guy, not before. You got it?"

"Sure, Snake. Sloppy seconds don't bother me."

Chapter Thirty-five

On his hands and knees, pulling weeds from the garden, Josh realized he hadn't moved. His mind locked on thoughts of Jolene. Three miserable days. He hadn't been able to reach her and she hadn't tried. She must be really pissed. He jerked a large weed, flung it aside, and then sagged dropping his head as he exhaled. Had he let something wonderful slip away?

Josh let the internal disgust build. He'd done it again. Caused problems where none existed. Why did he have to analyze things? He looked at the sky, as Resolve settled in. It might not help, but he had to try. He made up his mind. As soon as he finished here, he'd go back to town and make it right. His spirits lifted at the thought.

Then he heard Bo's low growl. Josh jerked his head up, instantly alert. Eyes squinted, he focused in the direction Bo looked. The unmistakable rumble of a single Harley Hog cresting a hill in the distance.

What the hell! He scrambled to his feet and sprinted for the cabin. As if practiced a thousand times, he snatched his Glock from the bedside table and dashed from the house and across the lane into the woods.

Son-of-a-bitch, I thought we were through with all this. The sound of the motorcycle changed to idling as it coasted down the final grade. So the rider must be easing in.

Slithering silently through the woods, Josh arrived at the junction of his lane and the logging road at the same time as the lone biker. Josh watched as the cautious rider nervously looked side to side, trying to see around trees to the cabin below. At the lane, the Outlaw shut the bike down and started waving a long pole with a white cloth tied to the end.

Perplexed, Josh searched for an explanation. He strained his ears for the sound of other bikes. Nothing. What the hell? This Outlaw must be even dumber than the others. Maybe he heard about the massive defeat of his brothers, and came out to surrender. No, this could only be about one thing. Jolene. He tensed, short of breath at that thought.

Josh crept within twenty feet of the biker and said in a normal tone, "Keep your hands where I can see them, and maybe you'll stay alive."

"Don't shoot," the man said, jerking in surprise. "I got a message for you."

Still hidden by thick pines and brush, Josh growled, "Talk."

"Snake's got the girl."

Josh's heart pounded. "What girl?" he said, stalling for time to think. His stomach cramped – they had Jolene.

"Come on man, you know what damn girl," the man said. "Snake said if you come in and give yourself up, he'll let the girl go."

"Who the hell is Snake?" Josh tried to control his breathing.

"He's the one running things here."

"And he wants to trade does he?"

"Yes."

"Well, since I have my own hostage, maybe he'd be willing to trade for you."

"I doubt it," the man said, getting some confidence back. "Snake couldn't care less about me."

"Who in the hell is this Snake guy anyway? And what's he want?" Josh demanded, seeking time to think what he should do.

"He's the leader of this chapter, and he wants you."

"Too much of a coward to come to the party last week with the rest of his boys, huh?"

"No. He was here. Told me he escaped during all the confusion, and he's carrying some buckshot to prove it."

"Were you here too?"

"Nope. I'm with the Boise club. Just helping out a brother."

"Big mistake on your part."

Quickly the biker said, "Snake said if I don't come back, he'll kill the girl. And he said to tell you he would do it real slow. Said he'd strip her skin off before killing her."

The thought of Jolene with the Outlaws sent a shiver through Josh. His legs felt weak, but he kept his voice level. "How many others came to help out a brother?" Josh asked.

"None," the man said, "only me."

Josh knew it was a lie, but continued. "What's he want with me?"

"You know. You're the one who wiped out his club. He wants payback. He's gone psycho, man. He wants you real bad."

"He'll kill her anyway even if I give myself up." Josh felt a weight pressing on his chest. He sucked in a breath.

"No man. Snake said he'd honor the code if you come in."

Knowing full well this too was a lie, probably on both their parts, Josh asked, "In where?"

"Okay," the man started. "You know where Blackfoot Lake is, up near Conda?"

"Yeah, I think so," Josh responded.

"Well there's a State Park there at the north end, right off the highway. He said to tell you to go there and wait by the public phone booth and he'll call you."

"When?"

"Ten o'clock tomorrow."

Josh calculated. A little over twenty four hours. He racked his brain. He'd need a car. "How the hell am I supposed to get all the way up there on horseback by then? That's clear the hell out of the county."

"I don't know. He said you'd find a way. He also said no cops, and don't bring no weapons. We'll be watching the phone and we'll know if the cops are near."

"No." Josh stepped from the thick brush with a hard penetrating look at the man. He'd noted the 'we' in the bikers answer. "I think I'll just kill you, and take my chances that the FBI can find the girl." The Glock was leveled at the man's head.

"Now don't do that." The biker pleaded with his hands up. "I'm just the messenger."

"Yeah, but that'd be one less I'll have to deal with later," Josh said coldly. "Besides, with you gone who's going to watch the phone?"

"No, man, that's not the way it is. A couple of his boys are still around. I won't even be here after today. I'm going back to Boise. Snake gives me the creeps."

Josh thought this too was a lie, but ignored it. After a pause, he said, "You tell this Snake guy that if the girl has even a small scratch on her, I'll hunt him down like the coward dog he is and make him wish I'd kill him quickly. You tell him. Tell him exactly what I said."

"I will," the man promised.

"And you tell him I'll be there, but I don't know if I can make it on time. It's a long way to ride a horse. If he has guys watching the park, they'll see me when I get there. But you tell him I WILL be there."

"Okay."

"By the way," Josh added. "I'll be armed before I get in to Platte just in case you assholes try any kind of ambush. I see any sign of anything unusual on my way in; I'll shoot first and won't even stop to ask later."

"He said no guns at the park," the man said, almost apologetically.

"I know. I'll leave them at the store. Just don't hurt the girl."

"Okay," the biker said. "Can I go now?"

Josh just faded back into the woods keeping the Glock aimed at the man's head. His own head filled with panic. Where are they? What have they done? How could he get her back?

When the motorcycle turned and eased its way down the logging road, Josh rushed back toward the cabin, forming plans and contingencies as he went. He had to get to Jolene before… His mind flitted rapidly over various scenarios and weighed the possibilities of each one. Damn, he thought. It's like every B movie of a kidnapping he'd ever seen. But he had to admit it would be tough plan to get around. He'd just have to follow their instructions and look for an opening.

When he got to the cabin he went immediately to his foot locker in the loft. There he gathered equipment he thought he might have use for. Josh pulled things from the trunk like a demented man, casting aside what he didn't need. His mind flooded with pictures of Jolene with the Outlaws. His heart raced.

He found his old ankle holster for his snub nosed revolver, and his off duty holster for the Glock. Rummaging through the trunk, he found his handcuffs and leather case. Most of the ammunition he had left from the shootout was still downstairs with his other weapons. There wasn't much.

When he'd gathered everything he could think of, he rushed to the barn where he put out extra rations of food and water, opened the stall doors, and the barn door to the pasture, and saddled Buck.

He led Buck back to the cabin and tethered him to the porch rail. He took a bucket of cracked corn to the hen house and left it. Putting a large bowl of the dry dog food and a pan of water down for Bo, he looked around thinking of anything he'd missed.

Bo sat with an expectant look on his face. "No boy, you have to stay here." He held his right palm to the dog and said, "Stay."

Tying the duffle bag behind the saddle, Josh mounted and heeled Buck into action. He headed for town as fast as he dared push the quarter horse.

Josh had to slow Buck to a walk on the downhill grades, but could put him in a canter during the uphill sections, and urged him to a full gallop over any level tracks of the trail. He kept constant watch on the horse's breathing to make sure he didn't push him beyond his endurance. Josh felt his own heart racing at a pace similar to the horse's.

Chapter Thirty-six

Buck galloped into the store parking lot before noon. Josh leapt from the saddle and ran up to the front door. Locked and deserted.

Josh sprinted around to the back apartment door. It stood open. The strike plate damaged from where the latch had been torn. His heart inched into his throat. Pictures of blood and gore splattered crime scenes flashed through his memory. What had they done to Jolene? What are they doing right now? He tried to vanquish those thoughts, but couldn't.

He hurried through the apartment. Jolene's bed a mess. Could have been a struggle. Josh scurried around examining everything for some clue to what had happened. Her clothes still hung over the silent butler beside her bed. Not a good sign. But no blood splatters. No destruction. He breathed a sigh, not realizing he'd been holding his breath. Maybe they haven't hurt her — yet.

Josh rushed to the table in the living room where Jolene had left Ross' keys. Pocketing the keys, he picked up the phone and dialed 911.

"Caribou County dispatch center." A female voice answered. "What is the nature of your emergency?"

"I need to get in touch with Deputy Zimmer right away!" Josh said in a rush. His feet shuffled back and forth as if wanting to start without him.

"That's not possible, sir. What is your emergency?"

Changing tactics, Josh said, "There's been a kidnapping in Platte Junction, and Zimmer is familiar with the case."

"Deputy Zimmer is off duty, sir," the dispatcher paused. "I'll send another deputy. Where are you?"

"No!" Josh said, unable to control the panic building in his voice. "I'm not going to be here. Look, just get a message to Zimmer right away. Tell him Josh Grant called…"

He slammed his free hand to the table, when she said,"Who?"

"Josh Grant, g. r. a. n. t." Anger seeped into his voice. "Look, just tell him Jolene Braxton has been kidnapped by the Outlaws."

"Outlaws?"

"Yes." Josh exhaled a defeated breath. "They're a gang. Just call Zimmer, he'll know."

"But sir..."

"Ma'am, please... Listen to me. Call Mark. Tell him I have to go to Blackfoot lake. I'll get information to him when I get it. You got all that, lady?" Josh's voice almost a growl.

She made him repeat the details while she apparently took notes. His body twitched.

"Did you say, Outlaws?" the operator again questioned, after his second explanation.

"Ah shit, never mind that," Josh almost screamed. "Just tell Zimmer." Then he softened his voice, "Ma'am, please call Mark. This is a life and death situation."

He hung up the phone, found a note pad in the desk, and hurriedly wrote a note to Zimmer in case he came to the store.

Mark,

Jolene kidnapped. Outlaws. Blackfoot Lake State Park. Public phone booth. Four o'clock tomorrow. Have to be alone. Guy named Snake wants to trade me for Jolene. Know it's a trap, still have to go. Don't go anywhere near that park until well after 10:00A.M. tomorrow. I'll try to leave a note in the phone booth.

Josh.

Josh hurried through the store aisles, ransacking shelves for additional supplies: bottled water, Beef jerky, and granola bars. He put the supplies in a paper bag, then spotted a scotch tape display. He snatched a roll and ran back to the apartment table to get the note.

Back through the front, Josh set the bag down and taped the note to the front door.

He stood on the porch, head cradled in both hands trying to think. He didn't want police involved until he knew where Jolene was, but he wanted them aware. Would this do it? Or would they rush to the park, sirens blaring? He knew cops.

Mark would trust his judgment, but if others get involved... "Shit!" If only he had time to set up a proper plan with the Sheriff's office. He couldn't afford to waste time thinking. He had to act.

Move, damn it. He unsaddled Buck and hobbled him in the field, grabbed the duffel bag from the saddle, and his sack of supplies. Josh strode long quick paces toward the large outbuilding at the rear of the parking lot, where he knew Ross kept his battered old pick-up truck.

He threw the supplies and duffel on the passenger seat, and fumbled with the keys until he found one that fit. When the old truck roared to life, he checked the gas gauge. Full. Thanks Ross.

Josh hesitated again, unsure if he were doing the right thing. Think, damn it, think. What else could he do? Is there a better way? He needed a plan. He needed details. Drawing a blank, he dropped the shift lever into gear.

At the last minute he decided to stop at Hannedy's place. Maybe Chad or his dad had seen something.

After rattling off what few details he knew about Jolene's kidnapping, Josh asked Chad, "Were you at the store yesterday?"

"No", Chad said. "Yesterday was Sunday and it was closed. I went over this morning, but the store was locked up. I thought Jolene might be with you."

"I wish she had been." Josh hung his head. "I shouldn't have left her alone again. Hell, I thought our troubles with those assholes were over."

"Not your fault," Ben Hannedy said.

"Actually, it partly is."

Josh told them to call 911 again and report the kidnapping. "And Chad, whoever shows up, make sure they contact Deputy Zimmer. I left him a note on the store entrance. I don't want any deputies to interfere until I know where Jolene is."

Josh didn't have time to go into more details. He knew it would take time for the Sheriff's deputies to coordinate with other agencies, and he had to do some scouting before the deadline.

"Chad, I left my horse hobbled at the store, Could you get him and keep him here until I get back?" Josh turned for the door.

"Sure, Josh. Where you going?"

Josh turned back. "Snake hunting."

Chapter Thirty-seven

Josh examined the Idaho road map he found in the glove box. He scrutinized the area and roads around Blackfoot Lake. The State Park was located in a remote corner of Madison County. Maybe that's why the Caribou County Sheriff's Department knew so little about the Outlaws.

Josh turned the old truck toward the highway and sped off. He wanted to arrive well ahead of the deadline, so he could scout the area, and maybe formulate a plan. They might expect him on horseback. This could give him an edge.

His nerve ends tingled, as he turned north onto Route Thirty and headed for Madison County. This entire section of southern Idaho was little more than mountains, wilderness forests, and winding roads. Small towns and settlements were few and far between.

Throughout the drive, Josh had time to reflect on recent events that had changed his life. God, I care for this girl. It felt so good being alive again, and now, damn it, I could lose it all… again. Everyone he'd ever loved had been taken from him: His grandparents, his mother and father, Ellen and Jimmy — killed. Even the job he had loved — gone. And now he could lose Jolene. His grip on the wheel tightened. He jammed his foot harder on the accelerator, and issued an intense prayer for Jolene's safety.

Come on Josh, think like a cop, he urged himself. Get that old edge back. Come up with a plan, Damn it. At every turn, his brain felt locked. No information to go on. What would they do? He could figure part of their plan. Call him and give him directions. Make sure he wasn't followed. Call him again, and so on until they had him. But what the hell could he do? The minute he got help, they would know. How could he get Jolene out? He knew they wouldn't just release her. She's a witness. He'd have to wait until he was with her and hope to find an opening before they were killed. He hated being on defense.

Back in Detroit he had attacked the investigation of Ellen and Jimmy's death with a vengeance driven by hatred. His involvement in that daunting task, the only thing that had kept him from going completely over the edge. Josh cringed at the thought of how close he'd come to going over.

The day Sam found him passed out in a puddle of vomit, pistol gripped loosely in his right hand, was the low point. He had no memory of most of it, but Sam had filled him in.

He awoke slowly to Sam's shouting, "Goddamn it Josh. I thought you were dead. You didn't answer the phone."

"What the fuck!" Sam screamed when he saw the gun. He snatched the Glock from Josh's limp hand. "I ought to pistol whip you with this. You asshole. Damn it Josh, no one's heard from you for days. You scared the shit out of me."

Josh looked up at him with blank expression – no comprehension.

Sam slapped him. "Wake up you son-of-a-bitch."

Josh's eyes narrowed as he jerked alert for a brief moment. Sam must have seen a spark of life still in there, so he softened his approach. "Look Josh, you might not care about living right now, but a lot of people do. I care. Tony called me and told me you haven't been to work for days. Hell, I had to kick your door in. I thought you'd really done it."

Sam busied himself making coffee and picking up empty whiskey bottles as he talked. "I guess it'd be hard to just drink yourself to death, but it looks like you tried. You ever try a stupid trick like this again, I'll personally kill your ass, and save you the trouble of doing it."

The painful memory of the cold steel Glock barrel in his mouth still haunted Josh.

"I couldn't pull the trigger, Sam." He had mumbled. "I tried, but just couldn't.

Sam glared at him. "Why would you even think about doing that, Josh?"

"I don't care about anything."

"The hell you don't. You may not care about yourself, but you care about Ellen and Jim."

"That's why I don't care. They're gone."

"Yes, and you can't change that. But you owe it to them to do what you do best – find the bastard that killed them."

Josh shook his head remembering it all. He had sobered up and set about his own investigation. Nine months later the gang banger responsible for the shooting was sentenced to life in prison.

Habeeb Rasheed Jones, an eighteen year old ghetto kid who had made bad decisions. The sentence brought no feelings of justice to Josh's aching heart. He'd accomplished his mission, but derived little satisfaction from it. Nothing could bring his family back.

What would the investigation of his and Jolene's death be like? The local cops would eventually find the Outlaws responsible and they would pay. But there would be no more satisfaction for the cops here, than there had been for him.

Less than an hour later, Josh pulled off the main access road to Blackfoot Lake State Park and hid the truck in the dense woods. He shook his head to clear the maudlin thoughts and opened the truck door. Josh crept through the trees parallel to the road until he could survey the parking lot. He saw only three cars in the lot. They were all near the boat launch ramps, and had boat trailers attached. He didn't observe any motorcycles or other suspicious vehicles.

Josh skirted the area trying to locate the public phone. He spotted it attached to a pole about fifteen paces in front of the restrooms. The phone was visible from all directions except from behind the restrooms. An observer could hide in that building and watch the phone. Probably too close though.

Hidden in the woods, Josh continued to scout the area around the asphalt lot looking for obvious hiding places for an observation post, as well as escape routes. He noticed several likely spots and marked them in his mind. When he completed his tour, he approached from behind the restrooms. Hurriedly skirting the building, he entered the men's room, and looked around for a hiding place.

The cinder block building construction allowed air circulation where the roof attached to the walls. Being open at the top provided a ledge where the rafters rested on the blocks. Josh hid one of the revolvers he'd taken from the bikers behind a roof timber. If they tried to snipe him tomorrow, he might be able to make it to the restrooms for cover. If they were in the building, he would have to run. No cover in the entire blacktopped lot. He'd be screwed.

He casually walked to the phone as if to make a call, and hid a pencil under the chained phone book. He then made his way back to the truck and drove toward the main highway. Along the access road Josh spotted a thick bush growing right next to the blacktop. He stopped the truck and looked around. Thick foliage canopied the road. Satisfied, he hid his duffel bag under the bush. They might search the truck tomorrow. If so, he could grab his weapons on his way out.

Cruising the back roads within a ten mile radius of the park, Josh looked for anything that might tell him where the Outlaws could be hiding Jolene. He found no obvious places, but noted several locations in his memory. He saw many farms with large barns, and crammed them into his jumbled brain.

He felt sure Snake would give him additional directions over the phone, leading him to another phone, or some location. They'd watch him to make sure he was alone, and not being followed by the cops. But in case they were really stupid and directed him right to their location, he wanted to be familiar with the area. They couldn't know he was driving Ross' truck until tomorrow, so he felt fairly secure on his scouting mission.

When darkness prevented him from seeing much, he found a deserted spot well away from the State Park and pulled off the road in a stand of pine trees.

Leaning back in his seat he relaxed his tense shoulders and tried to clear his overworked mind. He wasn't successful. He ate some beef jerky and drank a bottle of water. It didn't go down well.

He rolled his shoulders and laid his head back. He had to try to get some rest. He would need it tomorrow. Eyes closed, he tried to force himself to sleep. Instead his mind continually dwelled on what could be happening to Jolene. Hours later he must have dozed because he jerked alert when he heard a car pass. A few more tormenting hours filled with images of torture and rape, and he nodded off again.

Chapter Thirty-eight

Josh awoke with a scowl and a headache, amid chirping birds at daybreak. He was tempted to fire a warning shot. Damned cheery birds. His body hurt. Hell his hair hurt.

Two granola bars washed down with bottled water didn't come close to a steaming mug of black coffee. Josh looked at his watch. About four hours to go. Where were they? What were they doing? Images of Jolene being viciously raped and beaten flashed through his mind. Josh clinched his fists and forced those thought out. Had to focus on his objective. Find them. Don't think, move.

Josh opened the truck door and stepped onto soft pine needles. He relieved himself in the dense woods, and did a series of stretching exercises.

Back in the truck, he studied the map, then headed out to continue his recon of the area.

He again drove every back road he could find, familiarizing himself with the area. He expanded his radius to twenty miles around the lake. As he traveled, he marked spots on the map and in his mind. Each building he evaluated brought thoughts that Jolene could be inside, being tortured.

Josh spotted a roadside diner on Highway sixty-five near the park and stopped for breakfast. Greasy bacon and eggs didn't set well, but the coffee helped. He continued to scout the area looking for signs of motorcycles or likely hiding places, but stayed well away from the park entrance. He had to keep moving to keep his mind from dwelling on Jolene's condition.

At 9:50a.m. he pulled into the parking lot near the public facilities building and exited the truck. Again, there were a few cars with trailers all parked near the launch ramps. He saw no motorcycles or other suspicious vehicles. As he passed by the side of the restrooms, he casually strolled into the men's room. Empty. He reached into the roof rafters and felt the gun. So far so good.

Josh stepped out, zipped his cargo pants, for the benefit of any hidden watchers, and walked to the phone box. He casually leaned on the inside of the enclosure, turned and glanced at the restrooms. He couldn't see behind it but both sides were clear. He turned back, leaned into the booth, and waited.

Less than two minutes elapsed when the phone rang. Five minutes early. It confirmed his suspicion that a hidden lookout had reported his arrival, or perhaps the lookout was using a cell phone and called him directly. Either way he was being watched.

Josh took a deep breath and exhaled from his diaphragm to relax and focus. "Yeah," he said into the receiver.

"Well, asshole," a gruff voice said, "I see you got yourself some wheels. I was hoping you'd have to ride that horse all the way here."

"I wouldn't have made it on time."

"That would have been too bad." The voice hardened. "You ready to do the deal?"

"Is the girl alright?" Josh asked.

"Yeah, she's fine."

"How do I know that?"

"Because I give you my word," the man said.

"Are you Snake?" Josh asked.

"Yeah, and I bite."

Josh paused a second for effect, and then said, "I'm afraid I don't quite trust you yet. Let me talk to Jolene to make sure."

"No," Snake said. "Now listen up, asshole. I'm running this show and you'll do as I say or the bitch dies right now!"

"Okay, okay." Josh tried to exude some panic into his voice, "Just don't hurt her, okay? I'll do whatever you say."

"That's more like it," Snake said with satisfaction. "Now take your shirt off."

"What?" Josh asked.

"Just do it, asshole – take your shirt off."

"I'll have to put the phone down. Wait a minute."

Josh did as he was told, then picked up the phone again. "Okay, my shirt's off, but I don't understand." He knew they would be checking for weapons. That's why he'd hidden his duffel along the access road where they could be easily grabbed on the way out.

"Shut up and listen," the voice said. "Now step away from the phone and turn all the way around real slow, with your hands in the air."

Josh put the phone down again, and did as he was instructed, scanning the area as he turned. The park and lake were surrounded by thick forest, mostly pines. On an incline near the highway, Josh caught a reflection among the trees. Maybe binoculars or something chrome. He picked the phone up.

After a long pause, the voice said. "Now I want you to go to a rest area on Upper Valley Pike. You know where that's at?"

"I don't think so, but I have a road map."

"You turn right out of the park and take highway sixty-five. Go about six miles, then turn south on Turner Road. It dead ends into Upper Valley Pike. Turn east, that's right, asshole, and go another three miles. You'll see the rest area on your left. It's one of those old ones, but it's got a phone booth. Go there and wait for my call, and no funny business. You got that?"

"Yeah, I think so," Josh said, adding, "but I'm not going anywhere until I know the girl is okay. Let me talk to her, please?"

There was a long pause. "Okay," Snake finally said. "Since you said please. I told you you could trust me."

Josh used the time to scrawl a note on the phone book cover with the pencil he'd secreted there. Mark: Rest Area Upper Valley Pike. Stay well back.

After a brief pause Jolene's urgent voice said, "Josh."

Josh expelled his held breath. "Jolene, are you okay?"

There was a slight pause and she said, "Yes. No real damage."

Josh assumed she meant they'd roughed up a bit during the kidnapping. A pang surged through his heart, and anger grew in his gut.

He wanted to keep her on the phone as long as he could, hoping to hear something in the background that hinted where she might be. The kidnappers were probably listening, but he had to try to get some information. Josh said, "I had to borrow Ross's truck to get here. I hope it's alright."

After a hesitation she responded, "Of course it is." And then added, "How in the world did you find the keys? I hid them in that big woodpile?"

Josh cocked his head and mumbled, "Huh?" Her statement baffled him. Maybe she's been drugged. "Are you sure you're okay?" he asked again.

"I'm perfectly okay." She said with a lilt to her voice that confused Josh even more.

Snake's gruffer voice interrupted, "Okay, that's enough. You know she's alright, now do as you were told and I'll let her go when I have you."

"You promise?" Josh pleaded. He hoped Snake would interpret his attitude as weak. He needed any edge he could get.

"Sure I will. You just go to that rest area and wait for my call. When I know there's no cops around, I'll tell you where to come."

"Okay," Josh said.

"Hey motherfucker, If I see even a hint of a weapon, I'll pop a cap in her ass first."

"No weapons." Josh hung up the phone. Snake had said, 'where to come?' Would the rest area be the last stop?

The observer had to be in the woods near the highway so the box holding the public phone would partially block any view. Josh unhooked the receiver and laid it on the shelf. He quickly dialed 911, and turned to leave. He hoped the local 911 system automatically recorded the location of all land line phones, and someone would respond to check it out. He didn't know if the system did that with public phones or not, but he had to try every trick he could think of.

Hoping that would be enough, Josh picked up his shirt and put it on. He walked to the truck and drove from the park. Driving slowly along the left side of the wooded access road, Josh was able to open the driver's door and scoop his duffel bag from under the bush without stopping. The lookout would be near the highway so he could follow when Josh left. He wouldn't be able to see the truck until it exited onto the highway.

As he drove, he tried to make sense of what Jolene had said about the keys being in the woodpile. She knew the keys were on the side table – she had put them there. There was no woodpile at the store. She must be drugged, he thought. But then why would she say that, even if she were high? It was a completely off the wall statement. It had nothing to do with her situation. It made no sense. She sounded so normal other than that statement.

Josh continued to mull this over as he drove. A couple of times he spotted a motorcycle in his rearview mirror. He wasn't surprised, but thought this could mean there weren't many gang members left for this operation. Couldn't be many left after the shootout at his place. Probably wouldn't be anyone waiting for him at the next contact point either. The biker following him would probably report his arrival. The odds were looking better – still daunting, but better. The one following him would more than likely continue to follow him through any other detours until the final leg, and then follow him to the hideout, and act as a backup.

Suddenly Josh's mind cleared. He focused on Jolene. She'd tried to tell him something. What? She's sharp. She paid attention to things. She could think on her feet. She wasn't drugged. She had tried to give him a message. "Keys in the woodpile?" His mind raced. She knew where the keys were. Why did she say that? "Key." "woodpile." He struggled for meaning. His mind flitted to the various places he had scouted yesterday and this morning. He remembered an abandoned sawmill he had passed. There were several stacks of logs around a huge barn-like structure.

A picture of that old building lit up in Josh's mind like a comic book light bulb. He smacked his forehead with his palm. The key could be the woodpile. Had to be.

Should he chance it? The thought of something going wrong almost paralyzed him. But he had to do something proactive. He could either go on the offensive, and maybe get lucky, or he could continue to do as instructed, and be certain they would both be killed.

As he drove, his mind went over the roads he had traveled. He knew exactly where he was headed. His mind rehearsed the route and the various topographies. Slowly a plan began to take shape.

Josh approached the last leg of his instructions. As he guided the truck onto Turner Road, he made his decision. He remembered the road from his scouting trips. It was long and straight and gradually rose to a peak, and then sloped downhill all the way to Upper Valley Road. He looked for the following biker, but couldn't see him. When he turned onto Turner Josh accelerated as much as the old truck would stand. Just before reaching the crest of the hill, he again saw the motorcycle in his rearview mirror. The biker speeding to catch up. Good.

Josh topped the hill and slammed on the breaks while twisting the steering wheel sharply to the left. The old truck shuddered and slid sideways coming to a screeching stop in the middle of the road on the downhill side of the hump. Josh scrambled out of the truck and into the far side ditch with his Glock aimed at the truck. He could hear the roar of the Harley exhaust as the engine wound tight.

When the motorcycle crested the hill at about seventy miles per hour, the rider faced a stationary pickup truck blocking the entire road. The Outlaw never had a chance to react. The bike slammed into the bed of the truck, skidding the pickup several feet further on. The rider flew over the bed of the truck and onto the asphalt road, at least thirty feet further downhill. The biker slid and flopped like a dime-store robot down the blacktop another fifty feet or so. He lay still with limbs bent at extremely wrong angles.

Josh ran to the biker intent on questioning him. When he checked the vitals however, he knew questions would be useless. The Outlaw had a faint heartbeat but was unconscious, bleeding and broken beyond repair. Josh searched the pockets of the thug's leather jacket and found a cell phone. It appeared to be undamaged. He opened it and the screen lit. Fingers poised over the pad, Josh debated whether to call 911. He flipped the cover closed and pocketed the phone. Can't take the chance. He could be wrong about the sawmill, and if the cops came roaring through the area with sirens, Jolene would be in more danger. Even if right, it could still end in disaster. No he'd check first.

Josh dragged the biker off the roadway, and as quickly as possible. He moved the truck to the side of the road, and then pulled the motorcycle into the ditch. Didn't want some local crashing into the remains.

When he had the remains of the bike cleared, Josh started the truck and made a U-turn. He headed back to one of the side roads traveled earlier; the one where he'd spotted the sawmill. It would be a calculated risk. But the only one he had left now. He silently prayed he was right.

"I'm coming for you, you son-of-a-bitch."

Chapter Thirty-nine

Josh drove off the road into the woods well before arriving at the sawmill. He didn't want to take a chance. They might recognize the truck. Rooting through his duffel, Josh pulled out weapons, equipment, and his old duty belt, then stepped out of the truck.

When he swung the belt and holster around his body and latched it, he smiled, thinking of Ross's love for western gunfighters. Holstering his Glock and pocketing the S&W and extra ammo, he set off through the forest. When the mill came into sight, he cautiously circled around the building staying hidden among the trees.

Three motorcycles and a van parked in a stand of trees to the rear of the weathered old structure confirmed his decision. They're here. Relief eased into his mind, while tension surged through his body.

From the woods, Josh scanned the back of the building. Using binoculars, he examined each window on the upper level. No lights and no figures visible. Creeping slowly through the trees, he spotted a single window in the ground floor. It was encrusted with years of dirt.

Josh sprinted from the woods to the shadows next to the mill. Rubbing a small spot clean on the bottom corner of the lone window, he peered into a large warehouse like room. The room was dimly lit by several windows on the front wall. At one of those windows opposite his position, he spotted a man, highlighted by strong rays of sunlight. The man seemed to be observing the road. Due to the angle and the shadows, Josh couldn't see anyone else.

Further on, at ground level, Josh found an open hole in the foundation where a window or coal chute had once been. Looking in, he saw it opened into an unlit cellar. Couldn't see much other than dark walls and a floor covered with what appeared to be old dirty sawdust. Josh calculated his frame would fit through the opening, and crawled in. He dropped silently to the floor and looked around. A musty odor of fermenting sawdust assaulted his nostrils. Should he use the mini flash? Better not.

A wide wooden stairway occupied the middle of the room, angling upward toward the back wall. Ambient light dimly lit the area at the base. The faint sound of voices filtered down from above. He could distinguish at least two male voices.

At the base of the stairs, Josh took the cell phone he had confiscated and flipped it open. He scanned the list of recent calls made. Top of the list had to be the last number dialed by the lookout when he reported in. Josh highlighted the number and punched the send button, as he crept up the stairs. The same voice he had talked with earlier said, "Is he there?"

Josh muffled his voice and mumbled, "he's here, Snake." And then closed the cell and pocketed it. Figuring Snake would be occupied dialing the number of the rest area public phone, Josh continued to ease up the stairs walking on the outside edge of each step to avoid any creaks.

In his right hand, Josh gripped his Glock, and in his left he held his Smith and Wesson model 19. When his eyes rose above the level of the floor, he saw the man by the window still intently focused on the parking area. Josh scanned right and spotted another man with a cell phone to his ear. Next to him, Jolene sat tied to a chair.

A pang of guilt that he'd allowed this to happen to Jolene, hit him hard. Then seething anger replaces it. She was naked, except for panties. Her head hung down. She looked dirty and disheveled. He saw dried blood at the corner of her mouth, and spotted some bruises on her face and arms. His sinking heart changed to boiling rage.

The man with the phone was obviously Snake. A big man about six-foot four or five, and well over two hundred and forty pounds of what looked like solid muscle. He had long hair tied into a ponytail, and a large dangling earring in one ear. The big man yelled irritably into the cell, "Answer the damned phone."

Neither man saw Josh rise out of the stairwell. Josh pointed his right hand at the man with the cell phone and his left at the man by the door.

Stepping from the shadows, he yelled, "Freeze! Nobody moves – nobody dies!"

Neither man moved, except to look at Josh, and the two guns aimed at them. Apparently their brains temporarily locked in confusion. Without hesitation Josh further commanded, "You, by the door, get down on the floor. Do it now!"

The man didn't move. Josh pointed the revolver slightly left of the man and fired a shot into a support post. The man immediately dropped to the floor. "That was an intentional miss," Josh said, without taking his eyes off of Snake as he walked toward him.

Jolene's head jerked up, eyes wide. The big man stood close to her. Josh moved deliberately to them. "You," he commanded, "Move back!"

Snake moved back a few cautious paces, an angry glare on his face.

"Now interlock your fingers behind your head."

Snake dropped the cell phone and slowly raised his hands to his head.

Josh placed the S&W on the floor next to Jolene's chair and pulled a knife from his boot scabbard with his left hand. Eyes darting between Snake and the man on the floor, he kept the Glock aimed at Snake. Kneeling, Josh cut Jolene loose. "You Okay?" he asked, never taking his eyes off the Outlaws.

"Been better, but I'm okay now."

Josh moved nearer to Snake, gun pointed at his head. He leaned in and snatched the Colt Python butt protruding from Snake's belt.

He handed the weapon to Jolene. "Keep it pointed at Snake, and shoot if he moves." Josh used his free hand to unbutton the front of his denim jacket. "Here pull this off and put it on." He held out his arm for Jolene. With the jacket off Josh retrieved his revolver.

"Jolene, there's a pair of handcuffs in a pouch on my belt. Take them out." Josh's eyes shifted rapidly back and forth between Snake and the prone man.

When she had the cuffs, Josh said to the man on the floor, "You there, crawl to that post and hug it with both arms."

The man did as he was told. Josh said, "Jolene, take the cuffs over and clamp them tightly on each wrist. Move over and approach him from the front so you're not in my line of fire."

To the prone biker he said, "Move a muscle and you die."

When Jolene had the Outlaw trussed to the post, Josh said, "He's probably got a gun in his belt. Get it." His eyes now locked on Snake.

Jolene growled at the biker, "Roll onto your side."

The man complied, and Jolene removed a revolver from his beltline. He lay still on his side. Jolene eyed his exposed midsection. She snarled and launched a vicious kick like she was kicking a field goal through his gut. The man grunted in pain, and rolled back onto his stomach groaning.

Jolene returned to Josh's side. She squinted hard at Snake. Josh handed her Snake's Python, and motioning with his head to Snake said, "If this one twitches, shoot him."

"Do I have to wait for him to twitch?" The edge to her voice told Josh her spirit was intact. He smiled.

"Yeah," Josh said. "I don't want him to die quickly."

"Jolene, gather all the weapons and to move to that corner." Josh pointed. I'll keep him covered until you're in position." Jolene moved the guns and her chair to the back wall.

"Now keep that gun on this one at all times. If he manages to come out of this – kill him. I mean all six shots, and then use the Glock and the other weapons if you need to. You understand?" he asked.

"With pleasure," she said, staring hard at Snake.

Josh handed her his Glock, and the model 19. Jolene pointed the big revolver at Snake's head and closed her left eye.

A twitch developed over Snake's left eye that wouldn't stop ticking.

Josh unlatched his duty belt and dropped it to the floor. He withdrew a pair of skin-tight kid leather fingerless sap gloves from his rear pocket and pulled them on. An ounce of powdered lead in the palms and a half ounce ribbed over the knuckles both cushioned and added power to blows.

He deliberately headed for Snake. "I was going to hold you for the Sheriff, but I see you didn't heed my warning about harming the lady. So now you're going to pay."

* * * *

As Josh approached, Snake slowly realized he might have a chance. He smiled at the thought. He would squash this asshole, and work the fight near the girl, maybe shove the son-of-a-bitch into her, and get those guns. He was going to get his revenge after all. He rolled his neck as Josh approached. This idiot doesn't even have his hands up to defend himself. "Hey pussy," he said, "wanna know why they call me Snake?" He grabbed his crotch and squeezed it. "I'll show you later when I use it on the bitch."

* * * *

Josh stopped about two arm lengths away from Snake and waited. Snake crouched in a boxer's stance and circled. Josh turned as well, keeping his right foot back and his left forward in a modified T stance, hands open and relaxed at his waist. Snake feinted with a left jab, then lunged in throwing a powerful straight right aimed at Josh's head. The head wasn't there, but like a Cobra strike, Josh's left hand locked onto the wrist as it went by. Josh spun, turning his body and redirected the inertia of Snake's body until he was off balance.

Immediately changing direction, Josh brought his other hand alongside the wrist and bent it back toward Snake. Then with a circular motion forced the arm lock back in the opposite direction. Snake's head went down while his feet came up. His massive body did a complete flip and struck the old wooden floor. A plume of dust rose around Snake accompanied by a loud grunt.

Snake lay still for a time, then rose to his elbows and shook his head. Josh walked casually around Snake. The big man got to his feet in a rage and rushed in. Josh simply side stepped Snake and waited until he stopped his momentum and regained his balance. Josh let a smile play at his lips.

Snake grew more cautious as he moved in again. He tried a few more jabs with his left hand. They connected with nothing more than Josh's flicking hands as they blocked the punches. Snake rushed again. Josh backed a step for balance, and caught the heel of his boot on a warped floorboard he hadn't seen in the low light. Shit! Should've taken my boots off. Josh stumbled trying to regain his balance. Snake took advantage of the distraction and moved in.

Snake managed to grab a fist full of Josh's shirt and started to jerk him into a powerful punch. Instead of pulling back, Josh moved in with the pull, and at the same time brought both of his hands up and around the locked fist at his chest. Clasping the huge fist between his two hands he twisted it straight, immobilizing it in a wrist lock. Josh simply bowed at the waist and the big man screamed in pain as he went down to one knee to reduce the strain on his wrist.

Easily twisting Snake's fist loose from his shirt, Josh bent the wrist back toward Snake's shoulder while he held his arm straight at the elbow. When Josh applied pressure downward on the elbow, and in on the upraised wrist, Snake went on down, chin to the floor.

Josh applied more pressure to the bent wrist for an additional jolt of pain before releasing it. Josh was in no hurry. He wanted to humiliate this scumbag. Snake reacted quickly though, by rolling in Josh's direction and grabbing his legs. Josh went down in a heap with Snake's arms wrapped around his legs. Dust particles again danced in the sun rays.

Thrashing for a few seconds, they untangled themselves. Both men struggled to their feet. Before Josh could break completely free, Snake grabbed him from behind in a choking head lock.

Thankful for the boots now, Josh stomped down hard on Snake's instep. Snake yelped. Josh bent slightly, reached between his legs, and grabbed Snake's pant leg and lifted. Snake went down on his back and took Josh with him, but the fall broke the choke hold.

They both scrambled up, but Josh was too close to the more powerful man and couldn't avoid his grasp. The Outlaw tried to reach his large arms about Josh to apply a bear hug that would squeeze the air from his lungs. Snake's breath and body odor caused Josh to twist his head away.

Josh sagged, letting his weight pull Snake down slightly, then brought his right knee up sharply into the side of Snake's thigh compressing the Common Peronial nerve and causing the man's leg to buckle under him. As Snake sunk to one knee, Josh found the dangling earring in Snake's right ear, and yanked with all his strength. Snake screamed and grabbed his ear. He sat back on his rear holding his hand to his ear. He got up more slowly looking at the blood on his hand.

Josh pitched the earring at Snake's feet.

"Fight me like a man, you son-of-a-bitch." Snake said.

Josh smiled. He took a quick step to his left as if to fake, but continued to pivot left while executing a spinning back fist into Snake's jaw knocking him down again. "Like that?" Josh said.

Jolene screamed. Josh jerked around. What he saw took the air and energy from him. Another biker stood behind Jolene with a gun to her head. How in the hell had he gotten in here? Or had he been hiding all the while. Either way it looked hopeless again. As Josh tried to sort it out, he was blindsided by Snake.

The big Outlaw delivered a crushing blow to Josh's jaw, knocking him to the ground. He followed that with a series of kicks. A grinning Snake stood over Josh and said, "Now I'm going to soften you up a bit, but I won't kill you right away. I want you alive to watch me rape her, and then maybe I'll kill you both at the same time." He kicked Josh again for emphasis. Josh rolled more from the kick than with it, but he was able to see that the other man had moved away from Jolene, now that Snake seemed to have everything under control. It was now or never.

Josh's back was away from Snake. He sat halfway up and slouched over his legs as if groggy, which he was. He cautiously raised his left pant leg enough to grasp his snub nosed revolver in the ankle holster. He focused on the Outlaw near Jolene. With one quick motion he drew and fired three shots at the man with the gun. The man went down just as Snake kicked Josh in the head. Josh went down and almost passed out. His gun flew from his grip.

Still dazed, Josh expected another kick, Instead he heard another shot ring out. Had he missed the other biker? He didn't have the motor skills to roll or try to escape. But he wasn't shot or even kicked again. Regaining his senses, he looked around. He saw Jolene pointing the big model nineteen at Snake. She had his full attention. Josh got to his feet and tried to shake off the effects of the blows he had received.

Jolene walked to the wounded biker and picked up his gun while continuously watching Snake. She went back to her chair and said, "You okay, Josh?"

He nodded.

Jolene moved the chair further away and sat down. She casually waved the gun and said, "Gentlemen, continue."

Josh snapped a front kick to Snake's chest sending him sprawling backwards. "Like to kick, do you?"

When Snake got to his feet again, he found Josh right in front of him. Before he could react, Josh struck him with three quick jabs, then hooked off the last jab to Snake's jaw. When Snake crawled to his knees he was in perfect position for a strong uppercut to the chin. The crack of Josh's fist on Snake's jaw echoed through the room. Snack went over on his back like a load of wet cement.

Josh turned to Jolene. "Get one of those cell phones and call 911 now, and tell them we're at the old sawmill on Range Line Road."

When he saw Snake moving to get up again he continued, "I'm not quite done here, but I will be by the time they arrive."

Jolene found the phone Snake had dropped. As she dialed 911, Josh stalked Snake. All the anxiety of the past few weeks had built up and needed release. Snake held his hands out in front of him as if to say that's enough. Josh shook his head and said, "No. I still owe you for Jolene, and for Ross."

As Snake tried to stand again, Josh hit him with a straight right to the nose, shattering the bone and splattering blood. Snake staggered up, looked at the blood, and with renewed energy or perhaps panic, rushed Josh. Josh pivoted at the last moment, and grabbed the waving ponytail as it went by, again jerking the biker off his feet and onto his back. When Snake got up he wildly threw punches, like a third grader in a playground fight. Each ineffective punch answered by a stinging blow either to his rib cage or face.

Snake's power waned from the accumulation of body blows. Josh worked closer. Again Snake tried to apply a bear hug from the front. Josh grabbed the back of his head with both hands and pulled down at the same time jumping up and jamming his right knee into Snake's exposed jaw. His head snapped sideways as if on a bobble head spring. Snake was unconscious before he hit the floor. This time he stayed down. Jolene walked slowly to him and stared at the bloody man lying spread eagle on the floor. The temptation too much. She kicked him in the groin and walked away.

Jolene flung her arms around Josh's neck. "I was so frightened. They planned to kill both of us."

"I know." Josh stroked her hair. "It's all over now. We're okay."

Jolene buried her face into his neck. They clung to each other until Jolene pulled away smiling. "That woodpile thing was good wasn't it?"

Josh laughed. "It was real good, honey. Real good.

* * * *

Josh didn't recognize any of the deputies who responded to Jolene's call. Their shoulder patches were different than Caribou County. When he started to explain the situation to them, they said Zimmer had filled them in and was on his way here.

"But he's going to be disappointed," one deputy said, with a grin. "He told us to look for a lot of bodies. We only found these three, and two of them are still alive."

"Well, there is another one," Josh said, hanging his head. "He kind of ran into my truck over on Turner Road. He shouldn't be hard to find."

The deputy nodded and said, "Mark will be happy to hear that."

As the other deputies escorted the two handcuffed Outlaws toward their cruisers, one of them stopped and handed Josh his handcuffs. While they were paused, Snake looked at Josh through one eye not yet swollen shut and spat blood through split lips when he said, "Who in the hell are you anyway?"

"Just a farmer," Josh said, turning away.

Deputy Mark Zimmer pulled into the mill yard and got out of his cruiser. "Well, Josh, I see you're still at it.

Josh shook his head. "I sure hope this is the end of it, Mark. I'm getting too old for this shit."

"Not from the looks of things around here you're not. And why in the hell didn't you show up at that rest area, or was I too late?"

"No. I never made it there. I had to change their plans or we both would've been doomed."

"Oh well, it seems to have worked out. Were there only three of them?"

"No, four, but I got lucky again. If it weren't for Jolene saving my ass we'd both be dead."

Mark shook his head. You two are quite a team." The deputy started to turn then twisted back. "Oh by the way, my Sheriff wants to talk to you."

Josh bristled defensively, "Look, none of this was my fault. I just happened to be in the wrong place at the wrong time."

Mark raised his hands to calm him down. "Nothing bad, Josh, I think he wants to offer you a job."

"Well tell him thanks, but no thanks. I've done my time. I'm just a farmer and that's all I want to be."

"Well come in and talk to him anyway, I think you might like what he has to offer. I'll let you know when might be a good time, after we get this mess straightened out, and you've had some time to relax. Just sleep on it and at least talk to him. Okay?"

"Okay, Mark, but he won't change my mind."

Putting his arm around Jolene, he started to lead her to the old truck. He stopped and turned back waving to Mark, he called, "We gave our statements to the other deputies, so call us when you need us, and stop by for coffee sometime."

Mark waved then turned back to the Madison County deputies. Josh swept Jolene into his arms and started for the road where he'd parked the truck. "You're barefoot, he explained to her grinning face.

After driving in silence for a few minutes, Josh said, "Jo, I'm so sorry for all of this. If I hadn't left the way I did..." She reached her fingers to his lips, silencing him. "I love you, you know."

Josh slammed on the brakes and pulled off the road. He turned and looked at her, then finally said, "Are you sure, Jo."

She nodded her head with a completely helpless look on her face. "I'm sure. I think I'd like being a farmer."

He pulled her to him, "I've been falling in love with you ever since we met. I've had all these doubts and fears, but hearing you say those words just erased them all." He looked deeply into her eyes and said, "I love you too."

Jolene flung her arms around his neck and they kissed.

Josh started the old truck and eased back onto the road. As darkness settled around them, Jolene snuggled next to him, and they rode in silence toward Platte Junction.

Chapter Forty

Epilogue

Jolene brought two cups of coffee to the couch where Josh sat. "We've got some talking to do, buster," she stated. "And I don't want to hear any more of that crap about what's right for me. You got it?"

Josh gazed up at her with a wide grin and partially squinted eyes. "Yes dear," he mocked.

Jolene set the cups on an end table and playfully whacked him in the head.

He winced, and grabbed her wrists. His eyes locked onto hers. The mood changed. After a long moment, he said, "I'm forty-six, by the way,"

She looked at him, squinting her eyes, calculating. "Thirteen years, big frigging deal. When you're eighty-three, I'll be seventy." She waved her finger in a circle with an 'I could care less' look.

He pulled her down and hugged her tightly. They stayed locked together in thought. All the words and fears seemed to melt as they took comfort from the embrace.

After separating, Josh sat up and said, "I'm afraid it's too late for me to ride back to the cabin tonight." Then added with a grin, "I could sleep on the couch, if you'd like."

"Like hell you will."

They both laughed.

Josh wrapped one arm around her shoulders. "Wow. Thirty-three, huh? I had you pegged to be mid-twenties at the most.

"Thank you. When you had that beard, I had you figured for at least sixty."

"Ouch." Both hands to his chest, he affected a pained look, then laughed.

* * * *

That night in bed, basking in the afterglow, Jolene marveled at the deep satisfaction surging through her body. When she was married she thought she had enjoyed sex. It certainly hadn't been unpleasant, but nothing like this. She tried to remember what she had felt with Bradley. Nothing came to mind. Absolutely nothing.

This total involvement of mind and body felt so different yet so comfortable, as if her soul had merged with Josh's. Her mind couldn't find words that matched the mysterious feelings flooding her thoughts and nerve endings. Was it a different kind of love? Oh yeah. Had she even known what love was then? She thought she had loved Bradley at the time. Now she was certain she hadn't. Not like this.

After a while Jolene leaned up on one elbow, stroked Josh's chest and said, "Without thinking, Josh, tell me about you, just you."

"Reader's Digest version?"

"Yes."

"Well," Josh put his finger to his chin, "I like long walks on the beach, warm sunsets, esoteric conversations, and…"

Jolene pounded his chest, then fell onto him, laughing. "You doofus."

They rolled and laughed together, before she said, "Seriously, Josh."

"You already know everything important about me. I grew up on a farm, became a police officer, retired under stress, now I'm a farmer again… and very much in love. We'll have plenty of time for the small stuff."

"We will?" She leaned in and teasingly brushed her lips to his.

"Sure. Now you. Tell me something I don't know about you."

She thought for a moment. "I was a cheerleader in high school."

"Really?"

"Yep. Want to see me do the splits?"

He leered, wiggling his eyebrows, "I already have."

Again she hammered a fist into his chest where she had been stroking, and then eased her bare chest into his. They shared a long exploring kiss.

When they pulled apart for a breath, Josh asked, "Was it really so bad growing up here, Jo?"

Jolene rolled onto her back and rubbed her face with both hands. After a moment she propped sideways on one elbow and said, "No, not really. I'm starting to like it again." She smiled. "When I left for college I was homesick some. I thought I only missed Mom and Dad, and I did, but now I think I missed the simple life too. Wasn't much here for a young girl and I was so thrilled with the hustle and bustle of campus life. Then Bradley and I married and moved to Spokane and that was a whole different world. It seemed so exciting for a while. I thought that's what living was all about. Then after a while, the crowds, the fog, the rain, the crime... and then Bradley's extracurricular activities..." She paused, her face registered disgust.

"Well," Jolene took a deep breath, and continued. "lately I've begun to see the calm beauty of these mountains. And I'm starting to realize how good life can be with the simplest of things. Happiness doesn't depend on location or things. It depends on a state of mind and the people around you."

"You sure got that right." Josh sat up, and after a moment said, "I've been giving some thought to my living conditions lately."

"I like your living conditions,"

"I sure hope so, but just so you'll know, I have a pretty good nest egg in the Soda Springs bank. Some of my original investments from Detroit and the sale of my house, and most of my monthly checks stay right there. And..."

"I don't care about any of that," she interrupted.

"I know, but I think I have a plan. Since I don't need any of that money, I've been thinking... We could hire a crew to level some of the trail to the cabin, and even lay down some gravel.

Maybe we could get a new Jeep." Josh watched her with an expectant smile on his face.

"We?"

"Well, yeah." Josh affected a 'this is a no brainer' look.

When he was able to pry her arms from around his neck, he continued. "I also want to put in more solar panels or maybe a windmill turbine so we can install whole-house electricity. What do you think?"

"We," she wistfully said again, her face aglow.

"Yes, we. As in, you and I – forever."

END (maybe)